Fc

They took the same route as they had two years earlier. Legère was more animated than she had ever seen. He told her of his coup in hiring the best available men both last year in the west, and this spring in Montreal. He had eight canoes and plans for another eight when he returned east in the fall.

"It is a huge risk. I am counting on the war ending, and settlers rushing to get land grants in The Forks region."

The carriage hit a rut. Nettie reflexively grabbed Legère's arm. It felt good, and she remained that way, feeling a small thrill at this forward move. He stopped talking. She could see the tight line of his mouth and knew he was feeling the same sexual tension as she. The steady rumble of the wheels on the dry road accentuated it.

When it came, Legère's voice was hoarse. "Nettie…this year will likely be my last in a canoe. Others will…"

She put a hand on his mouth. "Don't say it!" Her mind raced. Not to see him again would be impossible to think about. She could not live with Thomas without even the infrequent hope of being with Martin Legère.

"Come to York with me." He said this, not pleading, but as an imperative. "We will go when I am back here in September."

The idea was delicious. I cannot wait that long, she thought. Then Lily's strange suggestion made sense. The wise old woman knew what both she and Legère wanted—needed.

"Up there by that bent tree—turn in." She pointed.

He obeyed, and the horse led them up a track until it could go no farther. Ahead was a dome-shaped structure covered in hides. It looked deserted, nestled in an attractive clearing surrounded by birch. Nettie had taken Carrie here many times to stay with Lily, learning the Ojibwa language and ways.

"Help me down," she said. He did, and she was in his arms. "I won't wait for autumn. I want you now!" Her own words amazed her, but had an electric effect on her body. She was burning.

What They Are Saying About

Forgotten Roots

Many people these days search for their family genealogy, but how often do individuals discover their true "history"? Wouldn't it be amazing if we could go back in time and "see" the happenings of our ancestors? ***Forgotten Roots*** had created that desire within me. Author Richard Whitten Barnes has created strong, interesting characters, and he weaves a story that keeps the reader guessing until the very end as to how these lives are connected. He writes both in the days of the early 1800s and in the present; he pulls those two eras together beautifully. When an author can use descriptive language to get his readers to places via visual imagery, he's done his job. He was able to wrap my heart around that of the characters, especially one, but I won't include a spoiler here. As a reader, I feel that I can describe both the world of the 1800's story and the present-day mystery included in the book, thanks to the wonderful writing of Richard Barnes. Readers who enjoy historical fiction and/or a great mystery will find ***Forgotten Roots*** a book of choice for their reading repertoire.

Joyce M. Gilmour
Reviews
www.editingtlc.com

Barnes's engaging novel written in parallel stories will keep you turning the pages until the stories merge to solve a family mystery. You'll learn a lot of history in an entertaining read. ***Forgotten Roots*** is a don't-miss story.

Cheryl Norman,
2003 EPIC Award winner

Other Works From The Pen Of

Richard Whitten Barnes

The Corydon Snow: In 1943, the SS Corydon Snow :sails from Pearl Harbor on a voyage that will take it to the most dangerous battle areas of the Pacific.

Brink: What happens when a respected scientist loses everything, becomes homeless, then when on the road to recovery—is charged with murder?

Bad Medicine: Inspector Andy Blake gets more than she bargains for when she returns to her Island home for R&R – a murder, and her old flame is in the thick of it.

Luzon: America has broken Japan's "Purple" code, and a captured U.S. Navy officer knows it. Someone has to make sure the Japanese don't find out.

Wings

Forgotten Roots

by

Richard Whitten Barnes

A Wings ePress, Inc.

Historical Fiction/Mystery Novel

Wings ePress, Inc.

Edited by: Camille Netherton
Copy Edited by: Jeanne Smith
Senior Editor: Leslie Hodges
Executive Editor: Marilyn Kapp
Cover Artist: Trisha FitzGerald

Wings ePress Books
http://www.wings-press.com

ISBN 978-1-61309-832-5

Published In the United States Of America

January 2014

Wings ePress Inc.
403 Wallace Court
Richmond, KY 40475

Dedication

"To the citizens of St. Joseph Island, Ontario, and their forefathers who strove to tame that harsh frontier into a jewel in the crown of the Canadian north."

Acknowledgements

Getting Historical Fiction right requires the expertise to whom I am grateful:

Sandra Rousseau, author of
American Attempt to Take Canada
War of 1812 – 1814
St. Joseph Island
Sault Ste. Marie

Britney Kyle McIlvaine, Ph.D.
Assistant Professor, Department of Anthropology,
University of Northern Colorado
Greeley, CO

Thanks also to the hard-nosed editing of Camille Netherton, who did a lot more than check for punctuation. Her literary sense and thoughtful suggestions were, as always, invaluable.

Prologue

July, 1814

She climbed out of the root cellar from her failed search for something to eat. The darkened cabin burst into light as the door opened, framing the huge silhouette of a man.

He spoke. She heard, but not the words, only the sneering intent, and watched in horror as he began to unlace his breeches. She made for the door, but his blow hurled her against the tools in the corner. *A spade!*

He was taking his time talking with someone. The door closed. Now, only the light from her lantern. She heaved the spade, and it hit him, forcing him to his knees. She swung again, but his big hand caught the handle. The last thing she saw was the edge of the spade flying at her face. Then, nothing.

One

Andy

Andrea Blake wrapped her shield and holstered weapon in a sweatshirt, and added them to the nearly packed suitcase. One last look around the bedroom to see if she'd forgotten anything. The framed photo of her son, Tim, in high school cap and gown grinned at her. Next to it, a small wooden box with her keepsakes. Not valuable, but sentimental. She slipped it into the pocket of a sweater hanging in the closet, a feeble gesture, she knew, in the event of a break-in.

As she shut the closet door, her image swept into view in the full length mirror. A few grey strands in her uncolored hair, and character lines at the eyes, but what the hell. The sundress with the short jacket for the plane ride looked good on her five foot-nine, forty-five year old frame.

She zipped the bag closed and rolled it out to the waiting cab. "Airport," Andy instructed the driver.

"Detroit?" he asked, eyebrows raised in anticipation of a big fare from Windsor to Detroit McNamara.

"No, just Windsor," earned her a shrug. At mid-morning they moved quickly through town, aided by the absence of school buses in July. She watched the familiar neighborhoods slide by, wondering when she'd see them again. This trip wouldn't have happened if a load of circumstances hadn't lined up.

Like her turning down the job—for the second time—to head up Investigative Services of the Windsor Police Service. Her boss Jack Carmichael's promotion vacated that slot, which was now to be filled by Bradley Smyth, a self-impressed stuffed shirt. She could not tolerate the man.

Then there was Grant Stacey. Weary of their long distance love affair, he'd been patient but anxious for her to quit, and do her thing in Northern Ontario where they both grew up.

A window of opportunity came when the Windsor and Detroit Chambers of Commerce joined to honor her for her leadership in breaking up the region's worst vice ring in history two years earlier. She used her notoriety to ask for and receive an indefinite leave of absence, suspecting her new boss Smyth was just as happy to have her gone.

The cab turned off Walker Avenue to the private air terminal where the sign read: 'Great Lakes Flight Service.'

She glanced at her watch—11:00 AM. Stepping out onto the curb, Andy gave a good tip in compensation for the cabbie's disappointingly short trip, and looked up into a cloudless July sky, half expecting to see Grant's newly acquired plane landing.

She wheeled her bag through the glass door where, inside, three or four men stood at the counter, probably filing flight plans. And there, sitting in the lounge area with his back to her was Grant, hunched over his flight log. His rawboned, six feet plus torso and dark black hair were unmistakable.

"You're early!"

Stacey spun around, flashing a toothy smile under a longish nose, dark brows, and deep set eyes. "Tail wind!" he laughed. "Come here!"

They kissed, holding their embrace. To Andy it felt good. Maybe she was doing the right thing.

"So…how much time will you have?"

"Not sure yet," she fibbed. Sill reluctant to commit to anything—anyone—even now, twenty years after her divorce. Or was it *because* she'd been independent for all that time?

Stacey made no effort to push the issue. "Let's get some lunch while they top off the fuel."

By half past noon, they were back in Stacy's new toy, a twin-engine Beech Baron G28.

"I'm impressed, Grant. Business must be humming."

They'd received tower instructions, and were taxiing to the runway. "She's pre-owned, a two thousand-six—but yes, the company is doing well."

Andy remembered two years ago, when Grant had purchased two huge road graders totaling hundreds of thousands of dollars for his equipment-leasing business. The company had grown from nothing after getting a start by the sale of acreage from his family farm. He'd grown his leasing business from one dump truck into the largest of its kind from Thunder Bay to Sudbury.

They were fourth in line for takeoff, and used the time to continue their conversation from lunch.

Stacey's voice competed with the engine. "Then what is this big project of yours you mentioned?"

"I want to tear down that dreadful barn." Grant had helped her make improvements to her family home on St. Joseph Island in Northern Ontario. The work had changed the humble farm house into a charming cottage. The 'barn,' which was a little larger than a single car garage, was truly an eyesore. The rusted tin roof was in peril of caving in. It was filled with old machinery of questionable value. Even as a girl, she had never seen it cleaned out. It had been left that way since the death of her parents several years earlier.

Stacy reached over, his hand on hers, as if to say *I hope that's not all you're coming home for.*

~ * ~

The two hour flight from Windsor to Sault Ste. Marie was uneventful. They cruised at fifteen thousand feet in clear skies, following Michigan's eastern shore along Lake Ontario. In the air, Stacey was all business. Andy knew he'd been an avid pilot since high school. She felt comfortable with him at the controls.

She was nodding off when Grant tapped her arm, pointing to his left. Below was the magnificent bridge spanning the Straits of Mackinac, clearly visible in the perfect sky. Just to its right lay the island of the same name, both properly pronounced *Mackinaw*.

He said something unintelligible into the microphone, and the plane began a shallow descent. Shortly he pointed to the right. "St. Joe," he said.

Andy recognized the oblong shape of St. Joseph Island from ten thousand feet, angling roughly northwest. She strained to see her home near the foot of the island but saw nothing but a patchwork of green forest and fields. Still, it brought memories of her last visit when she and Grant had rekindled the twenty-five year still smoldering flame.

Fifteen minutes later, Stacey lowered the wheels for the approach. Lake Superior's Whitefish Bay loomed ahead as the runway rushed up to meet them.

~ * ~

Stacey's Audi hummed east on the Trans-Canada Highway 17 through the Garden River Indian Reservation. Once free of the city traffic, they lapsed into silence, deep in their own thoughts. Andy watched the high bluffs slide by on the north.

Stacey broke the silence. “Missed having you up here last year.”

She didn’t respond immediately. “It isn’t like we haven’t seen each other almost every week-end since then, Grant.”

“I know. It’s just…”

She gave him a poke, making the car swerve slightly. “You just prefer your own cooking to mine!”

He smiled. “I admit I was getting a lot of flying hours clocked, but…”

She waited for him to finish the sentence.

“…I love to see you back home here on the Island. Go ahead, call me a provincial.”

She couldn’t find a good argument. After years with the Toronto Police, then the Windsor job and the headaches attendant with its proximity to Detroit, she was ready for respite.

That thought evaporated as Stacey turned south onto Highway 548 toward the Island of St. Joseph where the two were raised and fell in love. As they approached the graceful arch of the Island bridge, she asked him to slow down for her to enjoy the view that never failed to give her pleasure.

“I had no idea it would feel this good to be back,” she said as the car crested the bridge. The channel to the right was atypically smooth, while the current under the bridge swirled it into glistening ripples. The white towers of the range lights sparkled like two pearls against a green background in the afternoon sun.

Stacey beamed like a schoolboy at her words. "Really?"

"Don't jump to conclusions, Mister. I still have to make a living, and right now that's Windsor."

"Not if we'd…"

She put a finger to his lips. "I know, Grant."

They'd been dancing around the issue of marriage for two years. After being stabbed in the line of duty, Andy had taken some R&R to recoup and make some decisions about the old family homestead. What resulted was a renewal of the twenty-some year old relationship with Stacy, a renovated rather than sold house, and a huge pharmaceutical drug bust she'd led. Stacey had been flitting back and forth between Windsor and Sault Ste. Marie ever since.

~ * ~

The economy of St. Joseph Island largely consisted of maple syrup, logging, crushed rock, farming, and tourism. Its roads were configured more or less along its northwest axis, with Highway 548 forming a loop around the circumference. Andrea Blake's family home was situated at the southernmost part of this loop. It was a modest dwelling that at one time fronted a large garden from which her parents made their living. Beyond that now unused space, a narrow road served vacation homes on the water.

In the driveway stood a bright yellow Jeep Wrangler Stacey had insisted on availing her from the considerable rolling stock he maintained for his leasing business. Grant's hurry to get home left her no chance to thank him for that, nor the perfectly-manicured yard he'd paid someone to do.

Inside, it took her a moment to get accustomed to the changes she'd made to the place two years ago. The first eighteen years of her life were spent in a house where her parents had little time or money to spend on frills. She could still imagine the aroma of her mother's cooking, her father's pipe.

Her own handiwork of painting, drapery sewing, and accessorizing the place seemed foreign. She was surprised—like an artist who, years later, looks at something of his own, and admires it. *Yes, I could live in this house.*

With her bag still unpacked, she checked the fridge. Sure enough, Grant had it stocked. That cold Labatt's Blue looked inviting. She popped the cap, and wandered out to the back porch. Like the front, the grass was cut. It was mowed back to where her father had tended his organic garden. He'd sell what he could on the weekends in Richards Landing and Hilton Beach—the Island's two towns of any notable size.

The grass was neatly mowed right up to the walls of the old garage. She couldn't remember having ever looked inside the place on her last trip. It was in serious disrepair with its sagging roof, loose siding and boarded over window, an anomaly in an otherwise tidy setting.

She went back inside to unpack, sort out her clothes and, with any luck, sort out her life.

Two

Nettie

June 1801
Carlisle, Scotland

She had always found a way to get what she wanted. Not as a pampered child, but through the dint of her own perseverance. What she wanted now was Thomas Gibson, and seventeen year old Annette Duncan was about to get her wish.

Gibson was a man with a plan. He greatly admired the entrepreneurial spirit of the Scots before him, like Alexander Mackenzie and Simon McTavish, who had set out to the Americas to make their fortunes in the booming fur trade. McTavish's newly formed Montreal fur trading company was flourishing, and Nettie's father, Angus Duncan, knew McTavish. A letter from Duncan had procured a post for his future son-in-law with the North West Company, traders in furs, and competing vigorously with the older Hudson Bay Company.

Nettie stood before the mirror in her wedding gown cut high at the waist in the fashion of the day. Her plump five foot-three frame stared back at her with a look of satisfaction. She was neither beautiful nor homely, simply a fact, and she'd learned to live with it. Over her image's shoulder stood her mother, holding a small box.

Nettie turned. "Mother! Look at me. I am…so happy!"

Gwendolyn Duncan kissed her daughter's forehead. "I have never seen you so lovely, Nettie." She took a step backward, surveying the girl's pale yellow dress with the thin purple ribbon at the bodice. "When I saw your dress, I knew what to give you." She opened the box.

"Oh!" Nettie had seen the earrings before and always loved them.

"They are old, dear, but still quite fashionable these days, and they match the trim on your dress."

They were gold and amethyst with a shepherd's crook wire. Little more than an inch long, they were elegantly simple.

Mother and daughter embraced anew. "It's time, my dear," Gwendolyn Duncan said, and the two headed to the stairs where the girl's father waited to give her away.

~ * ~

The young Mrs. Annette Duncan Gibson stood in the window looking down at the wharf of Liverpool. So much ado in one place. The hotel's street was crammed with wagons, carts, horses, porters pushing barrows. Across a wide yard filled with barrels and crates stood the merchantman, *Penelope*, sails furled neatly on its spars. Stores were being rolled up her gangplank for the trip to Newfoundland and Montreal. It was cooler here by the ocean, and she returned to her still-opened trunk to retrieve one of her wedding gifts, a light green knitted shawl.

The wedding had been fine, if only a little anticlimactic after all the planning. Her father had held her hand for the longest time before offering it to the eager groom, possibly thinking how unlikely they would ever see the girl again. There, Thomas Gibson, a slightly pudgy man of average height, stood perspiring in the overwarm room. Nettie knew her husband-to-be was no Adonis, but knew him to be solid and purposeful. Her older sister, Kate, had made the mistake of marrying a man of her fantasy, only to soon become aware his shallow character. Such a fate was not in Nettie's plan.

They took the carriage from Carlisle south to spend their wedding night at a Penrith inn. Nettie was anxious. Her mother had tried to tell her what to expect, but it was less than what she had already heard from other girls—that her husband would be touching her in her private places, that she would come to know his body, as well. But that was the sum of her knowledge, and helped little to allay her unease.

They had a light meal upon arrival, nervous conversation throughout. After, Thomas escorted her to their rooms across the courtyard, then returned to their table, claiming a desire for a last sherry, ostensibly to give her time to dress for bed.

The accommodations consisted of two rooms and an inside privy, an extravagance from her parents for the occasion. Nettie had laid out her new nightgown and soon was out of her traveling clothes and ready for what lay ahead. She was barely in bed before Thomas returned.

She heard the door to the parlor room open and quietly close. Then, after what seemed an eternity, her husband of a few hours appeared shyly into the chamber. Nettie reached over and blew out the bedside candle.

The bed creaked as Thomas got under the coverlet. He said nothing, but she could hear his breathing.

"Thomas," she said, as if reminding him the next move was his.

He rolled to her and kissed her—a little too hard. She tried to respond to him, understand his groping hands. *There?* She'd had her own hands there, felt pleasure, but he was too rough. He was pulling up his nightshirt, and now at her underthings!

"Thom…" Her words were stifled by his mouth on hers, then his weight.

It became clear that he was not adept at this.

Let it happen!

She felt the penetration and cried out softly, a brief hint of pleasure, then it was over. Thomas Gibson rolled off his new wife, and exhaled a sigh.

Nettie retrieved her knickers, and tiptoed to the privy. Thomas was asleep when she returned.

Another attempt at their stay in Lancaster was better, then again last night. A*nd now she was an experienced, married woman*, she wryly thought.

There was a perfunctory rap on the door before Thomas entered. "We must hurry, Annette. The captain has sent a messenger. We must be aboard in less than one hour. I've a porter coming for this last wardrobe."

~ * ~

The city of Liverpool was literally named after the remarkable tidal pool on which it stood. The rise and ebb of the tide was of such proportions that dry docks were built there to accommodate the largest of ships. They hadn't been aboard the *Penelope* long before they felt the ship being hauled out into the outgoing tide which propelled them swiftly out into the Irish Sea.

Their accommodations amidships were shared with eleven other passengers. A long benched table served for a space to read, sew, visit, and have their meals. Their quarters were no more than closets lining either side of the table, and separated from each other by the thinnest of partitions. Privacy under those conditions was nonexistent.

The ship was well south of Holyhead before Captain Jeremiah Bell invited the passengers on deck. Below, Nettie had noticed Thomas' color was a bit off, but thought it might only be the poor lighting there. On deck he looked grey-green. His lips were tightly drawn against his teeth. His prematurely thinning hair appeared to be plastered on his perspiring scalp.

"Thomas, dear, are you ill?"

"Aye. I am that."

"Perhaps you should return below."

"Yes, I believe you're…" He lurched for the rail and gave up the biscuits and gravy proffered this morning by the hotel.

The trip was expected to take a minimum of sixty days. Nettie hoped this first experience on the relatively calm Irish Sea was not going to be the norm for the long haul across the North Atlantic Ocean.

~ * ~

They were three days out of Liverpool headed southeast around the Irish coast in a stiff northwest wind. Nettie was settling in nicely, making friends with the two other women on board, Ann Jeffries and Dora Boone, wives of Hudson Bay Company managers.

The *Penelope* was part of the British East India Company's fleet of merchantmen. At one hundred seventy-five feet in length, and over forty feet in the beam, she was larger than the typical vessel for North American service. She had been laid up in Liverpool, her bottom scraped and rigging replaced. The winter of 1800 had produced an abundance of furs that exceeded the capacity of previous ships. *Penelope* was dispatched to take on most, if not all, of that inventory.

Thomas was still sick, tucked away in their cabin with the sides of the bunk raised against the ship's constant roll to port. Since Liverpool, he'd eaten little except some broth and canned biscuit.

Nettie was in thrall over the workings of the huge vessel, never having been in more than a river punt. Yesterday, an ensign had taken some of the passengers on a tour of the ship, including a lecture on safety at sea. They were shown the officer's mess and quarters (excepting the crew's fo'c'sle), the gun deck with its fifty-eight cannon securely belayed. They toured the upper decks fore and aft. Nettie was impressed how labor intensive it was to make the slightest adjustment in the set of the sails on the three masts. Men aloft were adding sails above what the ensign called "t'gallants." They were the topsails. She held tightly to the rail in order to see all the way up to the top of the mainmast. It was dizzying.

The *Penelope* left a wake of froth back to England as it plowed its way at seven knots, and the red and white striped flag of the Honorable British East India Company waved farewell from the spanker. The air smelled fresh with hints of land as it washed over the hills of Ireland. *It's a good beginning for a new life,* Nettie thought on this fair day of 30 June, 1801.

Three

August 1801

Nettie gave up trying to sleep. At her side lay Thomas in fitful slumber. The expected sixty day voyage had already taken two weeks longer, and he'd been seasick the whole way. She had been awake for what seemed hours. Quietly she dressed, and went on deck.

Penelope lay hove to, the yards of its masts sheeted at cross-purposes. The eastern sky gave the first hint of dawn. The ship's first mate stood by the helm, and Nettie went to him.

"Good morning, Mrs. Gibson. Up early, I see."

"The rocking of the ship, I suspect, Mr. Turner. Where are we?"

"Just out of Sydney Harbor, Cape Breton, Ma'am. We're hove to, waiting for enough daylight to enter. We'll commence in just a few minutes."

"I'm surprised at the weather," she said. "So warm!"

"That it is. The ocean current here comes from the West Indies. You'll find Nova Scotia a temperate clime."

"How long will we be here?"

"No longer than the time to take on fresh water, and mayhap vegetables for the trip to Quebec. Tomorrow for sure." He touched his fingers to his hat. "If you will excuse me, Ma'am…"

The mate moved to the helm where his bo' sun and helmsman stood. Soon, orders were shouted to men on the deck and aloft. The yards of the foremast were hauled around, and the gallants unfurled. The ship ceased its wallowing, and listed to starboard as sheets were belayed. With spars creaking, the *Penelope* was once again underway. The sun peeked over the horizon, illuminating the topmost sails. It was thrilling.

~ * ~

Nettie was accustomed to beautiful scenery. Her home was in the well-known Lake District shared by Britain and Scotland, after all. But she was not prepared for the charm of the unspoiled, wooded hills rising high on both sides of the ship, as it entered the long stretch into Sydney Harbor.

The town of Sydney looked to consist of no more than a few hundred people. A few small boats were at the wharf, and a schooner lay anchored in the harbor. Surprisingly, piles of what had to be coal were neatly situated as if ready for shipment, but to where? Certainly not to coal-rich England.

"Quite an attractive place, isn't it, Annette?"

Nettie turned to find Thomas at her elbow looking quite chipper, whether from the calm waters of the harbor, or from the anticipation of setting his feet on solid ground, she wasn't sure.

The excitement of going ashore after more than two months was shared by the other passengers, and the crew as well. The *Penelope* was towed to the wharf, and the gangway set. The passengers swarmed around it, dressed in their best, despite the drabness of the little town.

When Nettie felt the ground beneath her feet, it was like walking on a moving surface, oscillating from side to side. Others among them were laughing and giggling at the phenomenon of regaining their land legs.

An enterprising innkeeper was there with a wagon fitted out with benches, inviting passengers to his establishment for their one-night stay.

"Oh, Thomas! Let's do!"

"A night off that ship? By all means!" He hailed the man on the wagon, and made arrangements for their stay.

~ * ~

The inn surpassed their fondest expectations. The place overlooked one of the many inlets that faced the northeast of Cape Breton. The night was warm, clear, and fragrant with pine. Their quarters looked down one hundred feet onto the inlet.

They'd bathed in fresh water, and spent the day and hour after a fine dinner strolling the wooded paths surrounding the inn.

"I could live here," Nettie said.

Thomas laughed. "Don't be impractical."

She took his hand. "You're right. Don't be angry. Come, it's time we retired. The ship will sail by the morning tide."

Later in bed, Thomas' recovery had revived his libido. Once more he fumbled for Nettie's drawers. This time she stopped him.

"Thomas, dear! Go slowly." She took his hand, holding it to her breast. They both softly gasped. She felt his hand on her nipple, felt him react. Slowly, she pulled him to her, guided him, felt his excitement, but slowed his entry. *So this is how it should feel!*

Her sensation increased toward some unknown climax, but Thomas exploded before she could know.

~ * ~

The overnight at Cape Breton, and the relative calm of the St. Lawrence estuary alleviated Thomas' sea sickness. He joined Nettie on deck more often then, but in the last few days Nettie had begun to have spells of nausea herself. The ship was eight days out of Sydney, and the passengers were impatient about the slow progress.

"The current is against us, and more so, the farther we progress upstream," Nettie instructed a group taking a turn on deck. She'd become the unofficial go-between for the passengers with the crew. "The captain says we should spy Quebec City by this afternoon."

The *Penelope* had the advantage of a southerly wind for the past few days, veering to the west by sundown. At those times the ship would anchor, and wait it out for the following day when the wind would back around to south or southwest. *Penelope* sailed close-hauled most of the time, hugging the shore with the least amount of current. As predicted, a high outcrop hove into view as the ship rounded a bend. From aloft came a shout. “Cape Diamond, ho!”

Two hours passed before the ship entered the wide mouth of the River Charles, forming a fine harbor for Quebec City. A sizeable part of the population was there to meet them. Gentlemen and ladies in the latest fashion frocks and livery, others in the rough dress of woodsmen, hunters, tradesmen and laborers, all anxious for letters or merely word from the old world. The ship had been hauled to the pier and the crew was busy with lines.

Nettie was impressed. “How large is this city?” she asked her husband.

“I’m told as many as ten thousand.”

“It’s like nothing I’d have imagined—all those spires!” Then a new wave of nausea erupted. This time it was different. She lurched for the rail in mid-sentence.

“Are you ill?” Thomas wondered. “Perhaps you should sit.”

“Yes—yes. I…Oh!” She doubled over in a violent retch. Little came up but saliva.

Two of the ladies preparing to disembark hurried to her.

"May I assist in some way?" It was the first mate.

"No," Thomas Gibson said. "I'm sure she'll be fine."

"This woman is seriously ill!" Mrs. Jeffries announced. Other voices joined in, offering the same opinion. Thomas was rebuffed.

The mate said, "There is a fine hospital, *L'Hotel Dieu.* It's nearby. I can see that she is taken there."

The small crowd, that by then had assembled, chorused approval, trumping Gibson's reluctance.

~ * ~

"I've seen this condition before. A severe reaction to a young woman's being with child. It is serious, and even fatal." The elderly nun spoke English with a pronounced French accent. She removed her spectacles, and placed a cool hand on Nettie's forehead "Some days of bed rest is what she must have now. It is all we can do."

Gibson was appalled. "No! I mean, we can't! The ship…"

"Sailing?" The sister confronted him. "You can wait for the next one, of course."

"That might not come for months!" he sputtered.

"Certainly not that long, but it could be weeks."

Nettie spoke up. "Don't worry, Thomas. I'm sure I'll be fine in a few hours."

"There! Do you hear? She's fine." Gibson reached for Nettie's hand. "There's my girl!"

The sister was adamant. “This girl is in no condition to travel. She is weak, dehydrated, and could lose the child she carries.”

Nettie watched as the old nun won a staring contest with her husband. He averted his eyes to Nettie. “Annette, my dear, I must speak with the *Penelope’s* captain. I’ll return this afternoon.” He kissed her cheek, and left.

Nettie closed her eyes, feeling exhausted. She had been taken to *L’Hotel Dieu,* a large hospital located not two hundred yards from where the *Penelope* tied up. She was in a ward of possibly forty beds. She could hear the rustle of the nuns’ habits as they went about their duties. *So it was true! “The child she is carrying...”* The sister said it. She drifted off into a dreamless slumber.

~ * ~

October 1801
Montreal

The hotel on St. Mary Street was a disappointment. The better ones, like the Pierre du Calvet were booked. Nettie was feeling better these past few days. Yet, the strain from the trip had been exhausting. She sat in a chair, still in her dressing gown, looking out onto the busy Montreal street.

In Quebec city, Thomas had plead with *Penelope’s* captain for a day’s departure delay only to find she was not expected to sail for another five to seven days while damage to the anchor winch was repaired. He’d been frantic to think they would have to miss the sailing due to his wife. He calmed down with the news that Nettie would be released before then.

On arriving at Montreal, Thomas was disappointed to find no one there to meet them. He'd sent a letter by hotel messenger to Simon McTavish, and received an invitation to visit the North West Company offices where he had now been for two hours.

By noon Nettie was dressed and hungry. Thomas had said nothing about when he might return, but she had assumed his interview would not last this long. All morning she'd had nothing to do but reflect on the life she carried in her womb. The prospect of being a mother was frightening. No one had prepared her for this. It dawned on her she was just seventeen, her family a continent away, and had already come to not expect much help from her husband in such matters.

The room was utterly silent—not the tick of a clock or the clop of a horse's hoof from the street. She had never felt so alone.

An hour later, there he was, crossing the street to the hotel. There was a distinct spring to his step. He reminded Nettie of a prideful penguin, with his mincing steps, white waistcoat with black frock coat, and the toss of his head. *The interview went well!* She was still suppressing a laugh at the open door when he arrived.

"Thomas! What is the news?"

"Never better, my dear," he said closing the door.

"Do tell!"

"It did not begin well. Mr. McTavish is ill. It was his nephew who led the interview, a man no older than myself. While he apologized for not expecting us so soon, it became clear to me that there will be much competition for advancement there."

"Oh dear! What do you mean?"

"Mr. McTavish has brought a good many of his relatives into the firm. His nephews William and Duncan McGillivray, his brother-in-law, a Mr. Chaboillez, and I believe others. These men are mostly my contemporaries, but as they are in his family, will have an advantage over my own achievements. It appears William is already assuming senior duties."

"But you said 'never better.' I don't understand."

"I have experience, Annette, in my family's granary doing accounts. They have a need for improving their system, and I am to be put in charge of it with a staff of two clarks! I had a brief meeting with them. They seemed competent, and assured me merit trumps nepotism at the company. Mr. McTavish's nephews will have to perform like anyone else. I am quite relieved."

"And what of our accommodations? Can we move to another hotel?"

"Better than that! They have secured rooms for us near their offices."

Nettie reached up to kiss her husband, who seemed to already have his mind on his new career.

Four

Andy

Andy guided the Wrangler down the long hill into Richards Landing. Last night a closer inspection of the pantry revealed a lack of some of her basic essentials, mainly vegetables. It was Saturday, and the farmer's market would be open. The town was bustling with tourists and the first of summer cottagers. After doing some banking at the credit union, she drove back halfway up the hill to the open market. There, several cars parked including a black and white Ontario Provincial Police cruiser. An officer was just returning to it. She recognized him, and called his name from her open window.

"Bert Wheatly!"

The broad-shouldered man of about thirty turned, hesitated, and then smiled broadly. "Ms. Blake…Andy. Good to see you!"

She scrutinized his uniform. "Well now! *Sergeant* Wheatly, I should have said."

He grinned. "You had a little to do with that."

"Me?"

"That drug business we broke up didn't tarnish my record."

"You did great, Bert. You deserve those stripes."

"Just back for a visit?" He tossed his bag in the cruiser and met her as she got out of the Jeep.

"Not sure," she said. "How did things work out with Sally?" Andy referred to a young girl who was a victim of the smuggling ring Wheatly referred to.

"I see her from time to time. Right now she doesn't want to rely on anyone but herself. She got her GED and has enrolled at Lake Superior State. I'm reluctantly giving her space."

The two had found feelings for each other at the time. Andy could see those feelings hadn't cooled for Wheatley.

"Nice to see you again, Bert." They hugged and he was off.

Inside, a half-dozen people were clustered around one of the tables. Andy could see why. It was filled with beautiful fresh lettuce, beans, potatoes, and more. There, making change and stuffing plastic bags, was Alice Graham.

Like Andy's parents, Alice (now in what must be her seventies) and her husband owned a small farm from which they sold produce. Andy knew from personal experience it was a back-breaking way to make a living.

When she had a chance, Andy said, "Hello, Mrs. Graham."

The woman straightened, pushed back a strand of steel gray hair. “My Lord! Andrea Blake.”

“I thought if I wanted fresh eggs and veggies, I’d better come early. When will the corn be in?”

“A couple of weeks yet, with this cool weather.” She reached for Andy’s hand. “Darlin’, I never set up shop here without thinking of your folks.”

“That means a lot. Thanks. Our place has gone to grass, I’m afraid. Not much of a farm anymore. I’m even going to tear down the old barn.”

Alice displayed a wry smile. “Things change, dear.”

Andy got her vegetables and headed for the Jeep.

“Excuse me.” A feminine voice made her turn. A tall woman held her own bag of green beans.

“Sorry, I overheard you talking. Your father was Earl Blake?”

Andy nodded. The woman, fortyish and bookish, looked very familiar, but no name came to mind. She seemed somewhat out of place in her hose and sensible heels.

“I was a year behind you in high school. I’m hoping I can talk to you about preserving what you can from that structure you mentioned.” From her purse came a business card that read: *Lila Knowles—Algoma Heritage Foundation.*

Andy stared at the card, then Knowles. The name and face clicked. “Oh, yes. Lila! It’s just an old garage-turned-shed. Why…”

"Look," Knowles said. "You're in a hurry, and so am I. May I stop by your place sometime this week and talk?"

"Well…sure."

And with that, Lila Knowles retreated back into the stalls to continue her shopping.

Andy took the long way home, which was to continue west on Highway 548, then south along the shipping channel that was the up bound lane for the huge ore boats returning to the Soo Locks and Lake Superior. She'd hoped to see one of the behemoths, but there were none. Still, the ride was her favorite, offering a different vista from the rolling farmland and forest of the Island.

Back home she put away her purchases and walked out in the yard to give the old building a closer look. Her best imagination could not conceive what that woman's interest was in the thing.

The siding might well date back from before the 1930s. The construction was spare and never meant to be anything substantial. The foundation was maybe a twenty-five foot square of field stones about a foot off the ground.

In any event, it was an eyesore, and she wanted it gone. Grant would know someone to tear it down and haul it off. She might have a fence built from the stone.

~ * ~

The highway that more or less followed the perimeter of the island changed names several times on its journey. St. Joseph Island gives singular names to its thoroughfares. Numbered "Side Roads" and lettered "Line Roads"—hence, the A-Line Road, or the 20th Side Road. Andy's house was on the U-Line, four or five hundred yards from Tenby Bay on the south shore. Tonight, on her way to Grant Stacey's for dinner –and whatever that might lead to—she turned off the rain-soaked 5th Side Road, and on to the P-line where his family farm looked down from a hill.

It had been a week since Lila Knowles had approached her at the farmer's market about her barn. Today, Lila showed up unannounced, and what she had to say was exceptional. Andy was anxious to discuss the matter with Grant.

She turned the Jeep up the long gravel drive that led to the Stacey farm. "Farm" no longer described the place. After the death of his parents, Stacey got completely out of the maple syrup business that had sustained the family for three generations. He converted the syrup-making building into a three car garage and a large workshop that was the envy of every handyman on the island.

She parked next to the garage, avoiding the drizzle under his newly-built portico connecting to the house some sixty feet away. She jogged around to the rear of the house to the patio where furniture was neatly stacked and covered. Through the glass slider she saw him in the kitchen opening a bottle of wine.

"So much for dinner outside," she said walking in.

"The front came through early, it seems." He handed her the glass just poured for himself, then poured another. "To summer," he said. He clinked her glass, then kissed her.

"Summer?" She looked through the rain-mottled window.

"It only *feels* like March." He followed her into the den where an impossibly funny looking dog sprawled by the glowing fireplace. The animal lifted his yellow head with droopy black ears seemingly sewn on each side. He was the image of Pluto, his namesake. Andy dropped to the floor to scratch him, and was rewarded with a drawn out groan of pleasure. One of Pluto's long legs kicked at the air. "That woman I told you about showed up at my door this afternoon."

Stacey returned a blank stare.

"Lila Knowles— from the historical society."

His face registered enlightenment. "Your barn!"

"Yes."

"Yeah, I meant to tell you I got a couple of young guys to tear that thing down. Remember Ronnie that helped me with your porch? He and his chum will do it for a hundred dollars."

"She says it's very old."

He shrugged, threw himself on the sofa. "Can't be too old. Those boards are standard one-by-sixes. The nineteen twenties earliest, I guess. There's a market for old barn siding. You could sell the wood for more than it costs to tear the thing down."

Andy shook her head. "She's interested in the foundation. She's afraid we'll tear it out."

"It's a lousy pile of field rock, for Pete's sake!"

"She's an archeologist, and thinks that pile of rocks predates the Rains Party."

In 1835, Major William Kingdom Rains and a group of speculators made a generally unsuccessful attempt to colonize the Island, setting up a sawmill and general store at an inlet not far from Andy's property. He named it Milford Haven. Both ventures failed before long, but Rains stayed on, and sired a large family, the name still known on the Island.

"And she knows this how?

"She's accounted for every homestead of the Rains group. As you know, only a few stayed for long. But earlier, when the fort was actively protecting the fur traders, there was a small community on the island."

"Your place is five or six miles from the fort," he said.

Andy sighed audibly. "Grant. I know it's all speculative, but I told Ms. Knowles I'd leave the stones intact until she could prove it's a real historical site. God knows I don't want a pile of rubble on my back lawn."

Stacey finished his wine, and gave her an inquiring look.

She held up her half-finished glass. “I’ll finish this with dinner. What do I smell?

“What else? Lasagna. That and salads are all I can count on turning out.” She knew that wasn’t true.

“Fishing for compliments again, I see.”

~ * ~

She slipped quietly out of Grant Stacey’s bed and drove home before breakfast. She couldn’t verbalize why, but it had to do with her not wanting to play the domestic scene with Grant, at least just yet. To do so would have her regressing to a place where she relied on someone else, or so it seemed to her. The abuse in her short marriage twenty-five years in the past was still like a painful bruise that wouldn’t stop hurting.

Five
Parcher

August 1801
Franklinton, Ohio Territory

A fly buzzed around the sleeping, unwashed, shaggy head and beard of Albert Parcher. When his eyes popped open, they were blinded by broad daylight. The sound of hammer on anvil at the forge amplified the pain in the back of his head. A blurred memory of last night was of the locked door to the cottage, and making his way to the stable.

Fuck! Parcher sat up brushing away the straw from his neck and a beard that was already thick despite his age of twenty years. He found his cap and replaced it on his head. The act of rising intensified the pain, the ale he'd consumed last night still affecting his balance. "God, I have to piss!" Which he did in the empty stall.

He walked the thirty some paces from the barn to the forge where Adam Varner was hard at it with a red hot iron in his tongs. A boy of maybe fourteen was watching.

"Who's this?"

Varner, half Parcher's size, but hard as the iron he wrought, raised his eyes, hooded under bushy, grey brows. They rested on Parcher and his partially unbuttoned breeches. "My new helper."

"What ya mean, 'new?'"

"Means I'm finally givin' up on you. Whole damn town calls me demented, keepin' you long as I done."

"You can't—you…"

Varner returned the hot bar to the coals, pulled a wrinkled envelope from his pocket. "I promised to teach you a trade when I picked you up out of the Pittsburg docks. Since then you done nothin' but lie, drink, and fornicate. I get more out of this here boy in an hour than you in a week." He held the envelope out for Parcher to take.

Parcher stared at the outstretched hand, trying to clear his mind, finally comprehending that Varner was getting rid of him.

"Then bugger you, Varner! I don't need to waste my time in this shit hole." Parcher snatched the envelope from Varner's hand, then hesitated, unsure of what to do next. The boy stared at him, wide-eyed. "Who in bloody hell you lookin' at?"

Varner put his body between Parcher and the boy. "You can get your clothes over there on the house porch. I packed 'em for ya at three in the mornin' whilst you were a-bangin' on the door."

Parcher opened the envelope. Four of the new United States three dollar notes were there. More than a month's pay. He turned, avoiding Varner's eyes, and collected his pack from the porch. A look back at the forge revealed the two back at work. *Look at them—lickspittles bustin' their arses for a few pennies. Not me, by God.* Following Varner up to this place in the middle of nowhere had been one of his dumbest moves, anyway.

At Varner's gate, he considered which way to turn. Maybe north to the Michigan territory? Or back down to Alexandria. Yeah, south. Lots of action in in the river towns for a man like me.

~ * ~

The driver of the wagon, grateful for company on the long trip, was getting on Parcher's nerves. Not content with his own boring stories, he insisted on prying into Parcher's life. Still, it was a ride, and all the way to Chillicothe.

His first day on the trail following the Scioto River south from the frontier village of Franklinton was mostly afoot. He'd found a shed last night for protection against the light rain. Then, first thing this morning, the man came along the puddled road in his wagon, intent on bringing two pigs to market in Chillicothe. Parcher spent much of the afternoon thinking of ways to steal the pigs for himself. He figured he'd have to kill the old bastard to do it, but in the end decided it would be less trouble to let the man sell the pigs, then steal his money.

As the wagon bumped along, Parcher wondered why he'd ever taken Varner up on his offer of an apprenticeship. Maybe just to get the hell out of

Pittsburg where that rape charge kept him looking over his shoulder. Women were all sluts, and nothing but trouble. Even his mother—whoring around. He would have starved if it weren't for his mates and him working the few people coming of the boats in Baltimore.

There was a knot in his gut every time he thought about coming home that night, just a thirteen year old kid, to find her gone. *Gone! Gone, without a goddam word. She thought more of that fat bozo that kept her likkered up than me. Well fuck her!*

The warm rain of the previous day gave way to clear skies by late afternoon, as the wagon entered the town. Stalls and pens were being set up for the Saturday market. He left the man to make his arrangements for tomorrow's sale, and found the town tavern where he slapped down one of his three dollar notes.

"A glass of ale."

The woman behind the rudely built counter pulled him a draft, giving him change in newly minted American specie. At a long table in the room, a dozen men sat in boisterous discourse.

"Who's that?" Parcher had spent the day listening to chatter, and was hoping for some quiet time to think about his next move.

The woman glancing that way, sneered, "Federalists—plotting against statehood."

Parcher had no interest in politics, but the subject of statehood for the Northwest Territory—

nominally Ohio—was on everyone's lips these days. The Federalist Party wanted to limit the proposed western border of the new state to the Scioto River, keeping them in political power there. They were in peril of losing control to the Democrat-Republican Party if the border was extended west beyond the Great Miami River. In any case, Chillicothe was expected to be the capital of the new state. It was ideally located on a waterway route to the Ohio River at Alexandria, and the new road being built that headed southwest.

The men at the table all looked well dressed in their waistcoats, cutaways and stocks. Some were in fashionable trousers, others in knee breeches and hose. Parcher took his draft to a small table near the group. From what he could make from their conversation, it seemed they were mostly from back east, probably Philadelphia or the new capital in Washington. They must be important men.

That night Parcher secured a bed in little more than a cupboard at the inn, owing to the visiting politicians' occupancy. From his eavesdropping, he'd learned they were returning the next morning to Alexandria on the Scioto River. A new idea began to form in Parcher's head, replacing the theft of pig money.

~ * ~

While there was a road south from Chillicothe, the preferred method of travel was by *batteau*, the shallow draft river boat that made movement from town to town practical, especially downstream. The long, narrow boats were of various sizes, often equipped with a mast and sail, but most often propelled only by men on the gunnels with long poles, another man at the stern guiding the craft with a sweep. A rounded arch of a shelter was often situated for passengers' protection from the elements. The boats were used for transporting almost everything the settlers needed for sustaining life in the Territory.

On this morning, only human cargo and two sets of wagon wheels were loaded on the thirty foot boat for the trip south. Parcher had wangled a job as a pole man, which was easily accomplished, the work being hard, and the pay low. Among the party headed downriver was a man Parcher had overheard the night before saying he had business in the booming port town of Cincinnati, while the others were headed back east to Pittsburg and beyond.

The choice was easy. Parcher had nothing waiting for him in Pittsburg but a charge of rape. No, he'd follow the portly, well-heeled gentleman west, and see what opportunities he might cause to develop.

~ * ~

It was a two day run downstream to Alexandria. Parcher made no effort to approach the passengers when they overnighted at the halfway house, other than a polite doff of the hat. They reached the Ohio River in the early afternoon of the second day.

Alexandria was a busy place with goods being unloaded from three keel boats newly arrived from

Pittsburg. These boats had made the trip together in safety against Indian raids that were a constant threat. Safety in numbers was advised for the long voyage.

Most of the group Parcher had observed in Chillicothe would have to wait one or two days for a keel boat to return upstream, but one of the boats had unloaded, and was immediately continuing on to Cincinnati.

It was time for Parcher to make his move. The little man who was headed west had bid goodbye to the others, and was struggling with a satchel and large portmanteau.

"I'll help ya with that, sir," Parcher offered, his knitted cap in hand.

"Oh, I'm sure I can…"

"Please, sir. No need strugglin'. Takin' the west bound keel, are ye?"

"Why, yes…"

"Headin' thataway myself, sir. No problem at all." He replaced his hat and took the heavy case. "Name's Parcher, sir, Albert Parcher."

"Well, thank you, Parcher. I'll be pleased to pay you."

"Nunna that, sir. Goin' to the North Bend, myself. Lookin' to find some work there."

~ * ~

The keel boat looked to be preparing to depart. The pole men were astir after a respite from unloading barrels of whiskey and flour. Parcher strode ahead with the luggage while the portly little gentleman held on to his hat and scurried behind.

Parcher hailed to a man seated in a rocking chair on the flat roof of the boat. A mug of something, likely a portion of the offloaded whiskey, dangled leisurely from the man's hand. He turned his head slightly toward the sound.

"Have two passengers for yer, Cap'n."

"How far?" The man's two words revealed a thick, probably French accent. He had dark black hair and bushy moustache to match.

"Cincinnati," the small, round gentleman replied.

"And who may you be, sir?"

"Oliver Gandy, ah…Captain, and this is my…ah…valet, Herbert."

"Albert," Parcher corrected.

"It'll be three dollar each," the man declared.

"That's bloody thievery, that's what!" Parcher said.

The moustache twitched in a smile lacking humor of any kind. The man turned his head away unconcerned, and took a swig from the mug.

"It's—it's all right," Gandy said, searching for his satchel. From a velvet bag with a draw string, he produced six Spanish dollars, or Pieces of Eight, which were still the preferred international currency and equivalent to the new US dollar.

That brought the man out of his chair, slowly descending the ladder to the deck. "You are wise to take this boat," he said as he ushered the pair aboard. “The river is alive with pirates from here westward. My men are used to dealing with them.”

The boat was newly built, by the look of it. Parcher strode the length in fifteen paces, which put it close to fifty feet long. Along each side was a narrow strip the crew called a “run,” which allowed them to pole the boat forward by six or eight of them pushing backwards, then scrambling back to the front of the boat and repeating the process.

The keel boat was an improvement over the flatboat—which was little more than a floating house—in that its narrow beam and shallow keel allowed easier rowing and poling upstream. The huge flatboats were more likely to be dismantled for their lumber upon reaching their destination.

They learned the captain’s name was Baudin, a Canadian who had quit the fur trade. His crew numbered sixteen, and a more disreputable group of characters would be difficult to find, unless it was on another keelboat. Riverboat crews were notorious for terrorizing the humble little port towns along the Ohio. Wild reveling, drunkenness, and debauchery were expected when one of these crews tied up.

It was inevitable that Parcher sought out a friendship with one of these, a Danny Kinch from the city of New York. Kinch was one or two years younger than Parcher’s twenty, and on his first trip down the Ohio. He was a pock-faced youth with eyes set wide and bad teeth. Like Parcher, he’d run away from poverty to find adventure in the wilderness of western Pennsylvania, finally being drawn to Pittsburgh, where scratching out an existence was possible for a boy of no experience, talent, or moral compass.

Soft bottom prevented the use of the iron-tipped poles, but the Ohio was not so tortuous west of Alexandria, and with the use of their long sweeps, they were at the village of Manchester by late evening. Here there was a solitary tavern where whiskey could be had. Three of the town's less respectable ladies were there to meet the crew, who, in turn, lost no time livening the establishment with fiddle and concertina. Uncomely as they were, the women were kept busy dancing, being groped and, later, offering comfort to those with money.

Parcher and Kinch were soon well lubricated, thanks to one of Parcher's three dollar notes. Somehow Parcher felt compelled to share with Kinch his plan to relieve The Honorable Mr. Gandy of his sack of silver. Kinch had had his bellyful of keelboat work, and agreed to disappear farther downstream together with his new friend after the theft.

Six

Cincinnati, Ohio

Cincinnati was a newly named town—after the Revolutionary War officer's Society of the Cincinnati, and the Roman Statesman Cincinnatus—composed of three villages between the Little Miami River and the Great Miami River to the west. Across, on the southern shore of the Ohio, the Licking River opened to Kentucky. All three tributaries to the Ohio were important avenues for the population of the surrounding area, and Cincinnati was booming with supplies and markets for the settlers.

They tied up in early evening, having made good time with a following wind and the sail rigged. Parcher was sick most of the journey, and was in awe of the crew's ability to function bright and early after a night of serious drinking.

The wharf was crammed with crates, barrels, wagons, horses, mules, and people. Many of the latter were there to meet Baudin's keelboat. The captain was impressed.

"*Dieu*! Six months past I was at this place, and it now must be two times the size."

Parcher had little to do with Gandy since Alexandria, but now needed to put his plan to work. The idea was to escort Gandy to his destination, likely an inn. Somehow he would separate Gandy from his satchel containing the sack of coins, allowing Kinch to steal them and divide at a place they had heard of from the crew's talk. If done right, Gandy would have no way of suspecting Kinch, and Parcher would be guiltless, lamenting the loss.

"Careful, sir," Parcher said as he led the way down the plank to the dock. He was carrying Gandy's portmanteau while the gentleman carried the satchel. After inquiring of the location of the Columbia Inn, they walked a distance up a considerable hill where a newly built inn and tavern sat. Workmen were there constructing a wooden sidewalk. Parcher stole a glance to make sure Kinch had followed.

"I would like to buy your evening meal, since you won't accept payment for your kindnesses, Albert."

"That would do nicely, sir. I appreciate it," Parcher said. "Here, let me take yer satchel while ye attend to lodgin's." To his delight, Gandy acceded.

He set the portmanteau and the satchel near the door to the street, giving a nod to Kinch lurking there. Returning to the desk where Gandy had engaged the proprietor, he shielded the door from the two.

"And now we'd like a meal after a long trip," Gandy said.

"Yes, Mr. Gandy. It's an honor to have someone of your stature staying at the Columbia. I'll have your luggage brought to your room. Take any table in the dining room. I'll attend to your meal, personally."

"I'd like to wash, first, if you don't mind," Gandy said. "Albert, order yourself an ale. I'll be with you soon."

Parcher looked around at the satchel, still draped over the portmanteau. Did Kinch have time to lift the sack of coins? A boy came from the rear of the place to retrieve Gandy's things. Parcher's instinct was to bolt, but no, he would be suspected for sure. He walked in to the tap and ordered an ale.

He was halfway through the ale when Gandy was back in a state of outrage, calling for the proprietor. *Kinch made the snatch!*

"Where is that boy who took my belongings to my room!" he demanded.

The innkeeper was struck dumb.

"Speak up, man!" Gandy was red-faced. "There was a pouch in my satchel holding more than sixty Spanish dollars that is missing!"

Finally, the man stammered, "Billy! No! He's an honest lad, sir."

"I tell you I had that pouch in my satchel when I left the riverboat. I personally carried it here. No one else had it but your boy."

The boy was brought in and accused. He broke down in tears, denying any wrongdoing. The innkeeper again vouched for the boy's honesty, saying he was the lad's own godfather.

The accusations and denials continued with ultimately no conclusion. The proprietor promised to forbear on any charges for the remainder of Gandy's stay if he would not pursue the matter.

"What will you do, Mr. Gandy?"

"I do have other funds, but that was ready money to be used until I settled here. This is a considerable inconvenience."

"Sixty dollars! I shall say so!" *By Christ, he suspects naut!* "I feel terrible about yer loss, sir!"

"Nothing to do about it tonight. I tend to believe the boy. Tomorrow I shall see what manner of law there is in the town, and pursue the matter. For now, I need a meal and a night's sleep."

They dined on brisket and potatoes. Parcher wolfed down his meal, anxious to meet Kinch and his share of the loot.

~ * ~

The constant drizzle early the following morning did little to stem the activity on the Cincinnati wharf. Baudin and his men were making preparations to cast off. Parcher hailed to them to wait.

"Where is Kinch?"

The previous night, Parcher had hurried from the Columbia Hotel to the Green Heron, the tavern he and Kinch agreed on as a meeting place. He unsuccessfully searched the crowded place for a glimpse of Kinch's red knit cap. Panic started in his chest. One by one he looked into the faces of the drinkers, searched the privy behind the establishment. Nothing!

Franticly, he returned to the keelboat where two well-armed crewmen lounged guarding the vessel, their drinking mugs and pipes in hand. They reported no sight of Kinch since leaving the boat earlier that evening. Parcher rushed back to the Green Heron, hoping for Kinch yet to turn up. It was not to be. He waited there until falling asleep, exhausted.

"Your *ami* Kinch has not returned," Baudin called down from his perch on the flat roof. "Or maybe he is no longer your friend, by the look of you."

Parcher looked up and down the length of the wharf for a red cap sighting.

One of the crew was untying the bow line. "He were useless as a pole man anyway."

"Likely he has joined a boat that has gone ahead," Baudin said. "If you are looking for him, I will take you as far as Evansville, where we turn back. It will cost you another three dollar."

Parcher shook his head. He'd spent all but a dollar on drink in Manchester, sure of his impending wealth. He watched the stern line being pulled in, and the keelboat drift out into the current. Neither Baudin nor his crew looked back as he watched them go.

Seven

October1804
Cincinnati

The three toughs shared a flask on the front steps to Bransky's Saloon, one of them in earnest discourse. They appeared to have little in common, save a disdain for hard work. Fletcher, the wiry man in the striped shirt and rodent-like face was a sneak thief and pickpocket. Barton was a thug who specialized in muggings. Passengers, or the lone besotted boatman off the keelboats and barges, were always good prospects. The third had turned to pimping. Actually, he was an assistant to the town pimp, Happy Jack Bransky, picking up a dollar or two by escorting clients to the back room at Bransky's. Later, he might be called into the service of beating up an unhappy client for lack of payment. The affections of the whores were a side benefit. His name was Albert Parcher.

For a while, Parcher schemed for a way to separate Oliver Gandy from the rest of his money, but was never able to devise an adequate plan.

Then, in 1802, the Honorable Mr. Gandy's bid for election was unsuccessful, and the man returned east.

Business was none too good for the three men. The wharf at Cincinnati was a dangerous place at night. Boatmen were the only people wandering about and then mainly in groups. Parcher's pimp was constantly at him for more patrons for the four prostitutes in his employ.

Barton snatched the upturned flask from Fletcher's mouth. He took a long pull, wiped his mouth, and continued with his proposal. "The flatboat what come in today is what I refer to, see?"

Parcher nodded. He'd been down to see it tie up, looking for potential clients. There were four families in the eighty foot barge along with every possession to their names, including two mules.

"They'll be pushin' off tomorrow or the next," Barton continued, "headin' down river, takin' their chances with the Illinois pirates."

Parcher looked at Fletcher. They both knew about the notorious pirates at the place called Cave-In-Rock, ruthless, unafraid to murder—even women and children—in quashing any resistance to their robbing.

"No reason why we don't get 'em first," Barton went on. "There's a place past North Bend I know of where the current pushes the boats against a shoal on the Ohio side. That's when we get 'em."

Barton gazed at the other two. "Are ye with me?"

Parcher didn't wait for Fletcher to answer. "By Christ, yes! I'm sick of bein' a lickspittle for Happy Jack. Been thinkin' of settin' up for myself down in New Orleans. I say we run that boat all the way down there, and sell it off."

"That's what I like to hear!" Fletcher piped up. "Lumber is hard to come by down there. Barge'd fetch a pretty penny. They's good livin' in New Orleens. You think we could take her down there, the three of us?"

Parcher, not knowing a thing about handling a barge, opined, "We take our time we can."

Barton grinned. "Then it's settled. Parcher! Go down there and find out when they expect to set off. We got plans to make."

They finished the whiskey.

~ * ~

Their high vantage was perfect, allowing a line of sight upstream for two hundred yards. Here the river took a sharp left turn. The current carved into the shore, forming a high bank, but immediately after shifted to the other shore. Light flotsam would follow the current downstream, but a gravel shoal tended to snare heavier objects. It was a well-known problem for the clumsy flatboats.

Fifteen minutes passed. Barton glared at Parcher. "I thought you said they was leavin' soon,"

"Keep yer blamed britches on."

Barton gave a shove to Parcher, who retaliated in kind.

"Think I see her," Fletcher said. "Yeah. It's her."

The others stopped their posturing. The huge craft hove into view like a house having lost its foundation in a flood. Long sweeps, fore and aft, were at work keeping the thing mid-stream.

"Let's go!" Barton whispered as if their prey could hear him.

They scrambled down to the shore. Fletcher was armed with two muskets, both primed, and ready to fire. Barton had gotten hold of a pair of dueling pistols, one in hand, the other jammed in his belt. He'd found a pistol and bush knife for Parcher.

To Barton's credit, his plan was well conceived. As expected, the current swept the big boat to the high bank of the Ohio shore. The boat's crew successfully fended off with stout poles, but had a more difficult time with the shoal that loomed ahead. The boat ground to a halt, and the men shifted their attention to the task of pushing off.

"Now!" Barton cried, and Fletcher fired a shot directly into the main structure of the boat. The pole men looked agape. "Off that boat, now—every last one of yer!" He leveled his pistol at an older man, perhaps a leader. Nobody moved.

Barton's pistol exploded, and the man went down. "We'll kill yer all, if yer ain't got no sense!"

That did it. Two of the pole men jumped down, calling for their families to follow. The third hesitated, but followed suit. Fletcher had reloaded and appeared from his place in the shore bushes, brandishing both weapons.

Crying children were being handed down from the grounded boat, mothers and siblings following.

Parcher was menacing the men with his bush knife, then spied a girl of about fourteen, her thin dress exposing the beginnings of maturity. He seized her, holding the big bush knife to her throat, his other hand busy at exploring her body. The others from the flatboat stood by, helpless.

"No time for that!" Barton yelled.

"I think we take this one with us!" Parcher laughed.

Barton got busy herding the men into a manageable group. Then,

'Crack!'

Parcher looked up to where the sound came from; saw a puff of smoke from the vantage place where they'd been, then down to where Fletcher lay face down in the shallow water of the shoal.

One of the men took advantage of Barton's distracted attention to grab his pistol arm. The two others wrestled him down.

Parcher panicked. He dropped the knife and splashed his way toward the shore. Another shot rang from the vantage point and chips of wood from a washed-up tree stump stung his face. From behind he heard another gunshot, but did not look back.

The thick brush of the shore soon enveloped him, but he kept scrambling up the steep bank and farther into the woods. Now came sounds of men's voices, many of them. *Who are they*? One thing for sure, he couldn't stay there. He decided his best chance was to make it back to town, as if he'd never left. Happy Jack would vouch for his being there all morning—he hoped.

~ * ~

He sat alone at a darkened corner table near the back room where Happy Jack Bransky kept two of his girls. Jack had said "maybe" when asked for an alibi, but Parcher was pretty sure Jack didn't want to train a new apprentice. Fortunately he'd found a new client for Tillie, one of Jack's girls in the shack she shared with another of the stable. Jack was in a good mood.

Parcher sipped at the horse piss Bransky's Saloon called beer. Even the good brews, by the time they made an August trip down as far as Cincinnati, were spoiled.

Four men—boys, rather—in uniforms of the Ohio Militia tumbled into the place. The previous year, a mandatory militia had been established in the new state of Ohio. All able-bodied men between the ages of eighteen and forty-five were required to serve. So far, Parcher had succeeded in avoiding service.

The four were young privates, full of conversation, and soon full of beer. It wasn't long before Parcher was aware they were talking about the attempted piracy this morning.

"...patched up and on their way," one was saying.

"Won't be pirating anymore, 'less it's in Hades."

"Cockchafers deserved it. Clean shot on the one, boaters got the other with his own gun!" Laughter.

"Corporal Sauer got a good look at the pot licker that skipped. Says he'll not get far 'less he's got a boat somewhere."

"I'd like to get that ass wipe!" said a towheaded boy.

"Yeah, do that, General!" More laughter.

Parcher abandoned his beer, and left by the rear door.

Eight

The smell and feel of autumn was in the trees as he walked. The road was newly built, largely replacing the twin Miami Rivers as a conduit north from Cincinnati. For the past four hours, Parcher had been on it at a quick march.

He'd panicked at the news about being seen by the militia soldier. Corporal something, Sour, it was. Odd name. No, he didn't have a boat. It was simply providence this road north was put in—all the way to the settlement of Dayton, some forty miles, he'd heard.

The lengthening shadows brought with them a chill in the air. He began to look for shelter for the night. Maybe a shed or barn in one of the new farms in this valley between the two rivers. Anything would be luxury compared to that shithole they called a jail back in Cincinnati.

~ * ~

The carriage bumped along a section of the road that had not yet been groomed, the wheel ruts dictating where two well-cared-for horses led an equally maintained rig.

Earlier, Parcher was rudely awakened by a farmer who, rising at dawn to milk his two cows, found him sound asleep. A pitchfork was enough incentive for Parcher to hit the road again.

Around mid-morning, the carriage returning from Cincinnati caught up with him. Parcher turned on the charm.

"Good day to ye, sir!"

The driver looked down from his perch, a serious looking sort, not in the clothes of a rural, but a businessman. "And where might you be heading on the Mad River Road?"

"Lookin' for work, I am, sir."

The man stared down at Parcher, his mouth pursed in doubt. "Should be plenty jobs back in town. Why trek up here?"

Parcher was thinking hard. "Well…ya see…" Then a thought. "It's all the vice and ungodliness there. I can't abide it, and aim to be free of it."

"You're a man of faith, then?" The pursed mouth softened.

"I am, sir, I surely am."

"I can take you as far as Franklin."

Parcher's first thought was of returning to Franklinton, but did not hesitate to climb up on the bench. "Name's…Goggins, William Goggins. *Franklinton*, you say?"

"John Shenk," the man said, did not offer a hand. "No, just *Franklin.*" He shook the reins, and the carriage lurched forward.

Shenk, it turned out, was the postmaster of Franklin, Ohio. He was returning from Cincinnati where he had picked up the week's mail from back east. Fortunately for Parcher, Shenk was a man of few words. Parcher had spent his early years in Baltimore. His limited experience with organized religion was through the Roman Catholic Church.

Franklin was not far from where Shenk had stopped. They soon came to a place where a general store stood across the road from a blacksmith shop. Another road trailed east and west forming four corners.

"Here we are," Shenk said, halting the horses in front of the store.

To Parcher's surprise, Shenk asked, "Have you nothing yet to eat this morning?

Parcher admitted he had not, and was promptly bid to come through to the rear of the store/post office. There, a woman was removing baked bread from a woodstove. The aroma was achingly delicious.

"This here is William. Could do with a bit of food."

Patience Shenk was her husband's opposite. Plump and pert in her starched house cap, she wasted no time engaging Parcher in conversation. As she pulled food from the pantry, her questions were innocent, but incessant, keeping Parcher busy making up one lie after another.

"And, you have no work, poor man," she lamented.

"No ma'am. I just couldn't face another day in that den of iniquity on the Ohio." He had heard the term during his brief encounter with the catechism.

"John!" she called to her husband who was sorting mail. He poked his head around the corner. "The new meeting house in Dayton needs a sexton."

John Shenk returned to his work with no comment.

"You're a big strapping lad…perfect for the job. Now sit down there while I feed you something."

Something turned out to be meat stew and a thick slice of the still warm bread. Parcher wolfed it down.

"This here sexton…" Parcher tapped his spoon in thought. "What might that be akin to?"

"Why you'd be in charge, so to speak, of the grounds, cemetery, and building."

He thought about that. *In charge.* There might some opportunities to line the pockets of a man "in charge."

"Where is this here meeting house?"

"Just this side of Dayton—no more'n nine miles up Mad River Road."

~ * ~

"You say John Shenk recommended you?" Pastor Eli Clemmons was a balding man of perhaps forty-five, his paunch protruding over his belt. He was obvious in his inspection of the rough looking man standing in the door of his newly-erected parsonage.

"Yesser." Parcher repeated his lie. In fact, Shenk had tried to dissuade his garrulous wife from going on about the position at the Dayton church.

The preacher nodded appreciatively. He was buying it. Mr. Shenk must have some influence here.

"Let me tell you what needs doing here, and you can tell me if it suits you." Clemmons grabbed his hat from a peg by the door, and led the way to the church.

There was much to do. Weeds were grown up around the building. Construction trash lay about. Inside, newly glazed windows were, as yet, unwashed. The pews, likely salvaged, were old and in need of attention. They looked out of place in the otherwise unfinished surroundings.

Clemmons showed Parcher the cellar where scythes for the weeds and other tools were kept. A corner was set aside for a cot, desk and washstand.

"Six dollars a month. I'll be willing to try you," the preacher said.

Parcher thought about his options. For certain, he could not return to Cincinnati, at least for a while. This was as good a hiding spot as any, plus he'd be paid!

"I'll take the Job."

~ * ~

March 1805
Dayton

The crocus had punched through the thin blanket of new snow, presenting its tiny purple bud to the world. Parcher paused for a moment from clearing the steps of the parsonage to study the flower. The snow reflected the sun, blindingly white, in this first cloudless day in weeks. The endless winter was finally giving up. It was time to make his move, and put his plan into action.

The five months here seemed like five years, and the winter had been a hard one. He had no stomach for footing it across Ohio in knee-deep snow. Once, at Christmastime, he'd almost been booted out of his job and lodgings.

At the congregation's yearly celebration, there was dancing—dancing and apple cider, a combination that encouraged a greater measure of familiarity among the parishioners than normal.

It was months since he'd held a woman, and the cider didn't help matters. Then that wife of Benjamin Carter asked him to dance one of those things where you swing your partner, and it felt real good. She seemed to like it, too. His hand just naturally dropped down to catch a feel. *Well, you'd have thought I'd taken her bloody maidenhead!* The bitch of a woman started screaming, and wouldn't stop! The music ceased and everyone stared at Parcher, including Benjamin Carter, a man half his size.

It was some very fast talking and apologizing that didn't have him out and on his way to who knew where in the dead of a winter night. Still, the attitude of the neighbors, especially Pastor Clemmons, was never the same. He'd kept his head down and done his chores, intent on making it through to traveling weather.

One of the first things Parcher had noticed about the meeting house was the lack of an organ, or similar instrument. Hymns were led without accompaniment by a member of the group. He'd asked the pastor about it, and was told there was a fund for that very thing. They wanted a good instrument that would require a sizeable investment which was being collected and held by the congregation's treasurer, Mr. John Shenk.

Every Sunday, Parcher watched them make a separate offering which was given to Shenk. He would carry a strongbox to and from the service. It was said the box was placed in the postmaster's safe. The practice had been going on for more than a year.

With real money, Parcher thought, he could live big in some place like Philadelphia or New York City. He'd had enough of frontier life. Maybe New Orleans, after all. It didn't matter.

Nine

Andy

She rushed to douse the two boiled eggs under the cold tap at the same instant the kitchen wall phone demanded attention.

"Damn!" She'd had maybe four calls in the three weeks there. *Now?* "Can you hold for just a sec?" She set the phone on the counter, and salvaged her breakfast.

"Sorry about that," she said into the receiver after the eggs were submerged.

"Andy, it's Roger Van Bourne. I heard you're back. For how long?"

Staff Sergeant Roger Van Bourne was the Commander at the O.P.P. detachment in Thessalon, about forty minutes east of St. Joseph I. Two years ago she had worked closely with him in uncovering the pharmaceutical smuggling operation in Ontario. It had its major transfer point right here on the island. One of his own men, a sergeant, had been implicated.

"I don't really know, Roger. I suppose it was Bert Wheatley who told you I was back on the Island."

"It was." He paused. "Andy…do you think there's a possibility of your returning permanently?"

"As I said…" She stopped short. "Why do you ask?"

The line was silent for a moment. "Ever think about working for the O.P.P.?"

That threw her. The question was from far left field. "O.P.P.," she stammered. "In what capacity?"

"Why don't you come on in and talk about it?"

"Roger! What's the job?"

"They're looking to fill a hole in investigations at the Sault Detachment."

She thought for a moment. "That guy Arnold something…'

"Terry. Arnold Terry." He finished her thought. "Yes, you'd be working with him."

Andy remembered the man from her telephone conversations only. She'd collaborated with him on the pharmaceutical smuggling case, and he'd been difficult, miffed over having to deal with her, the intruder from Windsor. Still, she had no doubt he was good at his job.

"Is it even done?" she asked. "I mean bringing someone in from the outside?"

VanBourne sounded confident. "At your level, it is."

"Wow. Let me think about this, Roger."

"Why don't you give us a visit? We can have lunch and talk more. Is Monday okay?"

~ * ~

Stacey showed up the following afternoon with two husky boys. Andy recognized Ronnie, who had worked with Grant to build the wraparound porch that had transformed her parents' farmhouse. The other boy was Darryl, his friend from the mainland. To call them "boys" was a stretch. They were as tall as Grant's six feet-two, and both well built.

After getting their instructions to dismantle the barn as carefully as possible so as to retain the lumber's value, they commenced to make short work of the project.

Andy had cleared out the largest pieces inside, most of which was immediately near the double door. But when the siding was removed, there was a considerable amount of rusted junk on the dirt floor visible through the exposed studs and joists.

What was left of the roof was broken down and dumped in Grant's F-450 Crew Cab pickup. Soon, the rest of the frame came down with a crash. By 4:00 p.m., all that was visible was a square of boulders delineating the building's foundation, and an embarrassing accumulation of countless years. Andy reasoned her father had given up using the barn for anything but a trash heap.

When Grant and the boys were off to the dump with the non-salvageable wood and roofing, Andy gave the interior of the foundation a closer look. An old and rotting plowing harness and horseshoes, for heaven's sake!—*I've never seen a horse on the property. Certainly Dad hadn't used one. The old tractor I sold after his death was the only plowing power this farm had known in my lifetime*—two oil lamps, a wash boiler—*I could salvage that for the copper alone*—the wringer for a laundry tub, a cracked grinding wheel, the collection seemed endless. It would take another day to sort this mess out.

~ * ~

The cold front that brought last week's rain brought the temperature back down to the realm of fleece and windbreakers. This first day of August felt like April. It was not a day she felt like mucking about outdoors, but Lila Knowles had called asking to see the foundation, and Andy wanted to clear out all that junk first. She steeled herself, and began to sort the mess out.

At first the task seemed impossible, but bit by bit she started to make progress. She used the triage method to divide the stuff into: trash for the dump, trash that might be someone else's treasure, and things she wanted to keep.

Among the latter was a pair of size-two figure skates she recognized as her own. She'd outgrown them into a series of hockey skates that ultimately provided her with a full athletic scholarship to the University of Toronto.

She'd accepted…a decision which, those many years ago, caused the breakup with Grant Stacey and her subsequent brief marriage to Tyler Adkins, who turned out to be an abusive narcissist. The man was still contacting her and her son after all these years, boasting about his life and making impossible promises to Tim. Before she allowed her mind to drift back to those anguished days, she blinked the thoughts away. Too many times she'd dwelled on the *what-ifs?* to no good outcome.

By 1:00 p.m. she had the area cleared out down to the dirt floor. It was time to get some lunch and a hot shower.

~ * ~

She was showered and cozy in sweats and her favorite fur-lined slippers. The minced ham on English muffin sufficed for lunch and the coffee tasted perfect for a change. She curled up on the love seat in the front room, hoping Lila wouldn't show up.

As if the thought were a trigger for the event, the crunch of tires on gravel announced company. The car door slammed twice suggesting multiple visitors. Sure enough, up the front steps came Lila Knowles and a bespectacled, small-framed man wearing a floppy wide-brimmed hat. Andy greeted them with an open door before the knock came.

"Afternoon," she said, holding up her coffee mug. "There's a fresh pot in the kitchen, if you like."

"Oh, I truly would!" Lila said. "This is Willard Tremblay."

They exchanged niceties, and followed Andy into the kitchen where she poured two more mugs.

"Are you with Algoma Heritage, too, Mr. Tremblay?"

The man had to look up into Andy's five feet-nine inches. "No. I'm from Ottawa, just passing through. Lila and I know each other from McGill. She asked me to come along. I hope you don't mind."

Before Andy could reply, Lila Knowles said, "Buck is a staff archeologist with Parks Canada in Gatineau."

Buck? Andy could not imagine a more unlikely appellation for this man. She assured them she had no problem with the added interest in her rocks. "I'm afraid it's not much to see. We tore the structure down this past weekend."

Tremblay peeked out the kitchen window at the square of boulders. "Well, Lila has a good sense for these matters, and I'm here, so we might as well take a look."

They finished the coffee and, once again, Andy donned her boots and jacket, leading the way outside. Tremblay walked the perimeter while Lila and Andy watched in silence. The wind had picked up, and the man held fast to his floppy hat as he returned.

"Have you had a fire?" he asked, pointing to the blackened stones.

"Not in the last forty-five years I've been alive, nor before that, as much as I know."

"Have you a spade?" He looked back toward the house.

"Why…yes. In fact, I just salvaged one from the old barn.

Andy walked around the corner of the house where she'd stacked her morning's work, returning with a rusty, wood-handled spade.

They followed Tremblay to the far corner of the stone square where he began to shovel sod, then dirt away from the stones. After about six inches of exposed boulders, he motioned for the women to come closer.

"First, I'd say the mortar looks really old. Second, the stones are blackened well below the current ground level. I'm sure this foundation is very, very old.

He continued to dig until the boulders were no longer charred—another few inches.

"How far down do they go?" Andy asked.

"Let's find out, Buck," Lila said.

After another foot or more of uncharred foundation was exposed, Tremblay stepped back, stroking his chin.

"What…?" Andy looked back and forth from the hole to him.

"I'm not sure." He stepped over the foundation to the inside of the square, and began digging directly opposite. The same pattern of charred foundation about nine inches below the surface, then a lighter color of rock until he stopped digging, giving Lila a curious look.

"Buck?" she said.

"I don't know. I hit something solid!"

Ten

Nettie

April 1807
Montreal

The candlelight tinged the child's blond curls to an angelic gold, a halo-like effect. Nettie lingered over the sleeping form, still amazed after five years by the mere fact of her being.

A last tuck of the satin-edged blanket, and Nettie took the candle into the sitting room where she found the book she'd been reading for the second time. It looked to be another night of retiring alone, an occurrence that was happening more frequently.

At first she wondered if it was the sign of an infidelity, but she had come to find out he was actually staying late at his office, sometimes returning after dinner. Recently, at a dinner given by the McTavish family for the employees, William McGillivray approached her asking discreetly if something was wrong "at home." She was mortified by the brash question, but McGillivray related to her Thomas' late, but unnecessary, hours at work.

"We've had nothing in progress that would require such effort," he'd said.

Nettie assured him Thomas was simply enthusiastic about his career, and only thinking of the best interests of The North West Company.

Thomas' increasing disinterest in the marriage bed was now, in a sense, even more troubling. She might be able to view an affair with another woman as a temporary bump in their lives. To not have a reason for his aversion to their intimacy suggested a permanent sentence of celibacy.

Nettie tried to read, but the words became blurred. She laid the book in her lap, scolding herself for such self-pity, being brought up to be grateful of the things she had been blessed with. Certainly Carrie, sleeping in the next room, a husband with a career, good health. No, she would shut out the mental images of his irritability, the signals of his disaffection toward her and lately, Carrie.

Nettie put away her book, stood holding the candelabra, surveying the well-furnished quarters of Mademoiselle Broussard's rooming house. They'd been fortunate the company had found such a decent place for them. The other guests were all of good quality, the meals more than acceptable. Yes, she could be grateful if she worked at it.

She left a single candle burning for Thomas, went into their bedroom to sleep and face another day.

~ * ~

Mademoiselle Yvonne Broussard was a third generation Quebecois. Her grandfather had been a successful trapper, setting his son up as an independent trader. Paul Broussard had married an Ojibwa girl. Together they had just one child fifty-eight years earlier whom they named Yvonne, and returned to Montreal to build a fine house in order to raise the girl. After the death of her parents, Yvonne sold her interest in the trading company to the Hudson Bay Company. She never married.

Yvonne Broussard loved people and lively conversation. Unfortunately, she was not quite accepted in Montreal society in that she was of mixed heritage, or as the French Canadians' termed, *Métis.* She took the snub in stride, opening her large home to Montreal lodgers, catering to the most interesting and diverse clientele she could assemble. It was only as a favor to the McTavish family that she accepted the young couple with their infant child in tow.

Evening meals at Mademoiselle Broussard's were a lively event. Guests were comprised of transient dignitaries, some eccentric local but fascinating regulars…and the Gibsons. The precocious little Carrie ate in the kitchen with Broussard's adoring staff, while the adults dined and delved into the issues of the day, both political and commercial.

In this environment, Nettie flourished. She was naturally outgoing. This combined with an inquisitive mind, and she was soon the belle of the dinner table.

Thomas was not enthusiastic about her popularity. At the table, he would offer terse replies to polite requests for his opinion of a comment, but little more. Lately, he might miss dinner altogether, having a small something catered to his office instead.

Two years earlier, Simon McTavish had died on a warm July afternoon. A week later, his will was read with a major condition calling for his nephew, William McGillivray, to succeed him. Thomas Gibson expected to move into the vacated spot held by William. It wasn't to be.

Thomas came home that day visibly upset, but it took Nettie a while to drag the news out of him.

"He said I was needed where I was," Thomas said after considerable prodding.

"Well, that's good!" Nettie said. "They value your work."

He exploded. "Damn! Don't be so naive!"

Nettie stiffened, unaccustomed to the profanity. "Did you not ask why you were not promoted?"

"Of course," he muttered.

She waited, knowing he would tell her.

"The fool said I lacked vision. Lacked vision! Damn that man! I put his accounts in order. No telling where the company would be had I not."

She listened as he went on with a litany of slights and perceived abuses he'd withstood with no appreciation for his many contributions.

This spring morning, Nettie had just returned from a stroll with Carrie. It was a brisk April day with winter still in the air, but the sun was already high in the cloudless sky. She was amazed to find Thomas in the parlor, speaking with Mademoiselle Broussard. He was glowing.

"Thomas!" She removed her shawl. Carrie ran into the kitchen for her morning treat.

"Annette! I have wonderful news!"

Mademoiselle Broussard kissed Nettie's cheek and quietly retired.

"Oh, Thomas! What?"

"I have been given the responsibility for the reorganization of one of our most important outposts! Our whole family is being sent."

The word "outpost" was not lost on Nettie. "Is this a promotion?"

"Oh, yes! I receive my present salary, plus a percentage of the profits there!"

"And what will be your position?"

"Um…I will be a…consultant at first. I am told if improvements are seen, then…"

She searched his face looking for clarity. "Then…?"

"For God's sake, Annette! Must you throw a pall over my good fortune? This is my chance to show those ba—those people what I can do."

"I am happy for you, Thomas. Where is this place?"

He calmed down. “Upper Canada, near the Michigan Territory. The duration could be for at least a year or two.”

Nettie, in her solitary, had had time to study a little of the North American geography, and had a good idea of the remoteness of Upper Canada. The “upper” connotation stemming from “upstream” rather than “up north.”

“Is this trading center, by any chance, Michilimackinac?”

“No, No! Nothing so remote. It is the Sault Ste. Marie post.”

Nettie looked around at her surroundings—the carpeted and draped rooms, the brocaded chairs, the crystal chandelier of the entry, the elegant pianoforte in the parlor—as if for the last time.

“And what of Carrie?”

“Caroline could stay here in boarding school. That might be for the best.” There was a lack of conviction in his voice.

“No! I will not be separated from our daughter!”

Thomas seemed to sense Nettie’s determination. “But the journey.”

“I know well what is entailed in such a journey. I won’t leave my daughter alone. I’ll school her myself.”

“Have it your way, then. If the girl comes to harm, it will be on you.”

Nettie knew he had to agree. They could not afford the cost of a truly good private school in Montreal. Besides, the best were run by nuns, and

Thomas' family were vehement anti-papists, going back to Mary of Scotland.

"When do we go?" she asked.

"McGillivray is arranging our passage on the next voyage west. I understand it will be within a week's time."

Eleven

Mademoiselle Broussard's elegant library included maps of North America, some quite recent. Nettie was fascinated by the maps, and on her solitary evenings would pore over them. Since learning of Thomas' new posting, her interest was rekindled.

The maps now looked more foreboding when viewed from the aspect of traveling with their five-year-old child. What route will we take? She'd heard about a way west on the Ottawa River. Another was a route up the St. Lawrence, but that did not connect well with upper Lake Huron.

The afternoon following Thomas' announcement, he arrived home again, this time in the company of William McGillivray. He was a handsome man of imposing stature. Reddish-brown hair and mutton chops framed a prominent nose. Nettie was having tea with Yvonne Broussard, and invited the men to join them.

"Thank you, no, Mrs. Gibson," McGillivray said. "In fact, I have come to see you about your coming trip, for I know it will be an arduous one for you. There are some things you need to know." Mademoiselle Broussard again excused herself, but McGillivray gallantly dissuaded her, stating there was nothing private about his visit.

"Please go on, sir." Nettie folded her hands in anticipation.

"Yes—then you may have learned from your husband that the North West Company competes by getting the best quality furs by trading in the Athabasca."

"Athabasca?"

"This is the region far to the west of the great Superior Lake. The fur pelts, especially beaver, are being overharvested. This requires us to venture far afield."

She waited for him to make his point, lifting her brow.

"Our company employs a class of men to transport our goods by canoe. They are the Voyageurs of whom I trust you have heard."

Nettie indicated she had.

"It is with these men your family will be traveling. They are a rough lot, and I imagine you will be concerned. The reason for my visit today is two-fold. I want to assure you that your family could not be more secure than to travel with these men. They are rude in both appearance and demeanor, but they are completely trustworthy. You have nothing to fear from them."

Nettie relaxed. "You said two things."

"I need to personally impress upon you the importance of the restrictions you must agree to, regarding what you bring with you."

She looked to Thomas, who merely blinked and turned his attention to his employer.

"Over the course of your journey, several portages will be necessary. Cargo is limited to what a man can carry, sometimes over several miles. I must insist your family items be limited to two chests not exceeding ninety pounds each."

The Gibsons had arrived in Montreal with two large wardrobes and a chest. Over the past five years they'd accumulated a few pieces of furniture and accessories.

"If you wish," Yvonne Broussard said, "you can store what you cannot take with you."

Nettie was still dealing with a word McGillivray had used—"canoe." She hadn't had time to process the obvious fact that they necessarily would be traveling in such a rudimentary way.

McGillivray stood, preparing to leave. "I will personally be here for you with my carriage on the day after tomorrow morning to accompany you to Lachine, where your voyage begins.

He bade the ladies 'Good Day,' and told Thomas to spend the meantime with his family in preparation for the journey west.

~ * ~

The carriage, drawn by two matched horses, swayed gently over the newly groomed road to Lachine. Two pine chests, identical in size, were strapped securely to the rear, having been supplied to the Gibsons for the trip.

The nine mile ride passed quickly. McGillivray was charmed by the precocious Caroline, who was holding a stuffed rabbit. It was a gift from Mademoiselle Broussard, and she'd named him "Mr. B." She kept them all occupied with her commentary on the passing scenery.

They came to a halt next to a fine stone building The North West Company had recently erected to warehouse their goods. Lachine was the westernmost spot on the St. Lawrence where a large ship could navigate, due to the rapids there.

Above the rapids was a group of perhaps a dozen men loading bundles and chests into a large canoe. One of them was approaching the carriage as the Gibsons and McGillivray were dismounting.

Nettie was intrigued by this man. He was dressed in a loose-fitting, long sleeved shirt over deerskin breeches with sashes at both knees. His shoulder length, dark hair was crowned with a loose fitting cloth cap that matched the scarlet of his waist sash. His shoes looked to be no more than beaded leather slippers. She felt herself blush as she lingered on his dark, handsome face.

"Monsieur McGillivray! *Bonjour! Vous êtes en avance."*

"No reason to be late, Legère. I've delivered your passengers, Mr. and Mrs. Gibson with their young daughter."

McGillivray introduced the man as Martin Legère, who wordlessly removed the two chests, strapped them together, and hoisted them on his back as if they did not weigh their almost one hundred-eighty pounds. They watched as he carried them to the canoe to be loaded.

"And now, my friends, it is time for me to wish you a safe and pleasant journey. Mr. Gibson—Thomas—I know you will find Sault Ste. Marie a challenge worthy of your skills. I look forward to your reports. Good luck."

He gave Carrie a pat on the head, tipped his hat to Nettie, and climbed into his carriage. With a knock of his stick on the roof, the carriage was away.

Nettie took Carrie by the hand. "Come, dear. Let us find what fun it will be to take a long boat ride on the river!"

Twelve

The only positive thing Nettie could see about the canoe was its considerable size. McGillivray had said thirty-six feet…somehow it seemed larger up close. The crew appeared to have finished loading and securing the cargo and was preparing to board. All the men were dressed much the same as the man called Legère.

She felt a little foolish in her long dress, cape, and stylish wide-brimmed hat. Thomas, in his knee breeches and hose, cutaway coat, stock, and tall hat looked equally ill-prepared for weeks on end in an open boat.

"Sir, you may seat your family in front of those pieces there." Legère pointed to a thwart running the six foot width of the canoe. Two large bundles were situated behind, acting as a back rest. He nimbly boarded, holding his hand out for Nettie, and lifted Carrie into her place. Thomas followed

Nettie felt awkward, the three of them there, all in a row, as the Voyageurs did their work. There were twelve of them, all holding a long paddle.

Legère was looking their way, smiling. He reached into a pouch he had slung at his side, retrieving something that looked like a long spoon or ladle.

"This is for the little girl, no?" He passed it down to Carrie.

It was a miniature paddle, the shaft beautifully carved in the shape of a slender beaver with exaggerated front teeth. The blade was fashioned to look like the animal's tail. Carrie was delighted.

He said to Thomas, "We travel first to Fort York."

"Fort York?" Neither he nor Nettie had heard of the place.

"It is upstream from here on Lake Ontario." Lake Ontario? Nettie was confused. "Then we will not travel the Ottawa River? I have heard it is the way west."

Legère grinned. "Ah *oui*, but that way is too difficult for our passengers, I fear. There are too many portages on that route for such a lady. This way is longer, but more comfortable for our guests, I believe. Do not worry. You will have your share of portages and other hardships on this route."

Thomas asked, "How long will it take for us to arrive at this fort?"

Legère pulled a face. "Mmm…maybe ten days, maybe more, depending on the weather." He said no more, returning to the task of pushing off.

The Voyageurs positioned themselves five paddlers to a side, with a man each at prow and stern. Nettie was busy looking at the intricate carving of the beaver-paddle in Carrie's hand before she noticed they were away. The light boat pulsed forward with the synchronized rhythm of the men's paddles. They immediately took up a song that matched their strokes. The shoreline flew by.

Now the reality of it all dawned on her. What on earth have I been drawn into?

~ * ~

The sun dazzled the river as it began to descend. The canoe surged ahead as if trying to race it to the horizon. Nettie had spent the day between observing the marvelous diversity on the banks of the St. Lawrence, and studying the strange men in her company. Her earlier assessment of their similarity of appearance was tempered by this inspection. She began to distinguish one from the other by interesting details.

Legère, standing at the prow with his long paddle, wore a beaded leather sash. Others wore woven sashes of worsted fabric, calico, or even silk. His red toque was knitted with a small knob at the tip which flopped down over one ear. Two of the others' hats were red, the rest blue, some knitted, some of felt, but all of the same shape.

The men decorated their apparel in some way. Most wore a large feather, either on the toque or shirt. All had a leather bag of tobacco hung from a leather thong from their necks. A pipe fashioned from clay or, perhaps, soapstone was looped through the pouch.

Their breeches appeared to be identical, possibly supplied to them by The North West Company. They were often further secured with sashes at the knees. But the shoes were unique to each Voyageur. Some wore moccasins that tied above the ankle. Other styles were not much more than slippers. Two of the men had cobbled shoes.

The canoe traveled rapidly. The coordinated, powerful paddle strokes were at an amazing pace of more than fifty per minute, kept on time by the tempo of the songs that were almost constant. Every hour the men would paddle to shore for a short rest. Out would come the pipes for a few minutes, then back to the relentless paddling.

Carrie showed the promise of being a good traveler. All day she had been engrossed with the abundance of flora and fauna along the shore and in the water. Ducks of all kinds, many with their first spring broods, skittered over the river's surface away from the canoe's prow. Mink and otter swam and patrolled the banks.

All the while, Thomas sat between wife and daughter, saying little.

"Le rivage, sur du côtė nord," Legère called. The canoe turned toward the north bank of the river where a natural clearing waited.

"It is still quite early to stop," Thomas said, loud enough for all to hear.

A voice from the rear responded. "It will be dark soon enough, sir. You will see." It was a giant of a man at the stern. Severe native features lined his face. Where Legère at the prow was called the Avant, his counterpart at the stern was the Gouvernail. His name was Henri, they'd learned, and would come to find out a full-blooded Cree Indian from the Athabasca territory.

Legère stowed his paddle, trading it for a long, steel-tipped "setting pole" to fend off the rocky shore. Finding a spot to land by the grassy clearing, he jumped out and guided the canoe up the bank. Others helped the Gibsons ashore.

Quickly, the entire cargo was unloaded and covered with an oiled canvas. The canoe was hauled ashore, and turned on its side. Another large canvas was rigged over the canoe forming a cozy windbreak for sleeping.

Thomas Gibson looked dubious. "Is that our accommodation for the night?"

Legère smiled. "For us, it is. Your family will be there." He motioned to where a tent was being erected.

"And where do we…" Gibson started

Legère was diplomatic. "Monsieur Gibson, you will have to use the facilities the wilderness provides. We will do our best to be sensitive to your privacy, especially to your wife and daughter. But it will be many days we are together. There may be times when your sensibilities are…challenged."

Nettie stifled a grin. She'd never even seen Thomas out of his nightshirt, despite his own desire to explore every inch of her body since the second night of their marriage.

She turned her attention to setting up the tent for the night. Carrie had already found it, and had a corner all staked out for herself and Mr. B.

The early spring night soon grew colder. They were drawn to the fire the Voyageurs had made. Miraculously, a fiddle appeared in the hands of Henri, the Cree Indian. A tune they called *M'en Revenant de la Jolie Rochelle* was struck, and the men were soon singing. They ate salted pork and sea biscuit for dinner. Any ocean sailor would have disdained the fare, but tonight, it was delicious.

Thirteen

Nettie was in a canoe paddling against a strong current to no avail. The voice of Legère was exhorting her to work harder. "*Madame* Gibson, *Monsieur* Gibson!" It took her some time to realize she was in a canvas tent, not a canoe.

"*Monsieur* Gibson!"

"Yes?" Nettie answered. Thomas coughed.

"We leave in less than one half hour." It was Legère.

"Yes, thank you."

Thomas rolled over on the thin mattress. "It can't be morning."

"I don't believe it is." She busied herself feeling around in the darkened tent for items to gather up.

Last night, after only a few songs, she was surprised to see the men begin to prepare for sleep. She took Carrie a short distance into the trees to relieve herself. "There is no need to empty the chamber pot!" They giggled at the joke. The child thought this adventure to be great fun. They settled in the tent and Carrie was immediately sound asleep.

Nettie and Thomas talked for a while; she about the exciting day just spent, he of anticipating his new duties in Sault Ste. Marie. “By Jove, my dear, I will make a success of this new trust in my abilities!” Soon, they too were overcome by sleep.

They were barely out of the tent than two of the men had it rolled up and stowed in the canoe.

“Is there no fire?” Thomas asked no one in particular.

“*Dieu, non. Nous allons maintenant*.”

“He says, ‘We’re leaving right away,’” Nettie translated. It was the fashion for a young lady of breeding to have, at least, some French. Nettie was grateful her tutor had been a stickler, and that her mother was able to hold a decent conversation as well.

There was nothing to do but climb into the canoe again, this time in pitch darkness.

“What time is it, then?”

“Almost three on a fine morning,” Legère said from his perch on the bow.

Out on the river, the outline of their course could be discerned. There was no moon, but the clear sky displayed the stars in clear contrast to the tree line

Soon the singing recommenced. The songs were of the same tempo, but more subdued, as if in respect for the quiet and beauty of the hour. The first bird had not yet announced itself to the day. Carrie slept, head resting on her mother’s lap.

The morning arrived with the sun at their backs. The late April chill gave way to warmth. The forest came to life. A fish jumped. Nettie was enthralled by it all.

This day was much like the one before, except they stopped for a brief breakfast ashore around eight. Then off again for an hour at a time, fifty to sixty strokes per minute, Thomas verifying it by his pocket watch. The rest stops were called “pipes,” since the Voyageurs invariably would use the time to relight theirs. In fact, distances were often measured in the number of pipes necessary for a leg.

The next four days were identical—ashore well before dark, sleeping soon after, then up by two or three in the morning in order to get twelve or fourteen hours on the river.

On the sixth day, their departure was delayed. Overcast sky made navigation in the dark too difficult. They waited for the pre-dawn light just after 5 a.m.

Around ten that morning, it began to rain. Legère called a halt while a shelter was rigged for the passengers. Still, they were not completely protected. Nettie’s clothes were becoming sodden. It was all she could do to keep Carrie dry. She saw Thomas was miserable, his woolen frock and linen shirt no match for the conditions. It began to rain harder, but the Voyageurs paddled on.

~ * ~

The sun had returned for two days by the time the river began to widen considerably. Occasional signs of civilization, a homestead, a plowed field, began to show along the shore.

"We must be getting close to Fort York," Nettie thought aloud.

"No, *Madame*," Henri said from the rear. "We are but little more than half way. What you see are farms, it is true, but only because there is a road now from York, the Dundas Street."

The St. Lawrence opened onto an immense lake she knew was Lac Ontario, but was completely unprepared for the experience. It was an ocean! Out here on the open water, the wind became a greater factor, today blowing from directly ahead.

Time enough had passed for clothes to be laid out to dry on shore and in progress. Nettie was in a new dress of a simple cut. One of the men loaned her a pair of moccasins—that surprisingly fit—and made a gift of a kerchief to use as a hat. He taught her how to tie and wear it the way the Voyageurs did. She joked about becoming quite the frontierswoman.

It was clear that the men's affection for her was growing. They seemed to respect her for never complaining about the hardships of the wild. Carrie, by now, was the darling of the canoe for many of the same reasons. She never whined or grumbled, happy to play games with her mother, or make up stories with her two friends, the stuffed bunny Mr. B, and the beaver/paddle she'd named Becky.

Over the span of their journey, Martin Legère remained aloof. This is not to say he was unfriendly or unhelpful to the Gibsons. Reserved might be a more apt word, perhaps to set an example of respect for a company executive and his family for the other men.

Nettie found herself fascinated by this man McGillivray called Métis, or French-Indian. *Where is he going after delivering us to Thomas' new posting? Does he have a wife out there in the western wilderness like the ones the others spoke of?* Would she even see him again? This last question alarmed her. *Why should I care?* Still, she could not take her eyes off the handsome, self-possessed man.

After eleven days and four hundred miles, they arrived at York. The "fort" consisted of a lone blockhouse unprotected by any perimeter of armed towers or the like. It stood alone by the natural harbor formed by a small river. Possibly a dozen recently constructed log houses stood nearby in neat rows. Another group of quite substantial houses lined a road that bordered the river. Already, there was a group of perhaps fifty people waiting to help pull the canoe ashore. A few women and children were among them. All were eager for any news from Montreal.

The sight of the Gibsons disembarking drew considerable attention, then disappointment on learning the new family would not be staying, but traveling on. Nettie especially, was besieged with admonitions about the perils and hardships of travel in Upper Canada, but a more hospitable reception she could not have imagined.

The Voyageurs planned to stay only the night while they added enough provisions for the next leg of the journey. Legère was conversing with an older man from the village, pointing in the direction of the British family.

Nettie held Carrie's hand as they walked up the several steps from the shore to the street level. There were more houses there than could be seen from the water. Roads extended both east and west from the center of town. It appeared construction of one heading north, into the trees was underway. She couldn't imagine this tidy village out here, hundreds of miles from Montreal. There were shops, a pub, the steeple of a church rising above the other buildings.

"Mrs. Gibson."

Nettie turned to see the man Legère had been speaking with, accompanied by Thomas. She smiled a response.

"I am Cyrus Dutton, a member of the town parliament. I wish to welcome you to York."

Nettie curtsied, and introduced Carrie.

"As you will be staying overnight, Mr. Gibson has consented to avail yourselves of our home."

She brushed back a disheveled strand of hair, looked down at her worn-in moccasins, her wrinkled frock. "Yes, Mr. Dutton, I think we'd be delighted."

~ * ~

The Dutton family carriage came to a halt the following morning, depositing Thomas, Nettie, and a sleepy Carrie at the wharf. Dutton had risen early to see them off. It was barely light but Legère, and another Voyageur named Émile, were waiting, anxious to take the Gibsons' chest.

"We shan't forget your kindness, Mr. Dutton," Nettie said as he helped her and Carrie down.

Their stay had, indeed, been delightful even if so brief. Nettie luxuriated in the first bath she'd had since Montreal. They changed into clean clothes in time for a fine meal in the Duttons' two-story, nicely furnished home on Front Street. The Duttons had two girls of twelve and fourteen who fell in love with Carrie. That night, Nettie replaced her good dress in the pine canoe chest, and laid out another more suitable for the next day's travel.

She emerged from the carriage wearing the practical moccasins, wrapped in a cloak against the frosty morning, surprised to see Émile go off with their chest, not to the wharf, but a two -wheeled cart drawn by a mule. Nearby was the cargo from the canoe, now including their own chests. Two smaller canoes lay alongside.

"I say, Legère, what's this?" Thomas pulled his coat collar up against the chilly morning.

"Mr. Dutton has offered you the use of his mule and Red River Cart. Otherwise the trail north would have been too difficult for *Madame* Gibson and the child all the way to Lac aux Claies. This street is new since my last time here."

"I thought we were seeking Lake Huron."

"We are still a long distance from Lake Huron, *Monsieur*," Legère said. "Now if you please—we are ready to leave."

Nettie, sleepy Carrie in hand, inspected the canoes. "So much smaller," she said to Émile.

"*Oui*, Madame. *Canots du Nord*. For the rivers. *Canot de Maître* too big," he answered in his limited English.

Henri lifted Carrie into the cart, and helped Nettie follow. "The smaller canoe is needed to pass the rapids and portages, as you will see when we get to Lac aux Claies."

"How far is that?" Thomas asked.

"Maybe sixty miles. We go first to the Pine Fort, then the last ten miles to Lac aux Claies."

Henri left when he heard the signal to go. He went to where the Gibsons' two chests were lashed together, and lifted them both off the ground and onto his back with a strap.

"My God!" Thomas' jaw dropped. He'd missed seeing Legère do the same on that first day. "That's one hundred-eighty pounds!"

Nettie saw the others carried at least one, ninety pound apiece. The canoes were carried upside down on the shoulders of two men each. Their cart began to move, as the mule followed Henri, unbidden.

"Is all well?" Legère asked on the first pipe break after two hours of walking.

Thomas answered. "This is not *Monsieur* McGillivray's carriage, but we cannot complain. I feel uneasy riding while you and your men walk with your loads."

"That is what we do for our living. Think no more about it."

Nettie said, "Is this route not a change in your plan?"

"Yes, *Madame*, but the construction of this Yonge Street is new. We could not have traveled the old trail with you and the child."

"*Young* Street?"

"It is recently built. The Toronto Carrying Place Trail has been replaced. This was not started when I was here three years ago." He told them how the trail was named for their destination lake the Indians called "Toronto," which the Voyageurs knew as Lac aux Claies. "It is now being called 'Lake Simcoe' by the English."

"I am concerned about Mr. Dutton's mule and cart," Nettie said.

"You need not be. There will be friends at the Pine Fort who will be happy to have a ride back to Fort York."

He left to call the men back to the road, and they were soon on their way.

Fourteen

May 1807

The trip to the Pine Fort took five days, during which April passed into May. The weather since York remained fair and had turned warmer, bringing an increase of annoying black flies. Carrie seemed to abide the pests, but Thomas was constant in his complaints. Nettie used her shawl to protect herself and Carrie, with limited success.

During the pipes and overnights, they learned more about Martin Legère. One night Nettie overheard him telling Thomas.

"I began trapping and transporting furs as a thirteen-year-old boy. Until recently, I was a Coureur des Bois. That means 'Woods Runner' in English, sir. I worked for myself, not an employee of a trading company, as are we Voyageurs.

"Now, since the game has diminished, it is harder for independent traders to compete. I joined the North West Company, and after two years with them, I am one of the few employees who know the routes beyond the Athabasca Territory."

The relatively easy travel along "Yonge Street," cleared and groomed by the occasional settler, worsened as they travelled north. Ultimately the way was little better than the trail it was designed to replace.

They arrived on the fifth evening at the shore of a stream the men said was Holland's River. It didn't look like much. Spring thaw had caused the banks to be littered with branches and deadfall. The water snaked around rounded boulders.

Nearby stood a log bunkhouse which Nettie surmised was the Pine Fort. It had been built by the same Governor Simcoe, then General Simcoe, while exploring the area ten years earlier. The place seemed abandoned, but for the Gibsons it would be a night of relative comfort, sleeping under a roof.

~ * ~

As usual, the canoes were packed and ready to launch well before dawn. Thomas held a still-sleeping Caroline in his arms while Nettie followed the short distance to the river.

The Pine Fort had been anything but abandoned. Inside they found traveling kits, men's clothing, evidence of a recent meal on the table, bedding in the dormitory. Shortly before dark, four men appeared, surveyors in the employ of Governor Simcoe. One was armed with a concertina which, with Henri's fiddle, provided entertainment for the evening. The officers' quarters were cleared for the Gibsons' use. Nettie was grateful for a real bed for the second time in less than a week.

Night crickets and tree frogs were still competing as they boarded the canoes. Nettie could just make out Legère, ankle deep in the water, steadying the craft as she and Carrie were situated in the center. Émile would replace Henri as gouvernail, who was avant on the second canoe in which Thomas rode.

The Voyageurs split up, six to a canoe. They waded out, dragging the boats over shallow rocks to deeper water, then boarded. The current was with them, and they swiftly bore away from the landing. Immediately, Legère was calling out orders in the dark "*Vers la droite! À gauche*!" as the canoe skimmed past obstacles in the water.

Slowly the morning dawned, and the river widened. The songs began in earnest. Sometimes the verse would pass from one canoe to the next. Always, the rhythm would set the pace of the strokes.

Before long, they arrived at a steep rapids. The canoes were unloaded, the Voyageurs called it a decharge, at a marked spot on the shore, and carried around the obstacle. It took two trips to carry the two canoes and cargo to the embarkation point, some two hundred yards downstream. Sun painted the tops of the pines. Lacy green was beginning to show on the tips of the maple branches. To Nettie, it was a fairyland.

While the men rested and smoked their pipes, one could hear and smell the forest. The song birds were mostly unfamiliar to Nettie, but she marveled at their abundance and diversity. Her upbringing as a young lady of quality had not prepared her for this. Carrie would spend her time on these occasions chasing toads and catching bugs of all shapes.

By noon, the river widened onto a larger body of water. She asked, “Is this Lac aux…”

“…aux Claies,” Legère said. “It is also called Lac Taronto and Lake Simcoe. No, this is Cook’s Bay, but in one hour you will see the lake.”

The morning warmed considerably. Some of the men removed their shirts, exposing muscular upper bodies with crude tattoos, mostly of symbols Nettie did not understand. Indian, she supposed.

They stopped for a rest at the end of the bay on an island someone had christened “Darlings I.” Nettie looked out on the lake and could not see the northern shoreline. “It is larger than I imagined.”

Legère drew on his pipe. “Maybe twenty miles to the north. We will reach the portage by evening.”

They followed the western shore, sheltered from the prevailing wind. They traveled abreast of each other. A new song Nettie had not heard them sing, *En Roulant Ma Boule*, began and they seemed to move faster than ever.

She continued to marvel at these men. They were all rough, crude individuals, but they were deferential to the Gibsons and their child. By and large, the men were not tall. Some were stocky, but never obese. Their arms seemed to be made of ship’s hawsers. Even through their shirts, she could see their shoulder muscles work, surging the canoe forward.

Twice on the trip to the north of the lake, they made landfall for a pipe. By now Carrie was adopted as the Voyageur's own. They would banter with her at these times, teach her French, and laugh at her antics. Nettie was starting to believe she could like living with people like this.

It was during the pipes that she began to know Martin Legère better. She was standing under an oak tree looking out onto the lake.

Legère sat nearby smoking, a small book in hand.

"I heard you telling my husband of your youth." It was a forward thing for her to do, but the man fascinated her.

"I was born far west of the Lac Superior on the Assiniboine River. Some call it the Red River."

"Your mother…"

He looked up at her. "My mother was the daughter of a Nakota shaman, my father, a trapper before he died when I was nineteen. I took over the traps and continued his trade."

It had become obvious to Nettie the other men respected Legère despite his relative young age.

"Forgive me for being forward, but I see you are…you can…" She pointed to the book in his hand.

"…read." He finished her sentence."

"Yes."

"My father taught me my letters and sums. The rest of my education is self-taught. There is ample time out here to read, and most of what society knows is in books."

She wanted to probe further into this fascinating man, but he abruptly rose and signaled to the others to continue on.

They made landfall at the top of the lake while the sun was still well over the tree line. "Landfall" was not quite the term for it. Lac aux Claies was separated from another smaller lake by a wide stretch of rocky land submerged in water, some places too shallow to pass without walking the canoe. The Voyageurs called this a demicharge.

Nettie was grateful for her moccasins as they guided the canoes over a hundred yards of rocky shoal separating the two lakes. She had to hike up her dress in the deeper parts, drawing a disapproving stare from Thomas.

"We will camp there, on that island ahead," Legère said to Nettie. "Then one more day's travel to Pentanguishene."

She gave him a quizzical look.

"A campsite on Gloucester Bay. From there we can follow the northern shore of Lac Huron to your destination."

The small islet had obviously been used many times before. A stone-rimmed fire pit was the focal point of a well maintained clearing. Henri explained the place was one day's travel from either Pine Fort, or Pentanguishene.

Fifteen

It wasn't quite daylight before the two canoes reached the north end of the smaller lake the Voyageurs called *Couchiching*. A current slowly caught the canoes as the lake drained into a river. They paddled for another half hour, coming to a prominent fir tree, its branches cut, all but the top ones. Nettie had learned they were called "lob trees," used to mark portage trails, camping sites, and in this case, forks in the river.

The river was the Severn—which seemed to be more a chain of lakes than anything else. The scenery was to Nettie more beautiful than anything she had ever seen, perhaps excepting her native lake country in England and Scotland.

But these forests and lakes were untouched by the hand of man—primeval trees, their ancient branches forming a canopy over the shoreline, green lace just emerging from them.

The beauty was not lost on Carrie. The child continued to be enchanted by every sensation this adventure offered. A pair of yellow butterflies was following the canoe, and one of them lit on the wooden frame of the hull. Carrie reached for it.

How it happened no one was sure, but Nettie heard a splash, and there was Carrie in the water! Instantly, she was yards behind the swiftly moving canoes.

"Thomas!" Nettie cried out to the second canoe.

The Voyageurs tried to turn, but traveling abreast of each other, there wasn't room.

"*Tourner autour de vous!*" Legère shouted.

Nettie, in her long dress and knickers, tried to jump in after the girl, but a Voyageur wisely restrained her.

"Thomas!" Nettie again called, but he sat, frozen.

Now Legère was in the water swimming awkward, but powerful strokes. Carrie went down, hands flailing. He dove after her.

By this time, Henri had his canoe turned, headed back. Legère emerged with a limp Carrie. Soon strong hands were lifting her aboard her father's canoe.

It was Henri who seemed to know what to do. Nettie couldn't see, but he was leaning over on the floor of the canoe as both boats were being steered to shallow water. Nettie got out and waded to her daughter, furious at the slow progress impeded by her cumbersome dress.

The sound of a child crying never sounded so sweet. Carrie was still coughing when Nettie arrived at the side of the boat. Carrie threw her arms around her mother, who looked up at Henri towering above.

"There was little to fear, *Madame*. The child was not unconscious long enough to…well, you know. It was Legère who saved her."

She stroked the child's sopping curls, kissed her forehead and cheeks. "How did you know what to do?"

Henri smiled. "Few of us know how to swim! I have done this before, but never with someone so deserving to live." That brought some laughs from the others.

Legère showed up, his toque amazingly still on his head but dripping copious amounts of Severn water.

"I say, Legère! Good show!" Thomas said.

Nettie put her free arm around Legère's waist, leaned her head on his shoulder and whispered, "Thank you!"

~ * ~

Little Carrie proved to all the resiliency of youth. A change of clothes was all it took to have her cheerfully chattering away again about this and that. They were soon underway.

The greatest challenge in these waters was to merely find one's way. The river was made up of a myriad of islands and small promontories that could lead to dead-ends. The lob trees helped, but years of experience reading the signs were key. It was dark by the time they emerged out into open water. The full moon illuminated the opposite shore, a dark line on the horizon, contrasting with the moon-dappled bay.

The Voyageurs paddled in earnest now. That they had an ounce of energy left from the long day was, to Nettie, hard to believe. It was hard paddling from the mouth of the Severn to Pentanguishene Harbor. The wind shifted around to the southwest, directly ahead. Nettie could not imagine how the men knew where to steer. On the dark line of the shore, there was no hint of where an inlet or harbor might be.

The canoes were almost completely across before she perceived a break in the trees, and protection from the wind. It was quite late by the time the canoes entered Pentanguishene. Legère said there were sometimes English ships moored in the harbor, but on this night there were none. "The barrack will be empty then." Sounds of approval came from the men. A cot and a blanket would be welcomed after this longer than usual day.

The small boats sliced easily through the now calm water, and were soon at a dock fashioned from rock-filled cribs of logs and sawn planks. The roof line of a low building could be discerned in contrast to the dark forest, as canoes scraped against the beach.

Émile held the sleeping Carrie with one hand as he helped Nettie ashore. Together, they walked up a path to the barrack.

"She has become attached to you, Émile."

"And I to her, *Madame*."

The accommodations here were much the same as the Pine Fort, except the Navy had left the place spotless, and apparently not long ago. The moon shown through freshly washed windows. Kindling and firewood lay near an iron stove. Nobody made an attempt to light a fire—it was far too late, and sleep was in the minds of all. An officer quarters was found for the Gibsons and the building was soon quiet.

Sixteen

The base at Pentanguishene had been established twelve years earlier to take advantage of the supply line from York for English ships patrolling northern Lake Huron. The harbor opened up into Georgian Bay, a major lake by itself. It was on this body that the canoes plied the next morning.

An overnight thunderstorm brought clear but cold wind from the north. Nettie and Carrie huddled beneath a huge woolen blanket, but the men seemed to bear the cold easily. They followed the shore of the bay, traveling northwest. After a late start, they had gone only ten miles and were ready for a pipe when a line of smoke rose on the rocky beach ahead.

"Indians," Legère said. "We'll stop and smoke. They'll be offended if we do not."

Nearing the shore, Henri said, "A fishing party."

There were no other canoes, so it appeared the natives were from a nearby camp in the interior.

Legère spoke to them in their language, which was similar for all northern tribes east of the Mississippi. "We are invited to smoke with them."

The four Ojibwa men had been using a seine at the mouth of a small stream with considerable success. By now their fire was smokeless and glowing. A part of their catch was roasting on suspended sticks.

Other than admiring Thomas' hat, they paid little attention to him, but Nettie and her rosy-cheeked daughter were objects of great curiosity. Nettie was put off by their unabashed staring. She put a protective arm around Carrie as one of them kneeled down, nose to nose with the girl, to touch a yellow curl poking from her bonnet. She relaxed when he stood, showing a smile of uneven teeth.

The warmth of the fire attracted the Voyageurs, and the aroma of the fish cooking was irresistible. More fish were gutted, and added to the fire. Henri was returning from one of the canoes with four sheathed knives as gifts. While the fish broiled, pipes were lit all around.

Carrie shyly inspected the nearest brave. He was totally clad in deerskin, although others wore woolen shirts. His leggings were beaded up the sides in blue and white designs. His pull-over shirt bore the image of a fox depicted in red dye, and bracketed by his loosely braided ebony hair. She reached to touch the fringe of his shirt, but Nettie pulled her hand away.

The Indian walked a short distance off the beach, and returned with something in his hand. It was a box, perhaps six by five inches, and four deep. A design of the same red fox was on the lid that had a clever bone closure. He handed it to Carrie, saying something in his language.

"For the little princess," Legère translated. "He makes things of wood for his tribe. They use no tools other than axe and knife."

Nettie could see the exquisite craftsmanship in the piece. "Tell him 'Thank you.'"

Legère said something that sounded like "*Mi-ig-wech.*"

The Indian smiled. Carrie's face was radiant. She clutched the box in both hands, holding it to her chest.

The men smoked their pipes, the Voyageurs the small clay ones they preferred, and the Indians, those they had crafted from wood. The fish that had been roasting when they arrived was offered to Nettie and Thomas. She could not remember when anything ever tasted so good. They stayed for a much longer time than the usual pipe. The fishermen talked with the Voyageurs, often pointing to the north.

"They say a boat with the red striped flag was patrolling nearby. It must be the Americans from Michilimackinac."

"Are they dangerous?" Thomas asked.

"They could be. They'll do what they can to disrupt English trade. We will stay close to the coastline. They cannot navigate among these small islands and rocks."

The roasted fish were consumed, grips of friendship shared, and the Voyageurs were again headed northwest on Georgian Bay. Carrie refused to let go of her box, despite her mother's exhortations to stow it for safekeeping.

~ * ~

The weather continued fair with the wind and seas abating. They made good time, averaging over fifty miles per day. On the third day out from Pentanguishene, Legère pointed out the French River estuary where they would have emerged from the more traveled, but arduous route.

The clear skies held until the morning of the fourth day as they were approaching a place called Weh-be-je-wung by the Indians, Le Petit Courant by the Voyageurs. The day dawned bright and warm, but Henri, leading the second canoe, pointed north where a dark line of clouds showed over the treetops.

Legère acknowledged, and the two canoes at once made a turn to the north for a small island just east of a narrow gap between two larger land masses. Though it was mid-morning, the canoes were unloaded as if camping for the night. Nettie asked Henri why the men were erecting the Gibsons' tent, and making overnight arrangements for themselves.

"The storm in the northern sky will be long and hard. We will have to wait until it passes."

"How do you know how long it will be?"

The big Cree was at a loss to say anything, as if he'd never considered the question. "I—know," was all he said.

The tent was no sooner up than Thomas went inside, followed by Carrie, still holding fast to her box.

Nettie saw the men had overturned the canoes on their sides, forming a protective barrier against the weather to the north. A draped canvas acted as a crude tent. No attempt to build a fire was made, but dry wood was collected and covered. Some flasks of whiskey magically appeared, and were passed around.

"There will be no traveling until tomorrow, *Madame*."

Nettie whirled to find Legère at her shoulder, a large bag of pine knots in his hand. "Henri says the storm could last all day," she said.

"Yes, Henri knows these things." He touched her arm. "How are you holding up?"

"Holding up? I have never felt so excited in my life! It seems I am…I don't know how to express it…"

"I understand." He seemed to be carefully studying her.

"I…should return." She made no move to leave. Legère's presence was magnetic, comforting.

"Yes, I am sorry to be delaying you."

"No, well…yes, then…I…" Her cheeks felt flushed as she turned and walked to the tent. What was she doing? Flirting? What was she feeling?

"Mama!" Carrie was in front of the tent flap. "Papa's sick!"

~ * ~

The storm front brought with it much colder weather, though sunny. The two canoes were holding close to the mainland headed due west on the North channel.

They had lost the previous day due to Thomas contracting a fever, Henri surmised it was due to an insect bite. Indeed, an angry welt rose on the back of Thomas' neck.

Nettie returned to the tent on that first night at Petit Courant to find Thomas shivering under a blanket, his face glistening with fever. She bathed his face with cloths the entire night, and into the next afternoon, while he fitfully slept in snatches of no more than several minutes. As the sun was setting, the fever broke. He—and she—slept at last.

Henri's canoe was taking the lead. Nettie could see Thomas ahead, hunched over under a woolen blanket. The trip was taking a toll on his health, while acting as a tonic for her. She continued to marvel at the stark beauty of upper Canada. Around every bend or island was a panorama of majestic rock formations, virgin forest, primeval wildlife. She delighted in her daughter joining the Voyageurs in song—she knew most of them—and truly thriving in the same conditions that were so debilitating to her father.

Nettie hoped Legère was right about reaching the Falls of St. Mary before another week passed.

~ * ~

On the morning of the third day west of Petit Courant, they set out from their camp, leaving the north shore in the darkened distance. As the sun rose, Nettie could see only a dim tree line to the north. Legère had said he wanted to make Fort St. Joseph by nightfall. To do that would require crossing the North Channel at its widest point.

For the first time on the voyage, Nettie's utter confidence in the Voyageurs waned. This was open, rough water…she held tightly onto her daughter, and saw the blood rush from her husband's face. The wind had veered around to the east, building large seas the length of the channel. The canoes had a difficult time steering, with much of the responsibility on the shoulders of the gouvernail at the rear. At times the canoes would surge ahead, as they surfed down the leading edge of a swell. The prow of the canoe plunged dangerously into the bottom of the trough. The tops of the waves were sheared off by the wind, raining down on them. These difficulties were rewarded, however, with increased speed. At last, by early afternoon they were just off the southern shore of the channel by the island they had followed since *Petit Courant* called Manitoulin. Once in the lee of that island, the seas were more manageable.

Again, Nettie marveled at Legère's ability to find his way. In these waters, forested islands sprung up everywhere against a background of other similar ones. Legère had no lob trees to guide him here, yet he led them unerringly.

Well before dark he called out, "The Fort!"

Ahead lay a point of land that had been cleared. There was a low structure that, as they neared, morphed into a palisaded log fort. A few small buildings were outside its walls, a thin line of white smoke rising from one. A wooden wharf jutted out from the eastern side of the point.

One by one, people emerged from the fort and the buildings to greet them. Nettie began to anticipate sleeping in a real bed tonight.

Seventeen

Andy

Grant Stacey's truck stood in Andy's driveway with an empty flatbed trailer attached. In the backyard, she stood with Grant, Lila Knowles and Willard Tremblay while a Stacey Enterprises backhoe operator carefully scraped away the top six inches of dirt from the interior of the foundation. The first bucket revealed small pieces of charcoal and severely burned wood,

"Save some of those pieces, please," Tremblay said. "We'll try to determine their age."

Earlier, further digging around the perimeter of the foundation had revealed the depth of the stones to be no more than eighteen inches with the exception of the corner where the first hole was made. There, the wall of stone extended down much farther. Just how much, they hadn't yet determined, but it appeared there must be a cellar of some type—probably a root cellar—in that area.

"It's strange," Lila said. "There's no record of anyone living on this land until the late 1890s when a Hector McVey built your house."

The name seemed vaguely familiar to Andy. She had never paid any attention to family history, particularly on her father's side. Her mother would mention her own grandmother, but not by name. "I suppose he built the barn, too."

Lila continued. "There isn't a clear history of every property on St. Joseph Island, but I suppose he had a deed of some kind, or maybe a grant. The first legal survey of your property isn't recorded until 1892.

"You've done your homework, I see," Andy said.

For some reason, Lila seemed uncomfortable with the innocent comment.

Stacey spoke. "It's the same with our farm. The original title is lost. I have no idea of its origin. One of my ancestors staked the property out and it's been handed down through the generations."

The engine of the backhoe throttled down to an idle as the operator jumped down. "Hit something," he called.

It was in the back corner where Tremblay had been digging.

"What is it, Jake?" Stacey said.

The man detached a hand shovel from the frame of the backhoe. "Dunno. Let's see."

He began scraping dirt from something that emerged from the layer of dirt appearing square and flat.

"It's a door!" Andy said

More dirt was shoveled away. The planks of a heavy door were revealed. Remnants of rusted hardware appeared on it.

"It *is* a cellar!" Lila said

The archeologist in Tremblay took over. "A broom! Can we get a broom, please?"

It took the better part of a half hour for him to carefully sweep away the dirt from around the edge of the door that lay flat on the ground. The sweeping also exposed charred pieces of flooring, possibly pine. The door was badly charred, but intact.

"This is pretty darn cool, isn't it?" Stacey said, looking at Andy.

"It's getting complicated," she said. "My new patio and sweeping lawn is turning into an archeological dig for a few pot shards and jars, if anything."

Lila put a hand on her shoulder. "Andy, whatever's there will help us determine the age of the site and give us a clearer view of the region's history. I hope you don't mind if we impose on you a little longer."

"Sure…uh, how long?"

Lila looked at Tremblay "Buck?"

"If we can get some archeology students in here to help, a month should do it."

Andy envisioned people crawling all over her backyard for a month. “If that’s what it takes.”

Tremblay brightened. “Let’s get a tent over the site! Lila, will you see to that??

The two continued in animated conversation, making plans on the way back to their car.

~ * ~

Andy pulled the visor down against the morning sun slanting through the windshield of the Jeep. She drove through the little village of Desbarats, and on to the slightly larger Bruce Mines where she could see the sprawling compound of Stacey Enterprises through the trees. She might have stopped had Grant not been at his Sault facility today.

Continuing on for another twenty minutes to Thessalon, she thought how little the highway had changed this far east of ‘The Soo.’ The thought of making the drive every day from her home to Sault Ste. Marie was less than appealing. Nevertheless, she’d promised Roger she’d come and talk, so here she was. She drove over the bridge spanning the Thessalon River, and made an immediate right turn where the modern looking O.P.P. Thessalon Detachment stood in its own cul-de-sac.

She announced herself, and was quickly directed to Van Bourne’s office. On the way she heard her name called. A familiar young woman in civilian clothes was waving from her desk. *What is her name?* Andy remembered her from the smuggling case.

"Ellen Bailey," the woman called out, rescuing Andy from the awkward moment.

"Of course! So good to see you again." They'd staked out a drug transfer together in Bailey's car.

"Here to see Roger?" Bailey asked.

"Yes, maybe we can talk later."

Van Bourne's door was open, and Andy stepped inside. He was standing behind his desk, tidying it up. There was another person in the room seated in one of the two visitors' chairs

"Ah, Andy!" he said, coming around to give her a perfunctory embrace. "Please—sit. This is Nolan Roberts. Nolan is Commander at The Sault Detachment."

She felt a little put off by Roger springing this man on her with no warning. They shook hands.

"Okay, Roger, what's this all about?"

He made a gesture for Roberts to explain.

"Orillio has given me the green light to expand my investigative service. Our case load has increased. Simple as that. Roger has recommended you. Your record in Windsor is well known. That's good enough for me, if you want the job."

Orillio was the O.P.P. headquarters on Lake Simcoe, an hour's drive north of Toronto.

Andy leaned forward in her chair. "I've got a little history with your Mr. Terry. He and I weren't exactly in love."

"I think you'd find you could handle Arnold."

"What about other candidates from your detachment?" she asked Roberts.

"All good young men, none who have the qualifications you'd bring. I can assure you. If I thought bringing someone in from the outside would affect my morale, I wouldn't do it."

"I'll have to think about it."

Van Bourne stood, removed his hat from behind the door. "Come on. I'll buy lunch, and you can think there."

They did, but on the drive home, Andy was as unsure as ever. She was disillusioned with the new regime in Windsor, and she loved being back on the Island in her little house. So what was her problem?

The image of Grant Stacey's face stared back at her. That was what! She truly loved the man, but she couldn't commit to a... *Say it! The word is "marriage*." The thought still scared her. *Tyler Adkins, you bastard! Will I ever get free of you?*

~ * ~

Andy sat on the steps of her back door with her morning coffee. The rectangle of stones that had been her shed seemed to mock her delayed hopes for a re-landscaped yard. "A month should do it," Buck Tremblay had said.

Yesterday she had returned from Thessalon, and hadn't been home an hour before Grant's truck pulled in.

"Showing up at cocktail hour, I see." She made a show of checking her watch.

"Got me dead to rights."

"Fine. I feel like a monster Manhattan to help me figure out a dilemma I have. The fixin's I have, the mixin' you do." She pulled a wheel of cheddar from the fridge and got out the Ritz crackers.

"What dilemma?" he said, searching for the sweet vermouth.

"I saw Roger VanBourne today. He…the O.P.P. wants me to take a job in The Soo." She watched him with his back to her, straighten, and then continue mixing the drinks.

"Oh?"

"I told him I'd think about it."

"And you want my *unbiased* thoughts on this?"

She laughed. "I guess that *is* pretty silly."

He poured the iced mixture into two large cocktail glasses garnished with maraschino cherries, handing one to her. "Let's have these on your fancy front porch."

They said nothing more about it through drinks, and later for dinner Andy scared up some leftovers.

"Gotta get up early. I'm off to Thunder Bay in the morning," Stacey said later.

She knew he desperately wanted her to take the job and settle on the Island. But he held back from pushing too hard. It was almost too charming for words.

Andy rose from the stoop and went back into the kitchen, dumped her coffee in the sink, and punched a number into the phone. "Sergeant Roberts," she said, after being put through. "I'll take the job."

Eighteen

Nettie

June 1807

St. Joseph Island

The fort was a disappointment. Nettie was told the fort, built in 1796, was strategically important. It was Britain's westernmost military presence, and was needed to maintain relations with the natives and secure trade from Sault Ste. Marie and points beyond.

The forts at Montreal and Quebec were impressive structures, built to withstand the ball of a cannon. This one was built of logs, close to the shore, and well within the range of a gun from the smallest warship. Worse were the soldiers…semi-retired men waiting for their pensions. She had never seen such slovenly men. Their uniforms were soiled, even threadbare. What was worse, no one appeared to care. War here was hardly expected.

"I expect it is not an enviable assignment out here away from civilization," Thomas said, when she mentioned this. "A good soldier is not likely to be posted here as a reward."

In contrast to the military were the civilians. Not only were there more people than expected living here, she and Thomas were welcomed with warmth and kindness. Carrie was an instant celebrity, showing off her box and dolls. Nettie formed an instant liking for one of the women, a dark-haired woman somewhat older than herself, named Madelaine. She was married to John Askin, the storekeeper on the island for the British Indian Department.

"You will stay with us!" Madelaine said with a hint of accent, probably French, Nettie thought.

The Askin house was a cedar log building some distance east of the fort near the water's edge. It was quite spacious with a spare room for guests which Madelaine claimed to be a common occurrence.

John Askin, Jr. turned out to be considerably more than a storekeeper for Canada's Indian department. He was in charge of the American holdings of John Jacob Astor's South West Company, and the safe transfer of their furs. William McGillivray had a share in the South West Company himself. Like most successful men in Upper Canada, Askin, who was one half native, had achieved a close connection with the Indian leaders, spoke their language, shared their trust. His house with four hearths was larger than Nettie would have imagined on such a remote island.

Madelaine was the de-facto nurse and midwife of the Island and its surrounds. She had been known to treat patients in her own home if necessary. Legère said her home was rarely free of guests or someone in need.

The Askins were aware of the Voyageurs preference for a pre-dawn departure. The Gibsons were given an early dinner of venison, apple cider and vegetables preserved from the previous autumn. Nettie watched Madelaine as she prepared the meal, wondering how a girl like herself, brought up in idle luxury, and having only lived as a married woman in a rooming house could ever learn to be so resourceful.

The fort's commander, Captain Charles Roberts, was asked to dine as well. He was a man obviously in poor health, having recently served in India and Ceylon. This post was meant as a place to serve out his enlistment, as it was for his soldiers, few of whom were combat ready.

Soon after the meal, they were shown their room and were asleep in minutes.

~ * ~

By first light the canoes were halfway up the thirty mile western side of the Island of St. Joseph. It had remained quite cold, and notwithstanding a cozy bed at the Askin home, Thomas was not feeling well. The fever had taken a toll on his spirits and strength. Nettie felt helpless to do anything about it.

This was the main channel of the St. Marys River. To the west lay land of The United States of America, only the previous year officially established as the Michigan Territory. John Askin had explained that the boundary meant little or nothing to the local inhabitants, whether European or native. International politics were trumped by the necessities of making a living in such remote circumstances.

At the north end of the Island, Legère stopped for their sixth pipe of the morning. Here the river split. He told the Gibsons there were now two ways to the settlement at the Falls of Saint Mary, as the English called their destination. The more direct route would be the left channel, while the easier paddling, but longer way, would be the right channel that included the wide and shallow Lake George.

Nettie was surprised when Thomas vehemently insisted on taking the shorter route. "I wish to be quit of this infernal travelling!" She was reasonably sure the Voyageurs preferred the lake route, but they said nothing, deferring to the supposed manager-apparent at The Company's outpost.

"How much shorter is this way?" Nettie asked, pointing left.

"About one, maybe two pipes," Émile said. He was showing Carrie some multi-colored stones from the rocky beach.

Legère shrugged "That's it, then. If we make good time, we should be there before dark."

~ * ~

As the canoes rounded the last bend of the St. Marys River, small huts and wigwams began to appear on both shores, America on the left, and Canada on the right.

Ahead were more substantial buildings, particularly on the Canadian side.

The river was cold and clear. The sound of rushing water accompanied the beauty of rapids sparkling in the sun setting over Lake Superior. It was a sight to behold, and Nettie held it until the last rays dropped out of the sky.

~ * ~

December 1807
Sault Ste. Marie

The house groaned when a gust of wind buffeted against its northwest face. The flame danced in the draft as Thomas lit the Yule candle. Carrie giggled in delight, having talked about little else but Christmas and the candle lighting for days. Although there was no tradition of gift giving in either Thomas' or Nettie's families, Nettie had made a mate for "Mr. B" to give to her daughter in the morning. Tomorrow would be celebrated with rum punch and a wild game dinner.

Until then, Nettie was happy to have a few minutes to relax, and watch her family in a rare instance of tranquility. Carrie was never idle, always curious and questioning. Her bright spirit made her constant probing bearable.

Thomas was another matter. Nothing ever seemed satisfactory for him, often complaining about a slight from someone at work, or his unforeseen hardships here on the edge of civilization.

For Nettie, the first few weeks were the hardest. The house the Company bought, from a trader returning east, was filthy. The man, a bachelor, had let the well-constructed home go to seed. Nettie almost cried when she saw it. It was in those first weeks, first cleaning, then having almost everything repaired, she learned she could cope with most anything that might follow.

Her greatest asset was her ability to get along with the Ojibwa community. She was fascinated with their culture. They sensed her admiration, repaying her with labor in the form of housekeeping and, just as important, purveyors of victuals. By the previous August, the house was sound and tight, a widowed Indian woman named *Waabigwan* was employed as a housekeeper/cook. Carrie had started her lessons at home from a primer Nettie had purchased at the last minute in Montreal.

The summer became autumn on a day in late September. Nettie blew out the bedside candle on a warm, sunny day to wake to a near-freezing morning. A scramble for warm clothes ensued. The house proved to be well insulated, though the wood stove in the kitchen and the hearth in the parlor were in constant use since that morning.

Carrie, who as a four year old in Montreal was never allowed out of the house alone, now had the freedom to play outside as long as she didn't go near the river. Her friends were mostly Indian children, but also one or two children of other European or Métis parents. One of these was Jane Johnston, two years older, the daughter of a successful independent fur trader. Thanks to Jane, and the others, Carrie rapidly became proficient in French-Canadian and many of the Ojibwa (*Anishinabek*) words children need for communication.

Thomas, upon arriving at the NWC office, was surprised to learn the current resident manager was a first cousin of William McGillivray's wife, and had no intention of stepping down any time soon. Thomas admitted McGillivray had made no promises, but was disappointed just the same.

The manager, Robert Logan, was a reasonable yet hard-nosed businessman.

He advised Thomas he would be put to use keeping tabs on the Company outpost at *Kaministiquia* River—recently renamed Fort William after William McGillivray—and a sizeable consignment inventory the company kept with the Americans at Fort *Michilimackinac*. That meant more canoe travel, something Thomas had hoped he'd seen the last of for a while.

His first trip to Fort William hadn't gone well, he admitted. The outpost was still using the inventory method he'd replaced years ago. The local manager, a crusty Métis, was not about to change a system he understood for one he did not, and that was that. Thomas' problem was that the post was well-managed in every respect, and vital to the NWC's ties with Grand Portage and the distant west. Thomas came home, tail between his legs, having accomplished little.

The visit to Fort *Michilimackinac* went a little better, but even there, his lack of rapport with the Métis and the Indians took the shine off any impression he would have wished to impart.

The success of Nettie's assimilation was largely due to Waabigwan. The old woman could hunt, trap, and fish with the best of the men. She was expert in herbal medicine and other healing techniques.

Carrie took to her at once, and began to call her "Lily" after learning the meaning of her name meant *flower*. The name hardly fit this sinewy, self-reliant woman, but it stuck.

Lily taught Nettie how to prepare and cook moose and venison to take away the taste of game, showed her how to clean the sweet meat of the pike so the tiny bones were removed. Lily taught her how to make lye soap from calcined limestone, where and when to pick the best berries and herbs.

Sault Ste. Marie with its two NWC warehouses, one on each side of the river, had ready access to the trade goods of modern life that made life bearable there in the dawn of the nineteenth century. But Annette Duncan Gibson, until then, had never lifted a finger in a kitchen, never held a feather duster, or scrubbed a floor. It seemed she was well on her way to becoming a frontier woman.

Nineteen
Parcher

April 1807
Chillicothe. Ohio

The "Court of Common Pleas" system in the Northwest Territory dated back only five years when the first sheriff was appointed for the river town of Marietta. Shortly other communities were afforded civil law with circuit judges travelling from town to town on horseback, from the new state capital of Chillicothe.

Not far from the courthouse stood a fine new jail from which one of its first inmates was, today, being released. Not that his sentence was up, it was a matter of freeing space for more serious offenders.

Albert Parcher stood on the wooden sidewalk outside the jail in the same clothes he'd worn the day he was arrested for the attempted theft of the organ fund from the Franklin, Ohio post office. In his pocket were twelve dollars. He was clean-shaven, and decided he fancied the look. Perhaps he'd keep it for a while.

The town was considerably different from the village he'd passed through six years earlier. The courthouse and jail were solid brick edifices as were several commercial buildings.

It was beginning to mist, and he set out to look for a place to sort out what to do next. By chance, he came upon that same inn where he'd seen Oliver Gandy and his fellow politicians gather. The establishment was much improved with a sign that read 'The Eagle and Spear.' Inside was an oak bar with fancy brass and ceramic towers for the ale. He plunked a coin down on its polished surface and asked for a draft. The man behind the bar looked at him, then back to the coin.

"It'll be three o' them, if you're wantin' a glass."

Parcher complied without a word, and took his ale to the same corner he'd sat in years before. He'd had twenty-four months to think about what went wrong that Sunday afternoon in the tiny settlement of Franklin, Ohio.

The plan had been straightforward. He would wait for the church service to start, saddle up Clemmons' horse, and make for Franklin to be there when John Shenk returned with the organ money. He knew all the money would be in the strongbox, because the church elders insisted on counting it all every Sunday.

Right on time, Shenk's carriage rattled into the yard. Patience Shenk entered the store, while John attended to the horses in their stall at the rear of the property. Parcher wanted to make sure the rig was put away, preventing Shenk from immediately using it to get help.

From his hiding place behind the blacksmith shop, he left his tethered horse, and followed Shenk into the store.

"William!" A beaming Patience Shenk greeted him. "So lovely to see you!"

"I…came to see Mr. Shenk."

"He's just in back having a cold glass of cider. You can join him if you like." She gave him a friendly pat on the shoulder to urge him on his way.

"Why…yes, I will have a glass"

Patience smiled, and returned her attention to the sorting of a display of notions.

He found Shenk sitting at the kitchen table with a glass of cider and, conveniently, the strongbox on the floor next to the chair.

Shenk appeared more dubious of Parcher's appearance in his home than did his wife.

"Goggins! What on earth…?" Parcher towered over Shenk, placed his hand on the man's chest to keep him seated. "I've had enough of church life, Mr. Shenk. Goin' to seek my future somewhere besides this little flyspeck on a map."

He reached down and picked up the strongbox. It felt satisfyingly heavy.

Shenk's face screwed up in horror, then in anguish. "You can't! That is the hard earned scrapings of honest Christians!"

"And who's goin' to stop me, Shenk? You? I don't think so. Now you just sit there. By the time you hitch up your rig, I'll be long gone to anywhere. Tell that cheap bastard Clemmons 'good bye.' My only regret is I didn't get a chance to bugger that young Mrs. Carter, her wantin' it like she did."

There was a familiar sounding "click" from the front of the store. Parcher turned to see Patience Shenk expertly holding a musket, and pointing it at his chest. Her usual sweet and doting countenance was replaced with grim determination.

"Set the box down, William."

Parcher was momentarily confused. This wasn't computing. Slowly he realized he had no option. She was too far away to rush, and he *believed* her. She would pull that trigger. Slowly he set the box on the table.

"John, unlock the shed," Patience said.

And that was how Albert Parcher was captured, arrested, and sentenced to five years of incarceration.

He looked at his already empty glass, and wondered what and where his next move would be.

~ * ~

"It's where I'd go if I were foot-loose," the barman had said. That was two days ago, in Chillicothe. The fast expanding town of Zanesville was rumored to be the new capital of Ohio. Its population was growing, and that meant opportunity for a man like Albert Parcher.

The new highway that folks called "Zane's Trace" was responsible for its influx of settlers and a new flow of money. Parcher wasn't impressed with the road. The empty cart that had been used to bring livestock to market in Chillicothe still had what looked like sheep droppings in it. The new road was still full of jaw-rattling ruts. There was no room in the bench up front with the big man and his son who spoke a language Parcher did not understand.

The cart stopped. The driver slapped his chest, and pointed up a trail to where his farm must have been. *End of the ride*, Parcher thought. He jumped down, rubbing his rear end. The farmer and his son laughed. *"Schlechte rida besser ols goot lauf!"*

Parcher didn't understand, and showed it.

The farmer pointed to his old mare. "More better," he said, then he used his fingers to simulate walking.

Parcher got the joke, but wasn't amused. He had no idea where he was. The cart rumbled away up the trail, and he had no choice but to trudge ahead. It was early afternoon.

In less than a mile, he topped a rise to see a sizeable town ahead by a small river. He wouldn't be sleeping in the open tonight.

As he entered the village, he noticed the signs on the shops were a mixture of English and some other language. One storefront with newspapers posted in the window had a sign emblazoned with an eagle that read: *Der Ohio Adler.*

He discovered the town had two inns, both with pubs. He chose the one that might best fit the budget dictated by the eight dollars he had left. He had only his bag and the coat and knit cap he bought from the Chillicothe jailer for a dollar. The room was small, but adequate. He was tired, but thirsty. The latter won out.

Back downstairs in the pub, the atmosphere was different from those he knew. Mostly older men, smoking pipes, playing an unfamiliar card game. He ordered a draft, but had to wait as the frothy light-colored brew the barman called "lager" was slowly pumped into his glass. It was worth the wait, much better than the ale of Chillicothe.

"What is the name of this town?" he said to a man of about his own age.

"Why, New Lancaster! Where have you come from?" He was dressed in farm clothes, and spoke English, but with an accent.

"Uh…Cincinatti."

"My name is Jens." He pronounced it Yens, and extended his hand. "Where are you going, now that you don't know where you are?"

Parcher wasn't sure how to answer. "I'm looking for work."

"Plenty of work in Cincinnati, yes?"

Think of something! "They say Zanesville is better."

The farmer nodded in agreement, asked Parcher what kind of work he did.

"I was a sexton in…Pittsburgh."

The other man's face registered approval. "Have you spoken with Reverend Sternkopf?"

"I only just got here."

"His church is on the east side of town on the right side of the road. You can tell him Jens Müller sent you." He took a last swig of his beer, smiled and left.

The germ of an idea hit him as he watched Müller leave. He took his glass to a table and hailed a bar maid. "What is that he's eating?" He pointed to the elderly man at the next table.

She looked at him curiously. "Why, it's a meat pie."

"I'll have one, and another glass of your beer."

Twenty

Up in his room, Parcher thought back to his encounter with the Jens Müller. Churches always had money. Gain the trust of the preacher and the deacons. That was the key. The mistake in Dayton was due to lack of planning. He'd had no idea what to expect inside Shenk's house, but went in nevertheless. His plan to steal the money was too spur of the moment. The trick is to be far gone before they know the money is missing.

This was a lot better than pimping for Happy Jack Bransky. This scheme could keep him in spending money as long as he moved from town to town every six or seven months. The roads were still rudimentary. Communication from town to town was slow, if not impossible. Yes, he'd take a walk tomorrow and pay the Reverend Sternkopf a visit.

~ * ~

Christ knew he didn't want to get up, but the beer from last night had to go somewhere. He found the pot at the end of the bed, and filled it almost half. Through the narrow window he could see people on the street going about the business of the day. It must be late, he thought.

Stepping into his breeches, he heard a woman's sharp voice outside his door. *A curse?*

He buttoned up and opened the door. A piece of linen was on the floor by a mop and wooden bucket. Holding the rest of the linen was a girl, curls of brown hair poking out from under a housemaid's cap. Her inflamed cheeks were separated by the slash of a mouth. Her eyes flashed in anger as they met his.

Parcher reached down to retrieve the sheet, soiled from the floor, offering it to her.

"I can't hardly take it with me arms full, now can I?" she snapped. He recognized an eastern voice, sounding much like the boys he'd met from the city of New York.

"Well bugger ye then, ya little tart!"

"I ain't no tart, ya fuckin' great oaf!"

"An a tart tongue, at that!" He took a better look at her. *Maybe mid-twenties. Pretty thing, if she'd wash her face.* He'd seen her type working for Happy Jack.

He followed her into the empty room across the hall where she unloaded her armful of bed linen.

"What might a girl who 'ain't no tart' be doin' here in the wilderness?"

"Nothin' you'll be needin' to know." She snatched the soiled sheet from him, and pushed back into the hall to finish her mopping.

"See it your own way." He returned to his room to finish dressing.

~ * ~

The girl was nowhere to be seen when Parcher left his room. A good breakfast would clear last night's cobwebs, but he had only a few dollars left after paying for a week's rent and last night's victuals and drink. First order of business would be to find a source of money.

The church was easy to find, just as Müller had directed. It was a fine, if modest, building. White clapboard, a spike of a steeple.

"Hello?" he called, after stepping inside the sanctuary. No answer after a second call. He went around to a house that stood juxtaposed, with the same white siding. He knocked.

An erect, aproned woman of about forty came to the door. She surveyed Parcher carefully, her eyes traveling up and down.

"Good morning, ma'am. May I assume this is the parsonage?"

She nodded, but said nothing.

"My name is Parcher, Albert Parcher, ma'am." He remembered to use his real name, the one he signed at the inn.

The woman inclined her head as a signal for him to state his business.

"I am a Christian, ma'am. A true follower of Christ, looking for honest labor. I was advised by my friend Jens that your congregation might be in some need." The years of hustling customers for

Happy Jack's whores was paying off in his ability for Irish Bull.

She returned a sly smile. "Jens, you say?"

"Indeed, ma'am."

"Not one's ideal sponsor. What type of work do you mean?"

"Anything Mrs.…Sternkopf, is it? I was a sexton in Dayton, but had to leave, as they no longer had funds for the position." He was pleased with his on-the-spot assembling of a story.

"Hmm. Wait here." She closed the door.

It was a long time before the door opened. A dark, handsome man with hair just greying at the temples stood in shirtsleeves. "I am Sternkopf."

"Ah, yes sir. Your wife…"

"Come around to the church. I'll try you for a day."

~ * ~

It was well after 5:00 p.m. by the clock on the steeple before Parcher set out to return to the Inn. The Reverend Sternkopf had a list of menial and not so menial jobs in mind. He began by having Parcher sweep, then mop the entire sanctuary, a much larger space than the one in Dayton. At noon the stoic Mrs. Sternkopf brought him a bowl of soup and a slab of buttered bread.

The jobs increased in responsibility, all inside the building, culminating with marking a new shipment of hymnals with the inscription NLEC1807, identifying the New Lancaster

Evangelical Church. He did this, after asking Parcher if he could write.

"I can print quite well, sir," he said. "Far better than I can read." Parcher was self-conscious about his reading ability, but thought it would be better to put the subject to rest. After showing the Reverend his careful, if childlike, lettering, he was given the task, his last for the day.

"You are a decent worker, Albert. Here is a dollar. Come back tomorrow at eight."

Walking back, he wondered if that little piece of trash would still be working this afternoon. *It would be nice to get into her knickers if she didn't want a lot of money.* That he couldn't afford. Not yet, anyway.

Tomorrow was Saturday. The Reverend would be preparing for the next day's service. A good time to learn about how the collections were handled.

Back at his room, the girl was not to be seen. He returned down to the pub for his dinner. There by the tap, Jens Müller was as he was on the previous night, his glass of beer half gone.

"Well now," Müller said. "The traveler comes. Did you see the Reverend?"

"I did, and have a job at least through tomorrow."

"Then?"

"Then we'll have to see. Tell me something."

Müller nodded.

"What are these people speaking?" He motioned to the room which was identically populated as on the night before.

“Something like German. Our people come from the south of Germany. Most to Pennsylvania, some farther west.”

“Why this town?”

He shrugged. “We followed the Trace. The Zanes sold parcels at a fair price here by the Hocking River. It is good land.

Parcher had no interest in any of this, but wanted to keep Müller engaged, a good man to know. He was a bit of a rebel, it seemed.

“There’s a girl that works here. Do you know her?”

Müller nodded again. “Flora. Been here a month. Keeps to herself.”

Twenty-one

The Reverend was in the church when Parcher returned the next morning punctually at eight. The day progressed much like the one before, finishing up the hymnals, then placing them in their pews. The carpet for the chancel had to be taken outside, draped over a line, beaten and replaced. He was shown the tool shed behind the parsonage and told to scythe the weeds that had grown up after the long winter.

At the end of the day, he had no more insight as to his long term goal of relieving Reverend Sternkopf's church of its ready cash, but he was reasonably sure he'd landed a permanent position there. And had gained the trust of the Reverend. As he walked home, he had another dollar in his pocket, and the request to return on Monday.

That evening, although his room had been cleaned and the pot emptied, the girl Flora was not around.

~ * ~

The sermon was good, he supposed, but Sternkopf spoke words and concepts that soared over his, and he imagined, the heads of everyone else. He'd had a hard time keeping his chin from dropping onto his chest. The last hymn was sung from the spanking new hymnals, and the little pump organ wheezed out the recessional march.

Parcher waited for the thirty-odd worshipers to make their niceties to the Reverend and he followed behind.

"Well, Mr. Parcher!" Sternkopf said, "I noticed you back there. I must say I am glad to see you."

"Thankee, sir. I was happy the sermon was in English, and not that old German."

That brought a wistful smile. "I believe we are Americans, and must speak English. It is a battle I have with some of my people. Our congregation has many who do not speak English at all, only what is called the Pennsylvania German."

The preacher seemed to want to continue, but Parcher's intent was only to let Sternkopf know he'd attended, a devout person. He definitely did not want to get into a discussion. He was happy to get away, wondering what to do with the rest of this day.

At the inn, the pub was closed. He trudged up to his room and immediately saw his door ajar. The four dollars secreted in the back of the washstand popped into his mind. He was sure he'd been robbed. Then, a soft noise told him someone was still in there.

With his foot, he bashed the door into the room, following as it slammed into someone by the bed. A high-pitched scream of pain was the result.

There, with one arm still under his mattress, was the girl.

He snatched her up by the hair. “Find what yer lookin’ for, Flora? That’s yer name, ain’t it?”

She stared back at him, holding her bruised elbow and fighting back tears of pain.

“Answer me, ya little cunt!” He slapped her hard.

“I found nothing,” she got out.

He pushed her back onto the bed, glanced into the hall before shutting the door. Then, a check of his hiding place to see if the four dollars were still there. He turned to stand over her as she stared back at him defiantly.

“Well now, Flora. What was it you were going to do with my money?”

“Get out of this…” She searched for a word.

“Piss-ant of a town?”

She nodded, looked away.

He laughed. “Ye won’t go far on my scrapings. Get up, ye little tart.”

“I ain’t no tart!”

He grabbed her arm, pulling her to her feet. “So yer want to be quit of this place?”

She looked down.

“What?” he demanded. He held her close, and felt himself getting aroused.

“Yeah,” she admitted.

"How bad, because if ya do, maybe we can work something out." He knew she could feel his erection through her thin dress, saw her nostrils flare, knew she was ready.

"I…" she began, but he covered her mouth with his own.

She responded eagerly, pulling him back onto the small bed as he fumbled with the buttons on his breeches.

~ * ~

Flora, as Parcher had suspected, was from New York. Her mother had been a camp follower, one of the group of women who follow an army from one battle to the next, selling their favors.

When the British army landed at Staten Island on that hot July day in 1776, few New Yorkers thought the Continental Army had a chance. Here was an opportunity for a penniless prostitute to make real money, selling herself to the highest bidders among the inevitable victors, the Red Coats.

Flora's mother was among these, following the successive campaigns of Generals Howe, Clinton, and Cornwallis until the British were cornered at Yorktown Virginia in 1781. Flora's mother was stranded and pregnant. Ultimately she latched on to an American corporal from New York.

Flora was born in June of the next year. Her mother went from one abusive relationship to another as Flora grew up. Finally, when she was fifteen, she bolted. The last straw was being forced to solicit men to keep the man her mother was with in rum. When she refused, he raped her.

Her next move was to flee New York. Somehow she got to Philadelphia, but it was the same there. She had no skills other than menial work; she'd seen what prostitution had done to her mother, and was adamant. It wasn't, she told Parcher, that it was immoral, the reason was much more basic. When she left New York, her mother was in the last phases of syphilis.

"If I want to have a roll in the sheets, I want it to be 'cause I like it, see?" She pushed off Parcher's bed, went to the washstand, and began to clean herself up.

Parcher watched her, nude, uninhibited. The girl had spunk. Maybe he could use her.

~ * ~

Once more, Reverend Sternkopf was waiting when Parcher arrived at 8:00 a.m. the next day. The building was already three years old, but only recently had the four stained glass windows been installed, two each on either side of the sanctuary. The trim around them had not been caulked nor painted.

"Follow me, Albert." He led Parcher around the side of the building where a ladder stood propped by the first window.

Parcher spent the morning with a trowel and a pail of caulk, frustrated by not working inside the building where he might get some insight into how the collections were handled. Yesterday he watched as the collection was placed in a nook under the altar. As the congregation was leaving, a deacon retrieved it and exited through a door to the left of the pulpit. He returned, empty handed.

At noon Mrs. Sternkopf came out into the yard. "Mr. Parcher, you are welcome to share a light meal with the Reverend, if you wish.

He accepted, happy to have time to discuss the workings of the church. He washed in a stand outside the kitchen door of the parsonage.

The day was quite cool. The severe woman was at the stove adding a log when Parcher arrived. The Reverend motioned him to a chair where mugs of cider and plates of minced ham and bread waited at two places on the maple table.

After a prayer, they ate in silence for a while until Parcher said, "The people liked the hymnals, I think."

Sternkopf smiled. "Yes, I did receive some positive comments on them. We have been singing only a few hymns from memory. It is good to be reacquainted with the other inspiring messages from our Lord."

"They must have cost you a great amount of money."

Sternkophf's wife raised her head slightly from some work at her sideboard.

The Reverend said, "We are fortunate to have a devout and generous congregation. The new prayer books are due, as well."

"And they are paid for, you say?"

Sternkopf dabbed his mouth. “When they arrive, they will be paid for, yes. Was the ham to your liking, Albert?”

Parcher testified as to the quality of the meal. *So the books will be paid for on arrival, which could be any day.* This meant he had to find where the money was kept without delay.

“I’ve only one half of the last window left to paint, sir. Should I clean the floor in the sanctuary, then?”

Sternkopf smiled approvingly at his wife, as if they had been discussing the worth of this man showing up off the Trace at their door. “That will be fine, Albert.”

The exchange of looks between the Reverend and his wife was not lost on Parcher. He decided he’d need to be very careful with this woman.

Twenty-two

The church, if not a humble edifice, was certainly not ostentatious. It was basically a rectangle, sixty by thirty feet with a ten foot square office addition to the left of the chancel. To the right, behind the reader's dais, was a bench for the eight-person choir. The way to the office led behind the pulpit. It was through there Parcher had seen the deacon take yesterday's offering.

The sanctuary was swept; the hymnals put back in order. It was a good chance to perhaps clean the office as well? *Something a conscientious sexton might think of, certainly.*

The door to the office was unlocked. Inside, the room was pristine. A small desk and chair with a chest of drawers behind. Two straight-back chairs with woven seats stood opposite. The pine floor was scrubbed almost white. A solitary cross on one wall.

The desktop was bare, save an inkwell, pen, and blotter. No drawer in the simple desk. The oak chest consisted of three drawers, the topmost one displaying a keyhole. He tried it, and yes, it was locked. Nothing of value in the others. Except for a window above the chest looking out on the rear of the church, there was no exit to the outside.

The money, then, *must* have been put in that locked drawer, at least temporarily. *But where is the key?*

~ * ~

That night Parcher returned to the inn. In front was parked an enclosed wagon drawn by a single horse tied to a post. White lettering on the wagon read, Wm. PIERPONT, MERCHANDISE.

Inside, speaking with the proprietor, was a man in long trousers, cutaway, and felt top hat, all showing the patina of time and miles on the road.

Parcher continued on into the pub, ordering a lager. He'd no sooner had it drawn, than the man was standing next to him, asking the barkeep for a draft.

"That yer wagon in front?" Parcher asked the man, possibly forty years of age with a moustache and goatee in need of a trim.

"Indeed sir, William Pierpont at your service. Friends call me Billy,"

Parcher wasn't sure he wasn't being condescended to, aware of his own soiled breeches and smock. He snorted and turned his back, tacking a long pull on his beer. He drained it on the second try, threw a coin on the bar, and returned to his room.

He found Flora there in his bed, a brazen smile revealing small, even teeth.

~ * ~

It was three days since, and the routine had been the same. He would come back to his room to find her there, ready for an hour of sex. She never spent the night for fear of discovery and losing her job.

He was dressing to go down for his dinner, all the while pacing up and down the tiny room uttering expletives under his breath.

"Ya been like an old woman frettin' for two days!" Flora said, sitting up. "Don't think I can stand it no more."

He stopped, stared at her, wondering if he could confide in her. "What would ya think about leaving here with me…and a lot o' money?"

"I thought as much!" she said. "What manner o' schemin' might you be up to?"

"Answer my question."

"Leave this grimy speck on a map? Nothin' keeps me here save a roof that don't leak, and the next meal."

He sat next to her on the bed. "Look here, Flora. I got this plan, see?" He proceeded to tell her about the church, the locked drawer, and the money.

"Why not bust the drawer open?"

"Don't want 'em to know they've been robbed 'till I'm long gone."

"Then pick the lock," she said.

He stared at her, shaking his head slowly. "Pick? With no key?"

She laughed. "I didn't keep my mum's drunken husbands in rum by spreadin' my legs! I stole for her. Not many locks I can't figure. All I need is a bent nail."

He tapped his foot on the floor, thinking. "How would you like to go into business with me?"

She got up to straddle him, her arms around his neck. "Well now, don't that sound like a fine idea?"

~ * ~

Parcher had just returned from the privies to his room the following morning. Down the hall, from the far end came William "Billy" Pierpont.

"A good morning to you, sir!" he greeted Parcher with a bright smile. He was freshly shaved, facial hair neatly trimmed.

"Uh…yeah." Parcher ducked into his room, wondering how long the fool would be staying. He wasn't sure why the man bothered him so. Maybe it was just the type, full of talk, mostly horse shit.

He had a half hour to go over what he intended to do to occupy Sternkopf while Flora practiced on the lock. The plan was to make sure her pick worked, then come back at night after Parcher made sure the office window was unlocked before Sternkopf locked the sanctuary for the night.

He needn't have worried. The plan went off like a well-oiled clock, thanks to Sternkopf, himself. On arriving at the church, the Reverend asked Parcher to accompany him to the parsonage to help install a new hand pump at the kitchen sink. It was a great luxury the congregation had donated, replacing the need to carry water from the well.

Sternkopf was a believer in leaving the sanctuary open during the day for the occasional worshiper in need of solitude and reflection. Flora would have access to the office with no one questioning her presence in the church.

The pump took almost all day to install by the time it was primed and working. Parcher returned with Sternkopf to lock the sanctuary, hoping Flora had done her job, and to unlock the window. To his horror, the Reverend continued on into the office.

"Sir! Uh…sir."

"Yes, Albert?" Sternkopf said without turning.

Parcher stood paralyzed as the preacher continued into the office, almost immediately returning.

"Glad I checked. The window was unlocked. So that's taken care of."

He headed for the narthex door, waiting for Parcher to follow, and locked it securely.

Parcher made his way home slowly, reluctant to disappoint his new accomplice after her good work. *Thank God he didn't check the drawer!* They would just have to wait until tomorrow…that was the fact of it.

Tonight he didn't stop at the pub, but went straight to his room to tell her—but she wasn't there! He checked the two unoccupied rooms off the hall. Not there, either. Then he noticed the door at the end of the hall was ajar. Pierpont's room. Curious, he quietly pushed the door open to peek inside.

It was empty. The peddler was gone.

Now what? He decided to have a drink.

Downstairs, standing at the tap was Jens Müller, jovial as ever.

"Ha! Here is the pious church cleaner!" he announced to the room.

A few heads rose from their card games and chess boards, then returned to what they were doing.

"How are you and good old Herman getting on?"

"Herman?"

"Sternkopf, and his cagey wife, Berta."

"Sounds like you know them well."

"Cousin. Berta, that is." Müller took a swig of beer. "I'm a bit of a black sheep in their eyes, I fear."

"I have no problem with them." Parcher nodded to the barkeep for a lager. "Have you seen that housemaid?"

"Odd that you ask. I came to town to buy a hay fork two hours ago, and saw her at the inn's stable talking to that peddler who was here. He was hitching his horse to the wagon. Must have been two hours ago. I thought it was strange."

"Strange? She's a maid, he's a guest."

"I'm sure you're right."

Still, Parcher finished his glass, and sought out the proprietor. "Has Mr. Pierpont gone?"

"Yes, indeed, sir. Earlier than I expected. He usually stays a few days, at least, while he makes his rounds."

"Can you have the maid see me? I need a clean towel."

"I'm sure you'll find her cleaning in one of the rooms upstairs, sir."

Parcher began to worry, wondering if she could have gone off with that fool Pierpont. *No, not with a share of all that money waiting to be plucked.*

Twenty-three

Andy

She had an appointment in the afternoon to sign the necessary employment papers with Staff Sergeant Roberts, the Detachment Commander.

"That's it then?" Roberts said when she returned to his office from filling them out with the Administration Clerk. "Let's go tell Arnold Terry he'll have someone to take over some of his cases. He's been griping for months about it."

"I saw him in the detectives' room. Would that be my desk opposite his?"

Roberts nodded.

"Let me surprise him."

She walked into the room where three desks were crammed. There, in a corner by the window a large man with the polished dome of a head was leaning back in his chair, a phone to his ear.

She waited until he put the phone down, then stood at his shoulder.

"Good to meet you at last, Detective Terry, I'm Andrea Blake." Though they'd collaborated two years earlier, it had been all on the telephone. Through it all he'd been a bit of a pain in the ass.

Terry pivoted around in his chair. "Excuse me?"

"Blake," she repeated. "Andy Blake. Two years ago."

Slowly light registered in his eyes. "The phony drug bust…so?"

She pulled back the swivel chair from the desk opposite, sat, and gave it a spin.

"What's on *your* mind?" Terry said.

"Thought I'd stop by and take a look at your case load." She propped her feet up on a drawer she'd opened.

Terry removed his glasses and rubbed his face. "What the hell'r you talking about, Ms. Blake?"

She reached in her purse and retrieved her five-minute-old O.P.P Shield. "Just sayin' that's all. Your troubled days are over. Andy's here."

~ * ~

Stacey was still out of town, giving her the chance to put away the several things she'd picked up at The Soo and spend a quiet evening by herself.

She pulled out the new shield, studying it, wondering if she'd done the right thing. Gritting her teeth, she picked up the phone, and touched a pre-set number. There was a wait while she was put through.

"Bradley, this is Andy Blake." She used Smyth's first name because the prig of a man would hate it. "I want to give you a heads-up that I'm tendering my resignation, effective in three weeks, at which time you can also terminate my leave of absence. I've cherished my years with Windsor Police Services, and wish you well in your new assignment. My written resignation should be in your hands within a week."

There was a short wait before a perfunctory "Thank you, Ms. Blake" was followed by the sound of the disconnect. She could not help but feel a smile spread across her face.

She found a book from her mother's collection she'd never found time to read, then poured herself a cold glass of iced tea. She read late into the night, feeling good.

~ * ~

Voices outside. Andy squinted at the bedside clock: It was 9:15 a.m. Last night's iced tea had graduated to wine. She'd read her way into the wee hours.

Dragging herself out of bed, she shuffled into her single bathroom, and shoved the window's curtain aside.

"Good grief." It looked like a carnival was setting up down there. A large tent was being erected that was easily four times the size required to cover the stone foundation. She brushed her teeth, and pulled her hair back into a short pony tail, choosing to ignore the strands of grey that surely must have popped up overnight. A pair of shorts and an old college sweat with BLUES emblazoned on the front, sufficed for the nonce.

Downstairs she started the coffee maker, and stepped out onto the rear stoop. Buck Tremblay's floppy hat was the first thing she spotted darting among workers struggling with the canopy. Lila Knowles was on the other side of the fray, writing something on a note pad. Having finished, she looked up to see Andy, and started toward the house.

"Hope we didn't wake you," Lila said.

"It's fine. I have some coffee on. Come in, and tell me what's what."

They sat in the kitchen while the old percolator began to gurgle.

"What do you know about your family, Andy?" Lila opened her note pad, and sat poised, pencil at the ready.

"My family?"

"I mean back in time, your ancestors."

Andy thought, while she got down two mugs. "Not much. I remember my maternal grandmother. She died when I was eleven or twelve."

"What was her name?"

"'Grandmother' to me, but maybe…Beth comes to mind."

"Could it be Bess?"

"Yes, I'm pretty sure that was it."

Lila was again making notes. "And your grandfather?"

"I have no idea. I don't remember him being talked about." Andy poured out two mugs of coffee.

"You never asked all these years?"

"As a kid I wasn't interested. I went away to school, and soon was a single mother with more on my plate than genealogy."

Lila smiled. "Sorry. I'm so deep into the subject, I forget people have other priorities."

"Why are you so interested in my grandparents?"

Lila blew on the hot coffee, and sipped. "I need to know more about the history of this site. Hector McVey built your house in 1892. That is the first deed that is recorded for the property. He and his wife Bess had four daughters. The oldest was also named Bess who married—" she checked her notes—"Arnold Bledsoe."

"Bledsoe! That's my mother's maiden name."

Lila nodded. "I was pretty sure."

"Seems you've been digging already."

"It's what I do,"

Andy was getting into this. "So, go on!"

"I'm afraid from here it gets more difficult. I've found Hector and Bess McVey's lineage, but there are three generations for both families between them and the burning of Fort St. Joseph. That means the original owner could have been anyone of at least twelve individuals, if indeed there is an unbroken line to your family. If not, then we may never learn the original owner of the cabin."

"Cabin? Seems small for a house."

"Yes, but the root cellar suggests otherwise—at least a cabin."

"What next, then?"

Lila closed her note pad. "More digging into the families. There's a lot of information available online these days. It'll take time to check out all the branches of your ancestors. Meanwhile, we might get lucky, and find a clue when we excavate the site."

There was a rap on the door. Andy opened it to find Tremblay staring up at her owlishly through oversized lenses. "Well come in, Buck. We have coffee."

Tremblay was irritated. "Those kids are running around the site like they were setting up for a rock band. No respect for the integrity of the dig at all."

"Oh, for heaven's sake, Buck!" Lila said. She peered down at him despite both were seated. "A backhoe has already scraped away a hundred years of dirt from the floor. What harm can they do?"

Tremblay accepted the coffee from Andy. "It's the principle of the thing. Those students need to learn how to properly prepare a site for an archaeological dig."

Andy changed the subject. "What do you do first?"

Tremblay said, "We screen every cubic centimeter of dirt your backhoe piled up back there. That will take a week. Also, I want to send char samples of rock and wood off for carbon dating. We won't start on the root cellar for at least a week, so my students can watch and assist."

"Where are you keeping the kids?" Andy asked. "There must be a dozen of them."

Lila spoke. "There's a music camp here on the Island. Their session is over for the summer, so we negotiated to use their cabins."

Andy could just guess what fun a co-educational group of college students would have being together at that old camp on the F&G Line.

~ * ~

That night her phone rang. It was 7:45 by the kitchen clock. Grant Stacey was on the line.

"What a trip," he moaned. "I took the plane, and got tangled up in that weather that just moved in. I'm glad to be home."

"Are you okay?" she asked. He sounded tired.

"Yeah. Good old instrument training. I'm just a little beat, probably hit the sack early tonight. What's new with you?"

She told him about the events in the backyard, then calmly told him about taking the job in Sault Ste. Marie.

"Ho-Holy shit! I'll be right over!"

~ * ~

Andy had a frozen pizza in the oven by the time he arrived. He was full of questions, talking excitedly, forgetting his weariness. The tension between them over the past two years was finally broken.

It was ten by the time the kitchen was cleaned up. Stacey made a move to retrieve his windbreaker

"Hold it, mister," Andy said. "You aren't going anywhere." She took his hand, and led him up the stairs.

It was the first time she'd made love in her bed where she'd fantasized the act as a girl. They both fell fast asleep after. She woke once, feeling him breathe. It was nice.

~ * ~

He was still sleeping when the alarm buzzed at 6:30. She got up, showered, and was dressed with morning coffee by 7:15.

"Grant!" She put a steaming mug at the bedside. "Grant, I've got to go. My first day on the job."

He opened his eyes, looking around the room to remember where he was.

"I'll call you sometime today," she whispered.

His hand shot out from the covers. She caught it, and he pulled her to him.

"Last night…." He searched for words.

"I know. For me, too."

Twenty-four

Parcher

Flora hadn't shown up in his room the previous night, a practice Parcher had come to expect. It was already time to be at the church. He splashed water on his face and got dressed, after a fitful night's sleep thinking of where she might be. As he stepped into the hall the proprietor's wife was exiting the room at the end of the hall—Pierpont's room—holding a laundry bag and a few clean towels.

"I'm just coming to your room, Mr. Parcher."

"Oh…ah, where is that girl Flora?"

"Disappeared, sir! Some say with that Mr. Pierpont. More work for me, worse the luck."

Parcher took the clean towel back into his room. He stood there, trying to understand what was happening, *No, she wouldn't!* But it was the only explanation. *She took the money! Shared it with that pot and pan peddler!*

He had to know for sure. Before he knew it, he was almost to the church, half running, half trudging along, thinking of ways to approach the matter without casting suspicion on himself.

At the door of the church, Sternkopf was there talking with a man Parcher recognized as a parishioner. He waited nervously as the two finished their conversation.

"Albert! You're late this morning. Is something wrong?"

"No, Reverend…I just…no."

Sternkopf stood motionless, waiting.

"Is everything all right then, sir?" At once, Parcher regretted the stupidity of the question.

"Why, what could you mean, Albert?"

"Nothin', I guess." He continued into the narthex, as if to flee the gaffe.

"The outside of the new windows need washing, Albert. That will be a good chore for today."

Parcher was about to reply, when they both saw Berta Sternkopf at the door to the office. Her face was colorless, her eyes blazing.

"Herman!" She fell into the language Parcher could only assume was the Pennsylvania German he'd heard about. Sternkopf answered her in kind. They went back and forth, the tone of the dialogue escalating from anxious to angry.

"What is it?" Parcher said.

"Albert! No one has been in the church office, have they?"

"No," Parcher answered. Perhaps a little too fast, he thought.

Sternkopf turned back to his wife, whose eyes were still locked on Parcher.

"What has happened?" Parcher insisted.

Berta Sternkopf's voice was low, almost a growl. "The entire six month's savings for the prayer book fund—gone!"

"It was locked!" the Reverend said.

"No more. The drawer and the lock box, both." Her eyes were still on Parcher.

"I…I should get started on the windows," he said, but couldn't tear away from the woman's glare.

"Yes, Albert," Sternkopf said. "No use your being involved with this."

He went to the shed to retrieve the ladder and washing materials. When he returned, he could hear the arguing still going on inside. The Reverend's baritone, his wife's shrill. Parcher was sure his own name was voiced by the woman.

Somehow that bitch knows—or believes—I have something to do with the theft. His mind seesawed back and forth between that thought and the idea that Flora had absconded with the entire loot, leaving him holding the bag. The more he thought of it, the surer he was the little whore had made a fool of him.

It had always been so. His mother leaving him alone to be with the sailors of the Baltimore ships. One of those big clippers would call, the crew flush with pay, looking for love. He hated the ships, the sailors, and most of all, the whores like his mother.

He hated them all, and now that little slut Flora was treating him the same way. If he found her, he'd kill her. He had no doubt of that.

Two hours later, he was almost finished with the windows when he noticed the deacon who handled the collections and two others show up at the parsonage. They were admitted immediately as if they were expected. *A meeting of some kind!* Soon, the whole town would be buzzing about the theft.

He'd made sure he had an alibi, but…*Jens Müller! I'm sure he suspects there is something going on between the girl and me!* He considered his options:

Get out of town.

Find Flora.

He decided to do both.

~ * ~

He'd accumulated just over eleven dollars. Not very much for travel. He certainly couldn't afford the luxury of paying for his room. Other than his coat, cap, and a satchel he had purchased to carry his personal gear, he had no luggage to draw attention of his slipping out of town. The question was, in which direction?

There was east to Zanesville, and west back to Chillicothe. A trail followed the Muskingum River north, but that led nowhere. He was so angry he couldn't think clearly. *Calm down! Get some information.*

He found the innkeeper, a humorless, harried man behind the tap in the tavern. The room had yet begun to fill for the evening. He was replacing a beer keg, muttering to himself.

"I'll have a glass, if y' please."

"It'll be a minute or two."

"No hurry. Where's yer man?"

"Sprained ankle. Says he can't stand on it all night. Same day the chambermaid disappears, of all things."

Parcher waited a moment before saying, "Heard she took off with that peddler fella."

The man responded with expletives as he struggled the heavy keg into place. Parcher walked around and easily placed the barrel. "Suppose they took off toward Chillicothe?"

"Not likely," the man answered. "That's where he came from. He'd be on his way back east. I thank you for the help, Mr. Parcher."

But Parcher was gone before the innkeeper reappeared from under the counter.

Twenty-five

Zane's Trace, in the central part of Ohio, is flat and straight, not having to contend with undulating topography, nor private property lines when it was laid out in 1797.

After a series of short rides and hikes on a two-day trek from New Lancaster, Parcher walked the final three miles into Zanesville. He could see the town across the Muskingum River, a background of hills in the distance. At the river, a simple rope ferry worked to and fro. The town couldn't be larger than a thousand souls, Parcher thought.

Stepping off the ferry, he was soon in the center of town. The place had the feeling of being newly built. Construction was in evidence everywhere.

He found Pierpont almost immediately. There was just one inn. Parcher inquired, learning that Mr. Pierpont was a guest there, but had had an unfortunate loss of his horse, and was negotiating for a replacement at the time. The clerk had no idea where that might be, but expected Pierpont would show up for his evening meal.

"Was he traveling with anyone?" Parcher asked.

The man showed yellow, uneven teeth as he grinned. "Might have sumpin' to do with losin' his horse! She was seen a-gallopin' down the road to Marrietta on that 'ol carriage horse."

Parcher asked around where he might buy a horse, and was told there were some likely farms on the Newark Road, north. He found the road, located a good vantage about a mile out of town, and waited.

As if Providence had written the plot, after a two hour wait he was rewarded by the sight of Pierpont on an old dray horse at a leisurely walk. He waited for the rider to pass, slipped from cover, and pulled Pierpont down hard. The horse dutifully stopped, looking around inquisitively.

"Where's my money, you cockchafer?"

Pierpont, his rump on the ground, looked up at Parcher in disbelief. "I don't…"

Parcher backhanded him across the cheek and nose. Blood colored his mustache and goatee. "One more chance before I kill ya."

"No, I really don't know!"

This time, Parcher's boot caught Pierpont's ribs with an audible crack. The man gasped, fighting to regain his breath. Parcher waited patiently for him to speak.

"She stole…stole it. Got my horse…"

"Where'd she go, ya snivelin' fuck?"

"Don't…know."

Parcher kicked him hard in the head. William “Billy” Pierpont spun like a top, landing face down in a rut.

Parcher pulled himself up on the horse, leaving Pierpont either unconscious or dead. He guided the horse back into town, asking directions for the road to Marietta.

~ * ~

He figured she had a day’s lead on him. She’d surely be looking for a keel boat, either east or west, on the Ohio. He’d seen Marietta when he and that old goat Varner traveled from Pittsburg, seven years earlier. Then, the city was only a few houses. He hadn’t any idea how many boats would call there these days, but hoped she hadn’t already found a way out.

The cursed horse had one speed—slow. He was sore as damnation, riding without a saddle, when he rode into the town nestled on the east side of the Muskingum River where it flows into the Ohio. The town was twice the size he’d remembered.

The wharf was alive with activity on both rivers. Any thought of finding her easily was now gone. *Where would a single woman go?* He tried an inn close by the river, but no one had seen a woman alone, much less one looking for a boat. *If she hadn’t found a boat immediately, she’d have to find an inn.*

He was right. A second, run-down place had taken her on the previous night, *a Mrs. Pierpont, no less. The cheeky bitch!*

"She ate a meal here around mid-day, then went her way," the innkeeper said.

It was late afternoon. *Three or four hours ago, then.* Parcher raced back to the wharf, leaving the horse tied at the inn. Frantically he asked anyone who would listen about boats departing since noon, going either way. It was maddening. No one knew anything.

He began to rant at whomever happened to be in earshot, berating them for not noticing a young, single woman requesting passage on the river. Eventually he had to give up. He tried the two ale houses near the water. It was at the second, on the banks of the Muskingum, where a large bosomed woman at the tap said a young woman had waited there for her keel boat to make ready. She had no idea which way, up or down river, she had gone.

At the realization of his defeat, a seething anger began to build, fueled by the perceived parade of women in his life who had brought him to this juncture. He ordered an ale, then a rum, then another.

Late that night—or early morning—the ale house closed, forcing Parcher out, stumbling drunk. Somehow he remembered the horse, and made his way back to the inn to retrieve it. It was gone, and he was in no condition to inquire about it.

He had no recollection where he'd slept after being in the tavern, but found himself on the streets of town the following morning walking aimlessly, his head a mess of cobwebs and throbbing pain. Passing a storefront proclaiming

'*The Ohio Gazette* and *Virginia Herald*,' a newspaper of the same name was posted in the window. His eye caught the word *MURDER* in large type. What he could make out in the story were references to Zanesville. Suddenly his headache and rolling stomach became secondary. He quickened his pace toward the wharf.

Twenty-six

Nettie

June 1809

Sault Ste. Marie

The large mirror that hung over her dresser table had been delivered only yesterday. It was in the hold of the British schooner *Calliope,* on a welcomed visit by a ship this far west. Thomas bought it for Nettie, she knew, as an atonement.

The previous month they had been across the river with the Johnstons celebrating the first leaves on the maples, and the warmer weather after a hard winter. Thomas had too much to drink, something that was occurring more often of late. The argument was over some trivial matter Nettie could barely recall. But the alcohol mixed with Thomas' growing melancholy proved disastrous. He struck her.

The gift of the mirror would normally have been a thing of delight, but now would always remind her of that blow to the cheek, and diminish her feelings toward Thomas.

Nettie stood back from the mirror in order to view her full form. The instance reminded her of that day, eight years ago, in her wedding dress. Was the image even the same girl? Where was that pudgy lass of seventeen? She saw only a trim, confident and—*handsome?*—woman of twenty-three. She gave one of her gold and amethyst earrings a flick of her finger. Now, instead of her mother's image over her shoulder, Lily's appeared.

"That glass will steal your spirit," Lily said.

Nettie turned away, embarrassed by her vanity. "I haven't seen myself in such a long time."

"You do not need that glass to speak of your beauty. I can do that."

Nettie flushed at the compliment, and changed the subject. "Our guests will be here soon."

It had taken almost two years, but Nettie finally had her home in a state where she felt comfortable reciprocating the dinners and parties they'd been invited to in the small European community. The Johnstons and the Logans, especially.

"Yes, and I have my nephew to serve the drinks and help in the kitchen.

Nettie was relieved. She wanted everything perfect. Lily had a girl from the tribe, as well, to help with serving dinner.

"Oh, Lily! What would I do, if not for you?" She embraced the older woman who accepted the gesture stiffly, unaccustomed to such effusiveness.

~ * ~

The guests arrived. First, Robert Logan, Thomas' immediate supervisor, and his wife. Logan was a man of few words, but sagacious when his opinion was requested. Marie made up for him. Always outgoing, she had been a great help to Nettie, lending the use of the minutia of household items a young family must acquire over time.

They were followed by the Askins, John Jr. and Madelaine, who had made the trip from Fort St. Joseph. Over the past two years, Madelaine Askin and Nettie had become dear friends, despite having seen each other only a half-dozen times. Madelaine made it her business to accompany John on his occasional trips upriver.

Last to arrive were the Johnstons, who lived on the American side of the river which, since 1805, had been designated 'The Michigan Territory.'

John Johnston was a man bigger than life. His presence filled any room he occupied. Johnston was an Irishman who arrived in Canada with means and influence. He quickly became involved with the North West Company, opting to become a "wintering partner," living near one of the company's outposts. He chose Sault Ste. Marie, assimilating immediately into the local culture. Soon after arriving, he married the daughter of a local Ojibwa chief. While it appeared to be a true marriage of love, the union was a major factor in Johnston's ability to deal successfully with the Indians. He later grew quite wealthy as an independent trader.

The Johnston home overlooking the south shore of the St. Marys River was always full of life, mainly of the eight children he sired with his wife Susan, but also with all manner of guests. Politicians, surveyors, traders, engineers, Indian leaders, made the Johnston home the center of Sault society. Nettie and Susan, whose Indian name was *Ozaguscodaywayquay,* had become good friends, tempered only by the river that separated their homes. They loved Carrie, and would send a batteau for her whenever possible.

Walking behind with Susan Johnston was a third person with his tall hat shading his face. When he turned, Nettie recognized him at once. Martin Legère!

He was dressed in European clothes, obtained from where, Nettie could not imagine. His lack of tuque revealed a shock of black hair down to his shoulders. His face was tanned and weathered despite his age Nettie knew to only be in his thirties. She felt a thrill ripple through her body.

"I hope you won't mind," Johnston said. "Our friend Legère arrived only last night. I believe you know him. Will it be a problem to set an extra plate?"

Normally Nettie would have thought, *of course it's a problem,* but Martin Legère? No.

"Monsieur Legère! How good to see you again!" She extended her hand which he proceeded to gently kiss.

"Mrs. Gibson, my pleasure."

The exchange lasted a trifle long.

Thomas piped up. "I say, Legère! You look the right proper dandy!"

They shook hands; Legère didn't respond.

"Come," Nettie said, "the others are inside."

Missing from the group were the Ermatingers, Charles and Charlotte. Ermatinger, a lawyer and gentleman farmer with a previous tie to the North West Company, was called away at the time. Like the Johnstons, their fine stone house was a popular center of social life in Sault Ste. Marie.

Nettie and Thomas made the rounds chatting with the guests. More accurately Nettie did the chatting. Thomas, uncomfortable with those niceties, hung back.

Lily's nephew, dressed in a ruffled white shirt over newly made deerskin trousers, passed punch for the ladies, and took orders of stronger spirits for the men. A side table of delicacies was available. Soon the home was alive with gossip and political talk of the day. Much of it consisted of the increasing tension between the United States and England. The Americans complained of English ships raiding American merchant vessels for un-naturalized English-born seamen to man their under-crewed Royal Navy in its current Peninsular war with France. That, and a myriad of complaints of the British impeding American trade.

It was close to an hour before Legère sought Nettie out. "I am sorry to inconvenience you like this. Mr. Johnston insisted."

She smiled. "Mr. Johnston knew I would be delighted to have you here."

Legère studied his glass of port for a moment. "I have thought of you…and your family often."

"Thank you. We have fond memories of our time with you."

"...and Caroline. She is well?"

"Oh, yes. She speaks of you, and big Henri and Émile!

I am sorry now that she is with our housekeeper's family for the day."

He nodded. "I know your *Flower*. She is in good hands."

"Will you be here long?"

"After tomorrow I shed these borrowed clothes, and continue on to the Red River country."

"Carrie will miss seeing you. Perhaps she might tomorrow?"

"We'll be at the landing, loading our canoes."

She turned her attention to Thomas' voice above the others.

Nettie joined him to suggest he announce dinner. Lily and she had prepared a special treat of Lake Superior trout, caught only yesterday.

Thomas was uncharacteristically holding forth. He appeared to be complaining about North West Company policy to an uncomfortable group composed of Mrs. Logan, John Askin Jr., and Susan Johnston. His speech was slurred.

"Thomas," Nettie broke in, "perhaps you can announce dinner."

"Must you always interrupt?" he snapped, loud enough for all to hear.

Nettie was mortified, the others wide-eyed. Conversation elsewhere stopped.

Gracefully as she could, Nettie retired to the kitchen to recover. To stay would have escalated the outburst, she was sure. It was true, she thought, he'd been relying on alcohol of late, particularly in stressful situations. He did not handle it well.

Sound from her dining room signaled the group was assembling. She joined them to find Thomas with another glass of rum in hand. Lily was doing her best to get people seated. Nettie came to her rescue.

The remainder of the evening of perfectly prepared food and gathering of good friends was unfortunately marred by Thomas' inane and often inappropriate commentary. Nettie wisely had Lily's nephew abscond with what was left of the rum, but the damage was done.

The evening was not ruined, but the company left earlier than they would have, giving Nettie sympathetic looks as they went.

Legère, last to leave, hesitated. "Madam… Nettie," he whispered. "Are you…content?"

Nettie was shocked. The question was so direct—*and so apt?*

"We are fine," she responded, a little too easily.

He stared at her for a moment, then gave a short bow and joined the Johnstons' carriage.

She shut the door and waited there, her head pressed against it, listening to the retreating carriage wheels on the bricks.

Twenty-seven

Bright sun slanted through the bedroom window, announcing another fair day. Nettie left the bed quietly, not wishing to wake Thomas. He'd found the rum bottle after the guests had gone, finished it and passed out in bed. Earlier, he had come into the kitchen brandishing the flask, as she and Lily were finishing up.

"Who does this Johnston think he is, inviting someone into my house without a word?"

Nettie headed him off, speaking quietly. "There was room, and enough food. John knew we'd be happy to see him."

He looked at her, petulantly. "He seemed happy enough to see *you*!"

That brought on a series of escalating accusations and denials, ending with Thomas stomping off to the parlor to finish the rum. Lily had respectfully slipped away, but not before giving Nettie's hand a surreptitious squeeze of support.

Still in her dressing gown, Nettie heard sounds of life in Carrie's room. There she was, so grown in the past two years. Now seven, she was reading everything she could get her hands on. She was getting down her copy of *A Pretty Little Pocket Book*, a collection of stories by John Newbery. Nettie had been reading Defoe's *Robinson Crusoe* to her, but she was reading the Newbery stories by herself.

"Good morning, Carrie."

"Mama," was her smiling response.

"You fell asleep, and Uncle White Deer carried you home."

"I woke up," she said. "You and papa were talking loudly."

The words stung. Nettie had heard her own parents argue at times, and hated it.

"Darling…" she began.

"I can't find *Little Goodie Two Shoes,*" Carrie said, oblivious to her mother's distress.

Nettie located the volume of the Newbery story and handed it to the girl. "Would you like to see some old friends of yours today?"

"Friends?"

"The Voyageurs are here."

Carrie lit up. "Émile? Henri? Martin?"

"And others, I am sure."

"Can we go now?"

"After we eat, and Papa is dressed."

~ * ~

Breakfast consisted of boiled eggs, toasted bread, and Carrie's excited chatter about the Voyageurs.

Thomas was irritable, and chided the girl for her lack of discipline.

"I have no desire to mingle unnecessarily with those types. I see enough of them on my travels."

"Thomas, you cannot mean that. Those men are our friends."

"Friends? They are our employees."

"Please, Thomas. It means so much to Carrie."

"It seems it means a trifle too much to *you!*"

Nettie sat up straight in her chair. Thomas ignored her stare.

"If it means so much to the girl, perhaps this afternoon," he said, sopping up the last of his egg, and muttering something about it being the Sabbath.

~ * ~

A breeze off Lake Superior brought a chill, countering the bright afternoon sun. Their carriage rumbled west over the rutted road to the docks above the falls. There, they engaged a batteau to ferry them to the American side. Nettie wore a simple frock under her shawl. Carrie insisted on a miniature version of her mother's ensemble plus her favorite blue bonnet. Thomas was for the occasion, and his stated lack of enthusiasm for the visit, a bit overdressed in top hat, white stock, cutaway coat. He even broke out his breeches and hose, a rare look in 1809 Sault Ste. Marie.

Halfway across the river, they could see three large *Canots de Maítre* at the landing with men working around them. As they approached, Nettie could see Legère and Henri making their way to the landing. Others of the voyage from Montreal began to join them.

Émile shouted, “Ha! There is our little Caroline, all growed up!”

Carrie giggled, thrilled to know Émile remembered her.

With the batteau tied up, they were helped ashore and led to where the three canoes were being laded. Questions about the impending trip were followed by reminiscences of their time together two years ago. Two of the boats would carry on beyond the Red River all the way to the Pacific Ocean. It had been three years since the Americans, Lewis and Clark, returned from an historic trip on a more southerly route to the mouth of the Colombia River, but the idea of such a journey was still unimaginable to Nettie.

“It is the trip we made after leaving you here,” Legère said, pointing to his canoe mates. “We will bid farewell to the other boats and return in two months.”

“I think it is time to go,” Thomas said, speaking for the first time.”

In unison Carrie and her mother cried, “Oh, no!”

All eyes were on Thomas. He looked from side to side. “Stay if you wish, I have a matter to discuss with Johnston. Annette, I’ll wait for you there. It’s but a short walk.”

They did not argue. At once, Carrie began to bombard Henri and Émile about what they saw on the trip west across the mountains to the west coast of the continent. Henri plucked her up, and sat her down in the canoe. He and Émile spoke to her in French about the Rocky Mountains, and the western Indian tribes. Others from the crew added their stories.

Legère began to walk with Nettie along the river. "I feel it has been too long since we talked. I enjoyed our *pipes* together."

"I too, Martin."

"I…asked you earlier if you were content here, and you didn't…"

"My life here is not what I envisioned as a young bride, but what in life ever turns out exactly as one plans? The people here in this little outpost are kind. My daughter is thriving here."

"And you. Are you thriving?"

"What do you mean?" She stopped walking.

"I am sorry. It was a presumptuous question."

She continued to walk, thinking of what to say, if anything. "I don't look happy?"

He stopped, looking down at her. "You look beautiful, competent, and…sad."

She thought about the image of herself in the mirror yesterday. He described the woman she'd seen, so changed from the soft, callow girl in Montreal—and yes, the look of melancholy around the eyes. His insight into her feelings had an odd sexual effect. She felt herself flush.

"Forgive me," he said, misunderstanding her silence. He took her hand. "You are upset."

Her cheeks were burning, and the touch of him was too much to bear. "No…no, I am not upset. I am…so unhappy!"

The words surprised her, as if someone else had said them. There was no taking them back.

"Nettie!" He held her arms, his face close to hers.

Two years of fantasizing about this man were about to climax into something that was irretrievable. She pushed away, looking to see if the scene had been witnessed.

"We must go back. Thomas will expect us."

"I'll go with you. I am staying with the Johnstons. There is something I must say first.

"Don't!"

"I've thought of you constantly since our time together, but when I saw you last night, it was agonizing. If you say so, I'll never bother you again. But if there is a chance I could make a life for you, I will do anything to make that come true.

Nettie began to cry, and could not make herself stop.

Twenty-eight

Andy

The morning drive wasn't as much of a pain as she thought. It was a good time to pull herself together, and think about the day ahead. She was thinking about working with that horse's ass Arnold Terry. *Better establish the relationship right from the get-go.*

She arrived at her desk before Terry, and was searching through it for items like paper clips, stapler, but found only gum wrappers, a four year old phone book, a sandwich bag, and erasure dirt.

"First day of school, eh?" Terry draped his jacket over the back of his chair.

"Who was the pig who had this desk?" she retorted.

"Dunno. It was brought in from storage when Roberts got the okay for another detective. You ready for work?"

"No. I need to requisition a firearm, and get some basic office stuff. Does this phone work?"

"Pretty sure. Here, start reading these. I'll get your stuff from stores while you do. You can get your gun later. I don't see you shooting anyone in here."

Smart ass, she thought, and took the three file folders he passed.

The first was a missing person—female. Husband reported her having skipped with her four-year-old daughter. He claimed she would never have left voluntarily.

The next was a simple break-in that was reported a week ago, and handled by uniformed officers. It turned to be two seventh graders who were playing in an old, abandoned farmhouse. She wondered why it was still open.

The third was more up her alley. Methamphetamine arrests were increasing. The analyses did not agree with samples from other cities. The US and Canada both assured one or two deliveries might get across the bridge from the states, but not a steady stream. Andy was not so sure, but agreed they could not rule out a lab right here in town.

Terry returned with a cardboard box and a new desk blotter. She sorted through the box, giving Terry an approving smile. "Aren't you sweet!"

"Don't get used to it. What do you make of these?" He indicated the files.

"The meth case looks delicious. A lot like the one we worked on together."

He uttered a few words of approval for her breaking it.

She continued. “The missing woman is probably at a relative, friend, or woman’s shelter. Does the husband have any priors, restraining orders?”

Terry shook his head “no.”

“This other one looks to be settled. Why is it still open?”

“You obviously didn’t read it.”

“Obviously, I did,” she huffed.

“Look again.”

She did. The same story—no, there was an added page. A note about one of the kids’ fathers calling to report an unusual item taken from the presumed empty house. The child’s father was a dentist, but had taken enough anatomy to identify what the boy had was what looked like a human rib. Police were sent to investigate, but found nothing at the house.

Andy mentally kicked herself for having missed the note. *Damn! Anyone but Terry!*

“Tell you what,” he said. “Old bones give me the creeps. I’ll take the missing woman, you follow up on the haunted house, and we’ll sort out what to do about the phantom meth lab together.”

Andy was issued a standard Sig P226 and two ten-round SW .40 caliber clips. She was provided for the day a patrol car and uniformed officer. His name was Anthony Crucianni, a second year patrolman.

"Were you one of the investigating officers, Crucianni?" she asked, as they were on their way north on Hwy. 17.

"Yes ma'am. The kids were seen coming out of the house. We talked to their parents, both nice families, about the danger of their kids poking around empty houses. That put an end to it, we thought. Then I got a call back from the dad of one of the kids, saying he caught the boy playing with a bone that looked human, and it came from that house. We investigated, but found nothing."

"Let's talk to the boy first," she said.

The boy was not at home, but his mother, Alice Woodruff, made a call, and had him there in less than ten minutes, along with another boy of the same age.

"Where did you find the bone, Brent?" Andy asked after his mother produced him.

"In the house."

"Yes, I know. *Where* in the house?"

"I don't know—in the attic, I guess."

Andy asked Crucianni if they'd looked there.

"My partner climbed up there with a light, and found zip."

She turned to the boy. "Where in the attic?"

He turned to his mother, who gave him a stern nod. "It was just sittin' there—on the floor. There was nothin' else up there, so I took it. I didn't know what it was, honest!"

Andy thanked the mother, gave the boy some obligatory words about breaking and entering, and they left.

"I've done worse than that as a kid," Crucianni said.

"So have I," Andy agreed.

They found the house on a dirt dead-end north of Fourth-Line Road, a bicycle ride distance from the boy's home. It was a two story affair, a typical farmhouse about the size of Andy's. The siding was of brick-textured tarpaper, and though the doors were padlocked, the windows had long ago been breached. The boys may have entered, but there was no breaking in necessary.

Andy hoisted through the gaping hole that had been the parlor window. Crucianni followed. The first floor was empty of anything but a few beverage cans, a faded pizza carton, and other trash. A hole in the ceiling showed where a heater or stove of some kind had been. Upstairs was much the same. Trash everywhere…an empty condom foil by a window glinted up at them.

"Check out the bedrooms," Andy said.

"We did," Crucianni said. "That one is empty, this one has an empty crate, and a chair."

Andy looked anyway, but it was just as the young officer said.

There was nothing in the bathroom—literally. The plumbing was entirely torn out.

"How did those kids get in the attic?" Crucianni wondered aloud.

"How indeed," Andy said.

There was a square in the ceiling exposing the roof rafters. "

"My partner is six-four. He just jumped up, got a handhold, and did a pull-up.

"But the kids?"

"Could have used that crate and chair in the bedroom."

He went back and retrieved them. Sure enough, it looked like an eleven or twelve year old could pull himself up by standing on the chair and box.

Andy eyed the rickety chair. "I'll opt for a hoist from you, thank you. Let me have your flashlight, and lift me up as far as you can."

Crucianni grabbed her around the waist, and lifted her to his full arm's reach. Andy got hold of the sill, and did a pull-up. Once there, she was able to work her upper arms into the space, and hoist herself through.

"Okay, I'm impressed," Crucianni called up to her. "What do you see?"

"Nothing," she said "…yet."

But there really was nothing. The attic was free of the junk that littered the rest of the house. She played the light on the rafters, thinking someone had possibly hanged themselves here. It was a common venue for such suicides, but she saw nothing. The attic walls were finished, not just bare studs, as in her own house. They were only about four feet high over the eaves, but Andy was able to stand at full height in the middle of the room.

At one end of the room she could see where the flue for the missing stove was enclosed, recesses on either side. Something about it looked odd.

Pushing away a spider web, she examined it more closely. One part of the wall behind the stack was deeper than the other. On the shallow side a crack of about one inch was where the wall met the floor. She shined her light there, but could see nothing. Knocking on both sides of the stack returned strikingly different sounds.

"Officer Crucianni, you still there?" she called.

A muffled, "Not going anywhere, Detective."

She walked back to the opening. "You have any tools in that prowler of yours?"

"Just a nut wrench, a jack, a pry bar…"

"Get the pry bar, and come on up," she said.

A few minutes later, he was handing her the pry bar through the opening. "I see what you mean about the crate and chair." He was five-eleven, and two hundred pounds, but surprisingly agile, and had no trouble working his way up.

"Take a look at this," she said, illuminating the flue.

"Painted a different shade than the other walls. Looks like this side of the chimney had some remodeling done."

"Exactly," she said. "You think you can pull that wall down without disturbing whatever's behind it?"

He took the straight end of the pry bar and jabbed the wall about head-high. It punched in a neat hole. "Dry wall," he said. "That's odd. Bet you a hundred bucks the other walls are lath and plaster."

He put the curved end of the pry bar into the slot he'd created, and pulled. A large piece came loose, and Andy ripped it free. Behind was the outside wall of the house. The space between was about ten inches.

"Keep going," she said.

Crucianni worked downward. Gypsum dust shown in the light.

"Hold it," Andy said, jamming the flashlight into the enlarged hole. She peered down into the space. A grinning face stared back at her enhanced by a gold inlay in one tooth.

She turned to Crucianni and said, "I think you'd better get on your radio and ask for the crime lab nerds."

Twenty-nine

September 1809

Thomas was ecstatic. For two years he'd been urging William McGillivray to instruct the post at Fort William to adopt uniform inventory and bookkeeping practices. The letter had finally come and Thomas was sent to implement the system. It would be a sweet revenge for months of resistance by the manager there. The five hundred mile visit to the northwest corner of Lake Superior would require at least a month.

Nettie came to the lower boat landing to see him off in a North West Company canoe, loaded with trade goods for the post, and manned by a full crew of Voyageurs for the *Canot de Maître*

"I am pleased that you will be with friends during my absence, Annette." Thomas kissed her. He was referring to an invitation John Askin had brought from Madelaine to join her on St. Joseph Island while John was in Sandwich visiting his father, and attending to business at Fort Detroit.

The boat entered the small lock barely large enough for the thirty-six foot canoe. It always intrigued Nettie how the system worked. A gate was closed behind the boat, and the upstream gate was opened, allowing water to flow into the lock, raising the boat several feet to the Lake Superior level.

She watched them as they swiftly paddled away. Thomas' drinking had gotten worse over the summer. Perhaps this good turn in his fortune would slake his desire for it.

Once home she began preparing for the visit with the Askins. Carrie and Lily would be with her. John was returning to St. Joseph by batteau in the morning, and she had packing to do.

~ * ~

It was good to be downstream on St. Joseph Island, away from the tensions of home life. This was Nettie's third autumn in Upper Canada, and the day was typical— still warm, but in the evening one could feel the fresh chill of the fall. Some of the maples were beginning to turn color. It was glorious.

"This may be my favorite time of year," Nettie said, watching Carrie and the other children playing on the beach.

Madelaine had led Nettie, Lily, and two other mothers on a picnic to a protected cove a considerable distance east of the fort. It was good to sit in the shade after a long, over-warm walk.

"I believe I prefer the spring," Madelaine said. "After such a long winter—what do you think, Lily?"

The stoic woman's lips formed a small smile. "There is good in all seasons the Great Father gives us. Good hunting in winter, good syrup in spring, good fishing in summer, good harvest in autumn."

Madelaine grinned. "I wish all our religions were that simple and pure."

Nettie loved Madelaine's way of looking at life. Her husband was posted on the most remote place she could imagine, yet her outlook was always positive. People gravitated to her.

"Why was John needed in Sandwich?" she asked.

"He was, until a few years ago, Director of Customs for Amherstburg. There are still some issues he attends to once a year. Also his father's health has waned of late."

"His father is in Sandwich?"

"Yes, a lieutenant colonel in the Canada Militia.

"Oh dear," Nettie said. "I do hope the talk of war is just that!"

Madelaine shook her head slowly. "It seems there is nothing that can satisfy the Americans. John is torn two ways—he is in charge of the Indian Department stores here, but also sees to the safe transfer of fur for the American, John Jacob Astor."

Nettie was scanning the large clearing. "What are those houses?" She pointed to two small structures well back at the tree line behind a neatly tended garden.

"This cove is one of the few places near the fort where the land is easily tilled. We keep this garden for fresh vegetables. Some of the harvest is kept there until needed. There is also a place to rest in the larger one."

Nettie excused herself, and walked up the incline to the little cabin. Inside were a washstand, and two cots. Shelves lined the east wall. Some tools were propped behind the door. A door to what must have been a root cellar was in the floor in the far corner. It was cool and pleasant in the place. Soft light shone through a single west-facing window.

Back on the outside, she surveyed the garden of mature plants, now mostly harvested, marveling at the industry of the St. Joseph inhabitants. Madelaine, she knew, had come from a well-situated family, yet was content, as was her husband, with frontier life.

She thought of her older sister with all her comforts, and how happy Madelaine appeared. She would be like Madelaine if only things—if Thomas…if Martin… She put the thoughts out of her mind.

~ * ~

Three weeks flew by. Nettie began to have thoughts of returning home in order to be there when Thomas returned. Also, Carrie was beginning to talk about her books at home.

The weather turned unseasonably hot. The Fort was on cleared land, offering little shade. Lily was watching the children splashing among the rocks along the shore. Nettie had on the simplest cotton frock she could find over light cotton drawers and a chemise.

"Lily, I'll take a walk in the shade if you don't mind watching the children alone."

"No, you go. The sun is bad for your fair skin." Lily returned her attention to the children.

The canopy of maples was a blessed relief. As she walked, her mind meandered over an array of matters. The most pressing was Thomas and his well-being. She and Carrie were secure only to the extent that Thomas was. His erratic behavior was unsettling. She prayed all had gone well at Fort William.

She hadn't planned to walk so far, but the relative coolness of the path lured her on. In time, she emerged from the trees to the cove where Madelaine had taken them weeks before. In the shade of a tree, she rested before returning home.

It was complete silence there, interrupted only by the buzz of a hummingbird or insect, and had a mesmerizing effect. The field smelled of the tall grass and something else—the water lapping softly on the shore. It was too tempting.

She walked to the shore, shed her shoes, then waded in up to her ankles, skirts hiked up to her knees. Minnows nibbled at her toes. It was wonderful.

"Hello!"

Nettie looked back to the path, but no one appeared.

"Here—out here!" The voice was unmistakable.

She whirled to see a canoe and a lone paddler. Martin Legère.

Her heart pounded. It was uncontrollable, and undeniable.

He paddled in to shore. "Lily guessed you might be here. I thought you might appreciate a ride back." He beached the small canoe, and joined her in the ankle-deep water.

"I—was cooling off. It's delicious." She took another step away from shore. "I see you have returned as predicted. What brings you to St. Joseph?"

He didn't answer immediately, seeming to be measuring his words. "You," he said, at length.

"Martin!" she cautioned.

"It's true."

"You mustn't say it. It's impossible."

He reached for her, but she backed away, misjudging the steep fall-off of the shore, and went headlong into the water. She came up, waist deep and sputtering. Her hair was plastered to her face, her sopping dress exposed to Legère. He gasped.

In her effort to get to shore, she slipped and fell to her hands and knees. He had her instantly in his arms.

There was no doubt in either of them of what would happen next. She had fantasized a moment like this and was powerless to prevent it.

He did not paw her, but caressed her breasts with such tenderness she audibly groaned, pushing herself to him. He lifted her and carried her to the tall, dry grass that grew beyond the beach. He laid her down, her arms still around his neck, and all she could utter was "Yes. Now."

His breath came in short rasps, as he tore at his belt. Nettie struggled with her drenched drawers that stuck to her skin. He seemed to get control of events, saying "Slowly, slowly."

And she too quieted, letting him take the lead. He lifted her chemise and took her nipple in his mouth. She cried out softly, feeling a sensation below that was entirely new to her. He was kissing her neck, and she felt him on her. She could not wait longer, and had her hands on his buttocks. "Oh, please."

He obeyed, but slowly. She felt herself soaring toward something totally foreign. Her nerves screamed with pleasure until she thought she could not bear it, and then a glorious release that left her in rapturous exhaustion.

She felt his heart beating as they both lay there, not wanting it to be ended.

Suddenly she became aware of her surroundings. The tall grass was like a wall around them, but the blue sky above gave her an odd feeling of exposure. "I think I am a wanton woman." She smiled up at him.

"You are the finest thing I know. Do not say things like that."

"Martin."

"Yes?"

"Thank you. I did not know what love was like."

"Come." He picked her up, she without a stitch of clothes, he looking foolish with one moccasin still attached. He carried her back to the water and waded in.

"Do you swim?" he said.

She gave him a nod.

"I do not, so we won't go far."

The water felt warm when he let her down. They stood in water up to her neck and his shoulders. She felt him again become erect, and they shared each other once more.

~ * ~

Laid out atop the high grass, Nettie's clothes were dry enough to don, nonetheless still damp and wrinkled. Great fun was made by the others of her story of taking a spill in the water. Only Lily gave her a look that said *there is more to this tale.*

She found Carrie in serious discourse with Henri, who had rowed downriver with Legère. "Mama! Henri has told me all about growing up in Athabasca! It's a distant land on the other side of the big lake. There are big herds of animals called bison, and…." She related everything she'd learned.

"That would be something to see," Nettie told her. "Perhaps we'll go there some day."

"Perhaps you can, Carrie," Legère said, looking directly at Nettie.

Henri's eyes caught hers, and she flushed, knowing Legère must have discussed his feelings for her.

"Carrie, Monsieur Legère has offered to take us home tomorrow. I want you to get your things together after dinner. We'll leave very early."

"Will Henri go too?"

"Of course!"

Carrie put her arms around the big man's neck. "Then I don't mind going!" she said.

~ * ~

By mid-morning they were resting at the far north end of the island. Ahead lay two routes home—west around St. George Island, or the more direct route to the east.

"I think we will take the long way. The current is not so swift against us, and Carrie will like to see the villages along the way," Legère said.

The men finished their pipes and set off again, the two women and Carrie propelled by Henri in the rear and Legère in front.

To the east of St. George Island lay a wide, shallow bay. Nettie could see the sandy bottom slide by in places. The paddles would stir it up. Here herons waded and kingfishers perched, ready to dive for a fish dinner.

As they rounded the island's north side, Ojibwa *wiigiwaams*, both domed and triangular, dotted either side of the narrow channel. Lily called out a few times to people she knew.

Since this morning, the consequences stemming from yesterday's lovemaking preyed on Nettie's mind. The closer they neared Sault Ste. Marie, the more troubled she became. What did she feel for Martin Legère? She knew she really did not love Thomas, but she'd taken a vow and had his child. Yes, she felt love for Legère, but what kind of life could she have with him? She did not regret yesterday, but could she live with tomorrow?

It was late by the time they spotted the rapids in the distance. The scene reminded Nettie of that day two years ago when she first saw the sun dropping into Lake Superior, and how much had changed since then.

~ * ~

It would be another week before Thomas returned. When they arrived at the landing, Legère insisted on accompanying them home. Lily, in her wisdom, found something to do with Carrie so he and Nettie could talk. He wasted no time.

"I want to be with you, Nettie."

"Martin…all day this has been on my mind. It cannot be. I cannot tear my family apart—take my daughter and live in the bush with you. She needs a proper home with books and music and culture, and…"

"I know!" He cut her short. "I love Carrie as well! I am aware of my life and the choices I have made. That does not change the fact that I love you and know you have these feelings for me. You cannot change your way of life, but I can change mine."

"What do you mean?"

"I am not sure what I mean, but I intend to have you one day."

He kissed her, and she responded in kind, despite her decision to break it off cleanly with him only a minute ago.

And then he was gone.

Thirty
Parcher

October1809
Portsmouth, Ohio

Albert Parcher was on the run again, and he was damn sick of it. He'd found a sweet arrangement in the newly rebuilt town of Portsmouth. Two years earlier, when he fled the murder charges in Marietta, he'd decided to take his chances in the spanking new town full of opportunity and unfamiliar faces.

Portsmouth stood juxtaposed with the old town of Alexandria, from where Parcher had accompanied Oliver Gandy to Cincinnati. Constant flooding of the Scioto River convinced the inhabitants to seek higher ground, and a re-naming of the town.

Things were good while they lasted. A scheme to steal a portion of everything offloaded from the river for the construction of the new town was the brainchild of Jonny Weaks, the leader of a gang that controlled the wharf in Alexandria and surrounding river towns. Weaks took a liking to Parcher, possibly admiring his utter lack of moral compass.

For two years, Albert Parcher was doing quite well with enough money for drinking and wenching. He'd been put in charge of distributing the stolen materials to builders of the new town at a discounted price.

Wells controlled prostitution for a twenty mile stretch along the Ohio. Parcher's abilities for procuring talent of that sort also appealed to Weaks. They became good, if not fast friends.

But good things can come to an end, and did. Word filtered down the Ohio that the new Marietta sheriff had heard the man believed to be the killer of William Pierpont was living in Portsmouth. A whore Parcher had nearly beaten to death for holding back on Weaks' fifty percent had gotten away up the river to give a description of her assailant.

"They say he has witnesses from the inns at Zanesville and Marietta. They claim they can spot the man who came lookin' for the girl when that man was killed," Weaks said.

It was agreed that Parcher best leave town, at least until there was a different sheriff in Marietta. Go back into the interior where the newly laid out counties had their own law. Chillicothe's Ross County had one of the first sheriffs after Marietta. The idea was for Parcher to see if there was some way for Weaks to extend his influence upriver. When Parcher arrived in Chillicothe, he was armed with the name of a man Weaks said would put him up and introduce him to some contacts. The man, Edward Kelso, was anything but inspiring.

Parcher found Kelso's house, no more than a shack on the far east side of town. He lived with an older woman he'd taken in to do his cooking when he had enough money to buy food.

After a week of looking for somewhere else, Parcher decided to spend the larger part of the two hundred dollars—he managed to scrounge before leaving Portsmouth in haste—on making Kelso's hut livable. *A major part of the improvement is to be rid of Kelso and the old skag*, he thought . He'd cook his own goddamned meals!

Thirty-one

Nettie

February1812
Sault Ste. Marie

First the snow, the heaviest Nettie had seen in this her sixth winter in Upper Canada. Then the bitter windless cold. Earlier in the day, she and Carrie had ventured outside on snowshoes Lily's nephew White Deer made for them. The snow squeaked under their feet, otherwise only the sound of a branch snapping, too brittle to bear its own weight. The cloudless sky was utterly devoid of anything but the achingly cold air.

They'd lasted only a few minutes before turning back, their muffled faces white with the frost from their breath.

Lily was waiting with hot broth while they unwrapped their scarves and outerwear. Nettie sat at the kitchen table, her hands wrapped around the steaming mug, and surveyed her daughter. Now almost ten, she was taller than many of the boys, and rail thin like her grandfather Duncan. How

Carrie had developed into this poised young girl was a wonder. Nettie had had only average interest in literature or science, but she was a persistent teacher and Carrie had consumed everything presented to her. There was hardly a boat headed east that did not have an order for a text of some kind for Carrie Gibson to devour. Carrie and Lily were Nettie's salvation. The short days and long nights of February were brightened by Carrie's positive outlook. She was constantly finding something to do, some way to delight her mother and those around them. She finished her broth, eager to begin a new novel by Jane Porter. *The Scottish Chiefs* had been published two years earlier following *Thaddeus of Warsaw,* which Carrie had read twice. Nettie wondered if even she could plow through one of those serious historical novels.

Thomas was no longer physically abusive, but he had become insular and generally unpleasant to be around, drowning himself in self-pity and drink. His drinking had not yet jeopardized his job, but Nettie could see it was headed that way.

Six months had passed since she had seen Martin Legère. Since that day on St. Joseph Island, he did not fail to see her in the spring and fall on his way through Sault Ste. Marie. Their meetings were usually in a public setting, excruciating for Nettie, except for last September. He had borrowed a rig to visit the house. Thomas happened to be at the Company post in *Batchawana Bay*, so Legère invited Nettie and Carrie for a ride on the new trail to the Garden River. Carrie had promised the Passeau family to spend the day, so it was just the two of them. Nettie's heart was racing.

Legère was not talkative on the way out. He stopped the carriage where the river bends, and stared across to the shore of St. George Island.

"Martin?"

Instead of taking her in his arms as she yearned for, he said, "I have something to tell you."

She looked into his face for a sign, waited.

He seemed to be choosing his words. "I have spent the last two years building a business of my own."

"Why that's…"

"Please. Allow me to finish. I cannot continue like this. I think of nothing but being with you, but not like a peddler passing through your village. "I want you to live with me."

"Martin, I can't! Thomas, Carrie…"

"Thomas does not love you. I love you. You know that! Carrie will thrive in any other city."

She was speechless, knowing what he said was true.

Legère turned the rig around, starting back into town. "The fur trade is dying. In the next twenty years, settlers will be moving west. They will need to sell their wheat, wool, livestock, They will need to buy tools, machinery, household goods. They have already started, and I have enough to stop what I am doing."

"Where would you live?"

"For a short time at Fort William, but soon in York."

"York?"

"It is where western business is sure to establish. I think you could live there." The last sentence was more question than statement.

"Oh, Martin! I must think!"

Again, there was little to say as they returned to the house. Inside, he kissed her, she responding easily. It was such a natural feeling to be held by this man. Their bodies seemed to fit together. The embrace grew in intensity before he stopped.

"I cannot make love to you in your husband's house."

She felt chastised, wondering if she could have.

Legère kissed her again. "Nettie, I must be helping the others prepare for tomorrow's trip east. I will tell McGillivray I am leaving the Company. I have saved enough money to purchase my stock for resale in the spring. When you see me it will be in my own canoes. Think hard, Nettie."

~ * ~

Lily sat down at the table with her own mug of broth. "You are thinking of the Métis. I can tell."

Nettie considered the older woman, so different from this Scottish lass from a privileged family—yet so adept at knowing her needs and desires. There was no use pretending.

"Yes." She covered her eyes with the palms of her hands. "Oh, Lily! I've been so miserable! What can I do?"

"You know what your paths are, little mother. Use your head…there is no risk, same life. Use your heart, there is big risk, maybe happy life."

"Maybe," Nettie echoed.

~ * ~

May 1812
Sault Ste. Marie

The return of a shawl Charlotte Ermatinger had loaned Nettie required but a short walk on this blustery day. A cup of tea and shared gossip in the stately stone mansion lasted an hour and she was on her way home, side-stepping the muddy patches from yesterday's rain.

Approaching her house, she spied a horse tethered there, and quickened her pace. She entered through the kitchen door to hear Thomas in conversation. It was Legère! Doing her best to straighten her wind-blown hair, she entered the parlor.

"Martin! How good to see you."

Legère performed a courteous bow. "Mrs. Gibson."

Thomas, in his usual Sunday smoking jacket held forth. "Legère here says he's quit the canoe paddling game—going into business. A jolly lark, I'd say, leaving the Company like that."

Nettie ignored the insensitive remark. "Do tell, Martin. How are your plans progressing?"

"I was saying to Mr. Gibson I am on my way west to recruit Voyageurs who have stopped working due to the decline of the fur trade. I have established a base of operations in York…."

Thomas broke in. "…to peddle pots and pans and gewgaws to whom? Bad idea for a business, I'd say."

Nettie could see Legère begin to respond, then change his mind. "I had best be going. I stopped only as a courtesy to our long friendship."

"Please stay!" Nettie said, a little enthusiastically.

Legère was already at the door. "Perhaps in the autumn when I return east."

Nettie watched through the window Legère on his mount, not looking back. It was crushing.

Thirty-two

Andy

Crucianni lowered the windows of the patrol car and unwrapped his sandwich. They sat in the cruiser waiting for the crime scene people to show. Andy had given him a twenty to buy their lunch while she police-taped the house and surrounding area.

"Pastrami!" she said, opening her own. "My breath will reek all afternoon."

"Perfume to a good Italian boy," Crucianni said, handing her the change.

"I figured you were, with a name like that, but the fair complexion had me wondering."

He grinned. "Hundred percent, Detective. Both sides of the family."

"Lots of Italians in the Soo," she commented. "Married?"

"Nah, You?"

Andy gave a negative shake of the head. "Was."

"Kids?"

“A boy, a year or so younger than you. Last year at Guelph.” She changed the subject. “What do you make of this…Tony, is it?”

He waited to swallow his bite. “Anthony, Tony,” he shrugged. “I just write down what I see in my notebook. *You’re* the investigator.”

“You have a brain, use it.”

He thought for a moment. “Seems like a lot of work and time for the average Joe to hide a body. Why not just dig a hole?”

“Exactly! Also, think about the logistics. That wallboard job would have taken, what, at least two of those big panels. How did they get through that small opening in the ceiling? They’d have to be cut into smaller pieces. That requires a lot of seams. We didn’t see any sign of that. The guy must have known what he was doing.”

“Didn’t think of that,” Crucianni said.

She went on. “So it seems we have someone who wouldn’t draw unusual attention to himself hauling in big pieces of wallboard, and a person who is pretty good at working with the stuff. Have you ever tried?”

“Yeah, it’s a bitch, especially the taped joints.”

She sipped her Slurpee. It helped to talk it through. She could think more clearly when she expressed her thoughts verbally.

“So what does that tell you?” Andy said.

“It tells me nothing, but *suggests* we’re looking for someone local who is handy with wallboard—or maybe a tradesman or handyman.”

"Right, and if we can ID the remains, that'll narrow it down even more."

A van with O.P.P black and white markings pulled in behind them. Andy got out of the patrol car to meet two women, one in her twenties, the other more Andy's age.

"Andrea Blake," she announced. She had her shield exposed on her jacket.

"Beth and Amie," the older one said, pointing to herself, then her partner.

"Did you bring a ladder?"

"In the van," Amie said. She handed a white overall and booties to Beth while Crucianni retrieved the ladder.

They had come well equipped. Camera, lights, and a power pack. It took them several trips back and forth to the scene to get set up, and was late afternoon by the time they'd carefully removed the remains and scoured the house and grounds for anything else. Andy was impressed.

"We'll keep the yellow tape up," Beth said, "but I don't think we need to put a guard on the place. It's pretty clean. That's your call though, Detective."

She agreed. It had been a long first day on the job.

~ * ~

Andy picked up a burger to go in Hilton Beach, and sped down the U-Line in her borrowed Jeep toward home. It was late. She'd stayed at her desk adding notes to the once thin file. She decided to name it the Woodruff file after the boy's name.

When she turned into her driveway, the front yard was crammed with vehicles. She pulled the Jeep up on the lawn, and walked around to the back.

Under the canopy was a grid of string, crisscrossing the entire floor of the foundation. Nineteen and twenty-somethings were on hands and knees, carefully trowelling down each two foot square a few inches at a time.

Buck Tremblay saw Andy, and came over. "Making good progress," he said.

"Good progress? Why aren't you searching the root cellar?"

"All in good time. We need to excavate the floor down to undisturbed soil—before human occupation."

"How long will that take?" This was getting outrageous.

"A few days."

"Have you found anything?"

"A few shards of glass, pottery. Hard to date them, though. What's left of the pine floor will be useful. I suspect it's from local wood, and will date from the late eighteenth century."

"The Fort was built in the late seventeen-nineties," she said.

"Exactly. Now, don't mind us. We'll be here until dark."

Andy went inside to eat her burger. *Maybe take a ride over to see Grant.* He'd be interested in today's excitement.

~ * ~

The following morning, Arnold Terry had just finished updating Andy on the missing person he was working. He said he couldn't determine if the husband was telling everything or not, and suggested Andy might sit in on the next interview.

Andy was surprised. First the office supplies, now this. Maybe he wasn't the grouch he seemed over the phone year before last, or maybe something happened in his life to change this outlook.

She opened the Woodruff file and recounted her day with Crucianni.

"I think we have some things to go on. I'll know more when I talk to the lab ladies."

"Meanwhile?" He pulled out a pack of Exports, and replaced them. Public buildings had long since been smokeless, but Terry's habit of forty years was engrained.

"Meanwhile, I've called the trade union for an expert drywall man to look at our evidence. He might tell us something."

Terry stood. "Let's take a hike—talk to Beth Stewart—see if she found anything."

~ * ~

Beth had a family emergency, and was not there, but Amie opened her laptop to display a series of photographs the two had taken at the scene. The first was of the flue and exposed hole as it looked when they arrived. The next showing the skeletal remains after they had carefully cut away the rest of the wallboard with a box knife. The bones were pretty much a jumble at the bottom of the space with the skull facing up.

The third was a close-up of the interior wall. It clearly showed what Andy was unable to see with her flashlight—a loop of clothesline through an eye screwed into the wall. A shoulder bone still dangled precariously from it.

Amie said, "We think the loop was used to prop the body while the wall was being made."

"The Cask of Amontillado," Terry said.

"What?"

Andy explained. "Edgar Allan Poe, only in that story, the victim was still alive."

A phone rang. Amie picked up, listened, and said, "the desk says you called for someone from the local trade union."

"Send him in here," Andy said.

A tall, gaunt man who introduced himself as Charles Shipley walked in dressed in work clothes. "Pulled me from a job," he said. "This take long?"

Amie produced the largest section of the wall.

Andy said, "What can you tell us about this?"

Shipley flipped the piece around back and forth several times. "Half-inch board, made in Canada, pretty good joint."

"Anything special, unique?"

He looked again, now at the back. “Kinda funny. Two joints in this small piece. Makes me wonder why. Maybe a repair job. Also, the board is almost twenty years old. See the code on the back? That’s the manufacturer’s date the day they made it.”

Andy did the math. “Actually, eighteen years and change. You say ‘pretty good joint.’ Care to expand on that?”

“Matter of fact, damn good. The guy knew how to apply joint cement so you don’t see the tape outline. It’s perfect.” He showed them the smooth side where two pieces were joined.

“That confirms what we thought about the person we’re looking for,” Andy said, after Shipley left. “He’s a working stiff.”

“Or was,” Terry added.

Andy noticed Beth had returned, putting her purse in a desk drawer.

Amie said, “Everything okay?”

Beth gave her a crooked smile. “My ten year old. Got his ears boxed by an older kid at the rink for smarting off. He’ll be okay.” She tapped a fingernail on the wallboard. “What’s new?”

They told her about Shipley’s comments.

“What have you learned about the remains?” Andy asked.

“A woman, we’re guessing about thirty. Some trauma to the skull. Likely the cause of death, but who knows? She could have been stabbed, smothered.”

“DNA?” Terry asked.

"No soft tissue. The remains are fifteen, even twenty years old. Probably picked clean by vermin."

Andy said, "It was a rat that must have dragged that rib through the hole at the floor." She pointed to the computer screen.

Beth continued. "We took tooth and bone samples, and sent them to Bay Street for DNA analysis, but unless our girl is on file, our chance of learning her ID that way is slim."

"Bay Street?" Andy asked.

Terry explained. "Centre for Forensic Sciences. The regional lab is here in the Soo."

"Anything else?" Andy asked, scribbling what she'd heard into her notebook.

"You'll be first to know," Beth said.

~ * ~

Andy and Terry returned to their desks. Terry had a map of Algoma tacked to the wall next to a whiteboard. Andy stared at it, as if the answer to the death of this woman would be there. "If we can learn this woman's ID, it will lead us to the killer."

"You have a good start on the guy," Terry said.

"Yeah, not many wallboard girls, but a shitload of wallboard guys. If I found whose bones those are, it'll narrow my search." She was aware of his raised brow at her vulgarity. *That's how I talk on the job. Bet you're worse.*

Terry said, "You only have all of North America to search for women twenty to forty years of age that went missing fifteen to twenty years ago. A snap." He rocked back in his chair, as if he, too, were studying the map.

"I start out in the city, and expand my radius. Only way I know how to do it."

He snorted. "And I thought my missing wife was a toughie. You coming with me to interview this guy?" He was getting his jacket on.

"Let me hit the Ladies' Room, and I'll be right with you."

~ * ~

They returned after lunch. Andy thought the husband's story was believable, but didn't like the way he blinked and averted his eyes when he talked. She'd found it a pretty good indicator of someone having something to hide.

Terry dropped her at the Detachment while he followed up on some other leads. She was glad for the time alone to think about the Woodruff case, and plan her next moves.

~ * ~

The rest of the week was crammed with the tasks all investigators hate, but almost always are the way cases are solved. Endless phone calls, and when necessary, follow-up visits.

She hunted down a dozen missing persons and runaways in the Sault Ontario and Sault Michigan records. It was late summer, and the bridge to Michigan could take well over a half-hour to clear customs. Much of her desk work was actually done inching along on that bridge to or from tracking down a Sault Michigan lead.

She'd hoped to get a lead on the killer by canvassing the neighbors of the farmhouse. There were only two who were in the vicinity. One was a house not much different from the abandoned one. The other was actually a church and parsonage.

The front yard of the farmhouse was mostly weeds. A scythe leaned against a railing for the steps that led up to a roofed front porch. Next to the door there was an overstuffed chair on which sat a large cat. It hissed and ran off. Andy knocked, and waited. The air was utterly still, heavy with the odor of mown hay. There was no car in the driveway. Possibly no one was home.

She thought to leave, but the door rattled, then opened. A man in overalls and undershirt appeared. He was sixty, or eighty, she couldn't tell. A stubble of white beard decorated his sunken face.

"Whacha want?" he muttered.

Andy showed her shield. "I'm Detective Blake, O.P.P. May I ask you a few questions?"

"What about?" His eyes showed—fear?—distrust?

"That house over there," she pointed. "Ever see anyone in or out of the place?"

"Never pay no attention. Can't stand lookin' at it anyway."

She looked over his shoulder. "Anyone else living here?"

"No."

"Well, thank you Mr.—I didn't ask your name."

"Barry, Wilfred Barry." He started to close the door.

"All right, Mr. Barry. I may want to talk to you again."

He shut the door.

Andy got back in the unmarked car she'd requisitioned, and drove a hundred meters down the road. She looked to see if Barry had a vehicle parked behind his place. There was none. He couldn't easily live there without transportation. *Somebody lives there with him, or at least visits him.*

The church was a large, well-maintained building. The sign in front announced services on Wednesday night and Sunday morning, the Reverend Paul A. Corinth, Pastor.

A huge macadam parking lot suggested a sizeable congregation. Across, a parsonage stood, built of the same stone exterior as the church.

There were no cars parked at the church, but two, a late model Volvo and a new-looking BMW sedan were at the house. She pulled in behind the BMW and walked to the door.

The yard was immaculate. A garden hose, neatly coiled on its reel, pine bark under the bushes, lawn perfectly mown and freshly edged. The doorbell did its version of a grandfather clock. Footsteps from inside were high heels on hardwood.

"Yes?" The door opened on a plain, but well-dressed woman in her fifties.

"Detective Blake, ma'am." Again, the shield flashed.

From inside the house, a voice said, "Who is it, Gwen?"

"It's the police, dear." To Andy, she said, "Perhaps you'd best speak with the Reverend.

Andy smiled and waited while "Gwen" retrieved her husband.

"Well, *hello!*" The smiling face of a man, late fifties, maybe sixty, greeted Andy. "What can we do to help the police?"

"Detective Blake, sir, O.P.P." Once more, the shield. "Like to know if anyone here has noticed activity of any kind at that farmhouse, the abandoned one."

He nodded. "Hmm. That house has been empty for years."

"I know, sir. Question was about any comings or goings over there."

"No not that Gwen or I know of."

"Well thanks, then… "Uh, I don't suppose one of your parishioners knows anything. How many do you have?"

He brightened, stood a little taller. "Three hundred fifty pursuing God's grace twice a week!" Pride filled his eyes.

"You might ask if anyone has noticed anything."

"I will indeed, Detective, and God love you."

"Why, thank you, Reverend," she said. "Oh! That other house. Know who lives there?"

"That would be Mr. Barry."

"Anybody else?"

"His son comes and goes, but doesn't really live there, I wouldn't say."

She thanked him again, and he quietly shut the door.

All told, pretty much of a strikeout, she thought, and drove back into town.

Thirty-three

Parcher

June 1812
Franklinton, Ohio

It had been years since Parcher was in the little town of Franklinton. There were rumors of the area being considered for the new capital of Ohio with the name *Columbus*. He recognized none of it. One or two familiar faces were all. Since then, the river had poured over its banks with such regularity the founder, Lucas Sullivant, rebuilt the town on higher ground the way Alexandria had, although the name of the town was retained. The recent declaration of war with England and Canada seemed to have no effect on the tidy little village, although the British were whipping up resentment among the Indians and raids on American forts in the region had recommenced.

Things had not gone well in Chillicothe. He blamed it on the war, and the fact that the state capital had moved to Zanesville the previous year. Fewer vulnerable outsiders were traveling to and through there these days, making it hard for a man of his vocation. The truth was that Jonny Weaks' estimation of Parcher's organizing abilities was exaggerated.

Parcher was a good follower, muscle man, and perhaps able to draw in an unsuspecting victim with his feigned sincerity. But he was no organizer or planner of eventualities. In time, Weaks ignored him, the invitation to return to Portsmouth forgotten.

Parcher was sure pickings would be easier back here in Franklinton, a place he thought he knew well. His idea was to revert to the church sexton scheme. It hadn't worked before, but not due to his lack of ability, only circumstances, he rationalized.

These reflections on the past eleven years, since Adam Varner plucked him off that wharf in Pittsburgh, were made in a tavern he'd come to frequent after arriving from Chillicothe. The ale was the same swill carted up the Scioto from the Ohio barges, but the major attraction was Patsy Kelly.

The girl's father, Elmer, was the owner of Kelly's Tavern. The place had a long bar hewn from a local oak tree. Two sets of beer engines served a large room that included a small stage on which a fiddler entertained on Saturday nights.

Patsy would help serve the tables on those nights when the place was crowded. She was a saucy one with a fast retort for the often-ribald remark directed her way. Parcher fancied she favored his advances. The problem was she was only fifteen. As a result, Kelly kept a sharp eye on her.

Parcher guessed she was big enough to know what she wanted.

Thirty-four

Nettie

June 1812
Sault Ste. Marie

Nettie was ending a lesson of French grammar with Carrie who was by now fluent. French was the preferred second language among the Ojibwa, and of course, the Métis. The girl had ample opportunity to practice. About to delve into another subject, she stopped when the front door burst open.

"Quick!" Thomas said. "Help me pack. A canoe leaves for Batchawana immediately!"

"Whatever for?"

"God sakes, woman! Have you not heard? The Americans have declared war. I am sent to secure our records and stock there and in Fort William."

Carrie was wide-eyed. "Papa! Are you going to fight the Americans?"

"Of course not, child. We have people for that if it is required."

Nettie began to help Thomas get ready for the expected rough journey up the eastern shore of Lake

Superior. “How did you come to know of this, Thomas?”

“John Askin brought the news from Captain Roberts at Fort St. Joseph. He is now with the Indians, hatching up some scheme or other.” He was pacing while Nettie packed his essentials. “Hurry! I expect a carriage any moment,” he chided.

War! Nellie thought her life couldn’t have gotten any deeper into turmoil.

And now this.

~ * ~

One could tell Lily was upset. Her stony, expressionless face was the same, but Nettie could tell she was preoccupied. After a morning of watching the older woman pace and stare in space, she asked if something was on her mind.

“White Deer.”

“What about White Deer?”

“He is too young to go to war with the English soldiers.”

So that was what Thomas meant about John Askin ‘hatching a scheme.’ She knew Askin well enough to be certain he didn’t do anything on a whim. Something must be happening, and soon.

It was late in the afternoon when she learned the whole story. Robert Logan stopped by to tell her Thomas had gotten off safely with a group of armed men in four large canoes.

“This word of war—is it true?” she asked him.

"Yes, my dear. The American President Madison has declared war on Britain and Canada. General Brock immediately sent fast riders and canoes to his outposts. We have reason to believe the Americans at Michilimackinac have not received this news. Captain Roberts has orders to attack Fort Michilimackinac at once. It will take us some time to build up a force. The soldiers at St. Joseph are few and ill-prepared."

Nettie knew this was true. The drunkenness and general lethargy of the Regulars there was well discussed. She noticed Lily listening to Logan, and asked for her benefit, "Who is this force you speak of?"

"Any able-bodied man who can fire a gun or carry a hatchet. I would volunteer, but the company…uh, you can appreciate. They are asking the Indians to volunteer, also the fur traders. We all have a stake in returning the fort back into Canadian control."

Nettie sensed Logan had sent Thomas to Batchawana to exempt him from the fighting. "Mr. Logan, thank you for your concern for our family at this time."

"Not at all, my dear. Now I must be off. Let me know of any concerns you might have."

When he was gone, she found Lily had left the house, likely to intercept her fifteen-year-old nephew. She was left with her own concerns about the war. Her husband's company was struggling with declining business before this, but war could shut it down completely. And Martin Legère betting his entire worth on a new venture. What would the war have in store for him?

~ * ~

July 1812
Sault Ste. Marie

Her immediate worries went for naught. Three weeks later, on an early morning, a flotilla consisting of Fort St. Joseph soldiers of the 10th Royal Veteran Battalion, one hundred-eighty angry whites and Métis plus over four hundred Indians from tribes as far as Wisconsin departed St. Joseph in seventy war canoes, ten batteau, and the brig Caledonia.

Under the cover of nightfall, they landed on Michilimackinac's north side, well away from the southern location of the fort. Through the night they struggled to haul their two cannon to the highest point overlooking the fort.

In the morning, they convinced a doctor stationed there to deliver the terms of surrender—give up without a shot fired, or risk having the whole population of soldiers and civilians hacked to death by the Indians full of spite for the fort's obstruction of their trade since American control there.

The commanding officer, Lieutenant Hanks, declined at first until other civilian reports of the British numbers were made. Although these numbers were likely exaggerated, Hanks conceded, for he was certain the British were not bluffing. A horrific slaughter had happened before in 1763 when the fort was located on the other side of the straits.

The majority of the invaders returned to their homes. The following week, Sault Ste. Marie was in celebration. It was an enormous victory. Word of it spread, and Thomas was soon returned home.

For Nettie, a troubling aspect of the raid was the abandonment of Fort St. Joseph. Captain Roberts had barely enough men under his command to hold Michilimackinac, the more strategic and better built of the two forts. With the soldiers gone, there was no need for civilian support at St. Joseph.

The Askins and other families abandoned their homes for new ones at the conquered fort. Nettie knew she would see much less of Madelaine now, living twice as far away. She knew both Askinses loved the life on St. Joseph, and wondered about their cozy home, now empty.

Thirty-five

Parcher

December 1812
Northern Ohio

The frozen night air clawed at Parcher's lungs as he ran. He knew he couldn't keep this up any longer. They'd be coming soon, and fast. Ahead was the gate to the Varner place. That skinny old bastard had a horse, by God!

Damn that Patsy Kelly, the little cunt! All that night he watched her joke with the other men in Kelly's Tavern. She'd laugh and sass them back. A few even gave her a slap on the bottom. His own advances were thwarted, though. The more he drank and watched her antics, the more he needed to show her what a real man was. He'd followed her to the stable behind the tavern, when her father sent her for a new keg. Bloody tart kept saying "no" when he knew damn well she wanted it. His big mistake was not hitting her hard enough. Hard enough to shut her up, and to keep her from getting away after he was finished with her. Old man Kelly would be on his horse by now with a load of his friends.

The Varner barn was close by the house that looked dark—the old man asleep. The snow muffled his footfalls as he entered the barn. Varner's mare nickered warily at the unfamiliar intruder.

"And you, old nag, you're goin' for a nice ride."

~ * ~

Parcher made his way as far north as Seneca, where he fed and rested the horse. Then, almost out of money, following the Sandusky River, and shivering from the cold, he continued to Lower Sandusky by the time darkness set in. Sounds of a concertina came from an inn with a sign swinging in the wind and announcing: 'The Goat and Anvil.' He handed the mare over to a stable boy, and pushed into the place where a number of patrons lounged at their tables.

"You look plumb worn out, sir," a voice from behind him said.

A rail-thin man stood wiping his hands on a white apron.

"What?"

"Needin' a room sir?"

"Well…I am that." The warmth of the place was delicious.

"As you see, we're crowded tonight, but I have a small room available, if it pleases you."

Parcher removed his hat, revealing his shock of black hair that drooped down over his dark eyebrows and side whiskers. "And how much?"

The innkeeper pointed to a sign next to a hutch. "These rates times two, sir."

"What do you mean 'times two'?"

The man walked over to the sign, as if protecting it. "It's the war, sir. The new dollar is becoming worthless."

Parcher didn't tell him he hadn't even the price of a room before the rates started climbing. "That will do. I have no bags. Lead away."

~ * ~

His last food was yesterday at Kelly's tavern and this morning in Seneca, only a piece of toast with tea. He washed his face in the basin by the small cot, and returned downstairs to the aroma of meat broiling. If he was going to slip out without paying his bill, he might as well include a good meal.

Despite the thin, tasteless ale, the cut of pork was good. Parcher pushed back his chair, calling for the proprietor. "Have you any spirits?"

When the innkeeper returned with glass and bottle, Parcher said, "Leave the bottle." The man shrugged and left.

Two or three glassfuls and Parcher was feeling restored from twenty-four hours of looking over his shoulder. He looked over the room: men mostly, engaged in their own meals, drinks and conversations. Two men dressed in rough attire were looking his way. One of them beckoned to him, motioning to an empty chair. Parcher grabbed his bottle and walked over.

"It's not good for a man to drink alone," the older of the two said. They both wore full beards, heavy grey woolen shirts. Piled next to the wall was their gear, consisting of rucksacks, cartridge boxes, muskets.

"Yer militia, I suppose," Parcher said.

"On our way north to join our company."

Parcher had succeeded in avoiding service in the militia which, since 1803, was required of all young Ohio men. "Where's your company?" he asked.

"We aim to join 'em at the new fort on the frozen Maumee River. Name's Drew." He held out a hand. "This here's Bass. Have a sit."

Parcher set the bottle on the table, and took the empty chair. "Help yourself."

Neither of the two men hesitated, pouring generous tots.

Bass wiped his mouth and beard. "And you—where to?"

Parcher hadn't considered that. His only goal was to get as far away from Elmer Kelly's tavern as possible. "Head'n yer way, I expect."

"Driftin'?" Drew said.

"More or less."

"Seem to be doin' all right, big pork dinner and all." Drew pointed to Parcher's bottle of good rum.

"Fact is, I'm not sure how I'm going to pay for it."

That earned a laugh from the soldiers.

"Might think about joining you boys…duty and all."

Drew gave Parcher a slap on the shoulder. “Well! Come along, then! There’s eight of us. Room for one more in the wagon.”

Parcher said nothing, his mind working hard. *Why not? Get the stolen horse off my hands. Maybe sell it. Then disappear into the militia, be sent to who knew where?* “I’ve got no kit,” he said, gesturing to their stash against the wall.

The two laughed. Bass said, “Gen. Harrison’ll be happy to take care o’ that for a pledge of a year or so’s service.”

They finished the bottle over the next hour.

~ * ~

The banging on the door slowly penetrated Parcher’s consciousness. He rolled out of the warm cot to pull open the door. Drew was there.

“Are you with us?”

“I need to piss and pay my bill.”

“We leave in less than half an hour,” Drew said, and disappeared into the dark hallway.

Parcher made his contribution into the chamber pot, dressed, and tripped down the stairs to where the inn’s proprietor was just tying on his apron. The semi-light of dawn illuminated the room through the single frosted window.

“I aim to settle up.”

The man smiled expectantly.

“I have no need for my horse now. She’s worth a week’s stay here. She’s yours for last night and another jug o’ that rum.

The deal was made and Parcher walked out onto the road where men were loading gear into a wagon drawn by two horses billowing breath in the frigid air.

~ * ~

It was as cold as Parcher could remember. He shivered under a blanket loaned to him by one of the men. A weak sun did little to warm the day. When the wagon finally jolted to a stop, he heard Drew's voice from the driver's bench. "Everyone dismount!"

The six men in the rear, including Parcher, tumbled out onto the ground to view the Maumee River clearly visible from the slight rise they occupied. At the river's edge near shore lay an unusually large enclosure, perhaps eight or ten acres, of perpendicular logs that looked to be still under construction.

"Line up!" Sgt. Drew ordered. "We're going to march in, and I want you to look like soldiers."

Drew went down the line adjusting belts, cartridge and powder cases, even the signature slouch hats of the Ohio Militia with the cockade and brass pin of their regiment. When he came to Parcher, he said, "Just follow us in as smartly as you can."

It had been an arduous route from the inn at Lower Sandusky. They'd followed a trail along a branch of the Maumee for the last day, and the horses were almost spent. They marched the last mile single file across cleared ground, with Parcher and the wagon bringing up the rear.

Entering the fort they could see structures as well as the fifteen foot walls were made almost entirely of logs. Parcher counted eight blockhouses. Some of the buildings still lacked roofs, or were in the process of getting one.

A Regular Army Lieutenant in his dark blue overcoat and gold epaulets hailed them. “You men! Militia?”

Drew saluted. “Yes sir! Where do we go?”

The officer pointed to a large log structure. “You’ll be reporting to Captain Stockton in there.”

On January 4, 1813, Albert Parcher became a private in the Ohio Militia. In under twenty minutes he was sworn in, given an overcoat and musket, and assigned guard duty for the eight to twelve shift. He was having serious second thoughts about his decision in that Lower Sandusky inn.

Thirty-six

Andy

The sun was still well up, but Andy arrived home later than usual this Friday night. Only two vehicles were parked in front of her place this time. She recognized both—Grant Stacey's Audi, and Lila Knowles' Corolla. She pulled around them, parking at the side of the house.

Grant, Lila, and Tremblay were there by the dig.

"Andy!" Lila called. "Grant just got here. We were filling him in."

"Well, start over. But first I want to sit down with something cold and wet. Anybody else?" They all partook.

Inside, Tremblay unrolled a chamois cloth on the coffee table where they'd gathered. A dozen objects lay on the open cloth.

"Most of this is junk. The shards of glass and pottery I mentioned earlier this week. This thimble is valuable, though."

"And this?" Andy pointed to a dark piece, about the size of a quarter in the shape of a bird with wings spread.

Tremblay flipped it over to expose a finding of sorts. "This is a medallion, either copper or brass, I'm not sure. The steel pin on the back has rusted away, but I believe it's part of a uniform."

"Whose?" Stacey asked.

"That's what I want to know. I've emailed photos to experts I know. It has to be circa 1812 from its location in the strata."

"That's all?" Andy said.

"No. We found some pieces of tools predating anything of modern manufacture, probably hand wrought. They're badly rusted, but recognizable. A hoe, a fork, and charred remains of a wooden rake. It doesn't look like this was a dwelling. We'd have found more domestic articles, and fewer gardening tools. The thimble was an anomaly."

Lila said. "We think the area may have been cleared for a garden…a big one. Notice the trees between you and the water—mostly pine and other evergreens. They're the first to grow. Trees on either side are mostly maple and other hard woods."

Andy nodded. "It's mostly summer cottages down there now."

"You'll be happy to know we've started on the root cellar, if that's what it was," Tremblay said.

"How long will that take?"

"We can't know. It'll depend on what we find down there, which is possibly nothing."

Andy asked Lila, "What do you *hope* to find?"

"Ideally anything that would tie this property to a particular individual. It would add a lot to our knowledge of the region's history."

"How do you go about excavating the cellar?" Andy asked.

Tremblay was in his element. He leaned back in the sofa, and crossed his legs. "We'll approach this as if it were an exhumation of a burial site. The size of the pit is not dissimilar to a grave. In these cases, trenches are sometimes dug juxtaposed to the grave to get a clear look at the strata. This was carried out successfully in the Bosnian mass graves. In this case I believe we'll do a top-down removal of each stratum, as there is no evidence of a burial."

Lila looked at her watch. "It's well past seven. We have to scoot. Buck is speaking to the Heritage Foundation tonight. Dinner at eight. We'll just make it."

Grant put his arms around Andy as Lila's Toyota was backing out of the driveway. "Couldn't wait for them to leave."

"I thought it was interesting, didn't you?"

"Yeah—I suppose. Some rusted tools and broken pieces. It doesn't make or break your week, does it?"

"I'll tell you what breaks my week!" She went on to tell of her initial progress on the Wodruff case, followed by a series of brick walls.

"But you're happy there?" He turned her around to face him.

"It doesn't matter now. I've quit my job in Windsor—but, yes, I like it well enough. In fact, I think the big grouch, Arnold Terry, likes me." She gave him a poke with her elbow, and began clearing the coffee table of glassware.

He followed her into the kitchen.

"You're hovering!" she laughed.

"Guess I am." He found a chair at the kitchen table. "I'm just glad you like your job."

The finality of her decision to quit in Windsor hit her with his words. "I'll have to sell my condo, move my stuff."

"Move to where?" he said.

"Why here, of course…Grant! Did you think because I'm living on the Island I'd just move in with you?"

He reddened. "I didn't know *what* I thought. I…guess I just hoped."

She dried her hands on a towel, reached down and kissed him. "You know I love you, Grant. The house means too much to me right now. It's more than that. You're talking about a commitment. I haven't thought that through. There's Tim to consider, too."

"Tim's almost a grown man," he countered.

"With thoughts of grad school. I'm still a mother first. Heck, he hasn't even met you."

"I don't see how that all connects to our mutual commitments."

"Maybe it won't. Give me some time."

He said no more.

~ * ~

Though badly charred, the door on the floor that led to the cellar was remarkably intact, hewn of thick hardwood. Andy watched as the team lifted it away the following morning. Inside, what she saw was an evenly distributed dirt floor about two and one half feet down.

Tremblay had a thin steel rod he used to probe the floor. He removed it, saying there was about three feet of soft dirt over a more solid level that was probably the original bottom.

There was only room for one worker in the pit at a time, so they worked in shifts. One experienced worker would trowel down three or four inches, passing dirt up to the others who would screen it for artifacts. It was slow going.

Andy watched them work for a while when her cell phone beeped. It was the duty officer at the Detachment telling her there was a large envelope that had been hand-delivered to her. She'd given instructions to be called when it came.

The union names! She decided to drive into the Soo and see what she could make of them.

~ * ~

Andy looked at the wall clock in the detectives' room. 3:45 p.m. She'd worked straight through without eating, and was hungry. The envelope had contained forty-seven copied personnel sheets for union members with drywall skills active between fifteen and twenty years ago.

She numbered the sheets 1 to 47, then found a map of the greater Sault area, and pinned it to the wall. She had a hunch the killer would have been familiar with the abandoned house, and therefore might have lived nearby. It had taken her all day to place a pin at the address of every name.

There was no pattern, but five of the names were within a half-mile of the house. Nothing solid, but a good place to start. Pin number three was closest to the house, in fact, very close. The name was David Wyse, and the address familiar. She checked her notes, and stared in disbelief. It was the house of the old man, Willard Barry.

~ * ~

Driving out to the Barry place, she noticed the yellow tape at the murder scene was still in place. As she approached Barry's house, she noticed a man on a big Harley motorcycle was just roaring off. They passed in the street. He had a full black beard and a cycler's leather jacket. She tried to read the name of the club on his back, but failed. He looked to be in his forties.

The house seemed even more forlorn than before. Again, she had to wait for her knock to be answered. When it opened, Willard Barry was dressed as before, but with his suspenders hanging down. He said nothing, waiting to hear what she wanted, staring at her with rheumy eyes.

"Mr. Barry. Hello, again."

No response.

"Seems I need some more from you, sir. Do you know a David Wyse?"

"What if I do?"

"Does he live here?"

He hesitated. "No."

"I need to know how you know Mr. Wyse. He gives this as his address."

"That's a goddam lie. He don't live here."

Andy caught herself. That could be true. The record was written fifteen years ago. "Was this ever his address?"

Again, hesitation. "Maybe."

"What is Mr. Wyse's relationship with you?"

"Married my girl, is all."

"And what is their address?" She got out her notebook.

"Ain't no *they*. She run off a long time ago."

"How long ago, Mr. Barry?"

He made a derisive snort. "Must be fourteen, fifteen years or more. She's long gone, and good riddance."

Andy knew she was on the right track. "And her name?"

Barry uttered something, and Andy had to coax it out again.

"Alice."

"Was that your son-in-law who just left?"

Barry indicated with a nod.

"How can I reach him?"

"What for?" Barry said. "What the hell for?"

"He may have noticed something at the house over there."

Without a word, Barry left the door ajar, and retreated inside. A minute later he returned with a creased business card announcing G&K Cycle Shop with an address on the Soo's west side.

Andy copied the information. "This is his store?" She returned the card.

"He works there is all."

"You've been most helpful, sir. Thank you."

She returned to her car, leaned back in the seat. Years on the job, yet it always felt special when a case was breaking your way.

Thirty-seven
Parcher

February 1813
Ft. Meigs, On the Maumee River

In the month of February, General William Henri Harrison was still assembling his army for the intended invasion of Canada. The losses to the British of Fort Michilimackinac on Lake Huron followed by Fort Detroit just two hundred miles north sabotaged the American's plans for a swift victory.

Harrison's regular army was in dire need of reinforcements. Ohio's Governor Meigs was helping by supplying his militia, but it was not enough if Harrison were to successfully dislodge the British entrenched with Indian troops of Chiefs Tecumseh and Round Head at Detroit.

The militia troops were treated poorly by the regulars. Most of the menial chores were assigned to these conscripts, completion of the fort's construction being paramount. Parcher and his fellow Ohioans were put to work. He was assigned to a permanent detail building a parapet to buttress the outer wall.

"This is worse," he told Bass, "than my jail time in Chillicothe. At least there I was warm and better fed."

In late February, stragglers from a sortie that had been one thousand troops to capture the British Fort Amherstburg returned. Fewer than twenty men. Low morale at the fort sank even lower. Parcher considered deserting, but he was far from familiar territory now. Indian raids were common in the villages and on the roads. He'd become deathly afraid of them as stories of their savagery abounded.

By the end of April, most of the construction was finished. Parcher was reassigned to one of the blockhouses guarding the north wall overlooking the river, and beyond. It was a position to clearly view what happened over the next several days.

Harrison by then had received intelligence that the enemy was on their way from Fort Amherstburg to take Fort Meigs. More reserves were called up, increasing the garrison by another thousand men. Also a brigade of Kentuckians was expected.

Parcher took the news of the impending battle in stride, feeling safe inside the fort. The feeling was short-lived.

~ * ~

May 1813

On the first day of May on a high bank across the river, red uniforms began to appear. The alarm was given, but no order was heard from the officers. Parcher could see cannon being rolled into place.

"Why don't someone go out there and stop them?" he said aloud.

It soon became obvious the fort was surrounded. Indian warriors were brazenly showing themselves in the clearings on all sides.

A puff of white smoke across the river followed by a deep throated bark was Parcher's first taste of warfare. There was the *thump* of a ball hitting the earthen embankment. He was petrified. He could see gunboats downriver, and more activity of battery emplacements on the opposite bank. The reality hit him that he might actually have to do battle.

Over the next few days, shelling of Fort Meigs continued, but little damage was sustained. Sorties were sent out to harass the enemy, but Parcher was kept at his post. Then the Kentucky brigade that had since arrived was sent across the river to drive the British from their positions. At first, the surprise attack had the enemy reeling, but they soon recovered. Indians hiding in the woods opened fire, drawing the brigade into the thicket as they retreated. It was a slaughter. Meanwhile, British artillery was decimating the other Americans on the open field right in front of Parcher's eyes. In the end, the Kentuckians lost over eighty percent of their nine hundred men. If this was what war was, Parcher wanted no part of it.

Still the fort held after a siege of five days. Prisoners were exchanged, and the British retreated, having no adequate supply chain. Weeks later another half-hearted attempt was made in late July, but given up after a day's shelling. Fewer Indians were engaged this time. Parcher hoped this was the end of the fighting.

Soon after, Parcher was ordered to join a contingent of regulars and militia for an unnamed assignment. Corporal Drew and Private Bass were among those chosen.

Parcher was leery of leaving the fort's confines. "Where are we going?" he asked Drew as they formed up near the gate.

"Dad Blamed if I know, Parcher. Just do as yer told!"

The main gate opened, and five horse-drawn wagons rolled in. The lieutenant Parcher had seen on his first day rode ahead on a dappled mare. He was resplendent in his white breeches and blue coat with gold epaulet on one shoulder. His new rank of captain was emblazoned on the saddle cloth.

The officer cantered up to the detachment. A sergeant ordered "Attention!

At once, the captain, Parcher did not know his name, ordered them "At Ease." The wind played with the red and white plume of his tall hat.

"Men, you are about to partake in an important venture. It will be dangerous. If any of you believe you do not have what it takes, you are free to decline. The mission is voluntary."

Parcher looked to his left and right, not daring to be the only one to take the coward's way out. No one said a word.

"Excellent!" The officer reeled his horse around. "Sergeant!"

"Yessir! You men—load up. Twenty to a wagon!"

Less than a half hour later, the convoy was headed east.

Thirty-eight

Aboard the American Brig Lawrence
August 1813

The sun was unrelenting. The second drill of the day, and Parcher was spent. They arrived at Sandusky to learn they'd be placed aboard ships of the American fleet for an anticipated battle bolstering the fleet's dearth of able-bodied seamen. Most of the duties were grunt work, as was Parcher's of feeding the heavy shot to the guns. The fleet's commodore, Oliver Perry, had prevailed on Harrison to loan him the bodies, anticipating the British attempt to break the blockade the fleet was imposing on Fort Amherstburg.

Most of the militia was assigned to the brig *Niagara*, as were Drew and Bass. Parcher was sent to the *Niagara's* sister ship, *Lawrence,* the commodore's flagship, though he rarely saw the man from his place on the gun deck. He felt ostracized among the predominantly naval crew, some of whom had been sent from the famous *USS Constitution* while she was laid up for repairs in Marblehead, Massachusetts. The ship was like an oven, even at night. He would never get accustomed to the constant motion of the deck. The days dragged on.

~ * ~

Late in the month, the *Lawrence* returned to its base at the island of Put-In-Bay, just off the Ohio coast. It was to be a short time in the harbor. Two hours later, anchor was weighed, and they were at sea. Parcher caught a glimpse of the commodore as he returned. He seemed quite young for a position so lofty. Whatever he learned at Put-In-Bay must have been important for the ship to take to sea so soon. The other officers took on an air of urgency. Something was afoot.

~ * ~

The wind shifted. Parcher could feel it through the starboard gun ports. Aloft, and on deck there was a cry of "hurrah!" Parcher looked to the grizzled gunner from the *Constitution.* "What?"

"We've got the gauge, I expect." The seaman went on to explain it meant the enemy fleet was downwind and at a disadvantage. The information did not assuage his unease.

For the past hour, the ship had been called to battle stations. Tensions increased. Parcher heard orders on deck for sheets to be hauled. The ship heeled sharply to port. Something must be happening, but all he saw through the gun port was sky. More orders, increasing in frequency. He could hear the strain in the barked orders.

The order to ease sheets came. The ship settled on even keel. The order to "Fire as she passes!" came. In succession, the eight starboard thirty-two pound cannons let loose their deafening blasts, shaking the boat as they racked the target. Parcher could not see from his vantage. The call for reload came. He and others passed the heavy balls to the loaders.

Before another volley, he could hear return fire. The ship shook badly. *They've hit us!* More blasts from *Lawrence's* guns, more cries for ammunition. Again, the ship shivered as something aloft was hit. Then a loud crash. *A spar hitting the deck?*

The ship heeled sharply as the order to open the port gun ports was shouted. Parcher was shifted to that side. Another crash as the *Lawrence* was turning. Cries of wounded and dying men. Again the ship settled. The port guns fired. They were giving as good as they got, he hoped. The battle continued furiously for what seemed hours. Parcher's arms and shoulders were leaden from passing the heavy shot.

Then the hull exploded. Huge splinters of wood flew in every direction Daylight from the hole exposed mangled bodies of at least ten men in varying degrees of wounds, from decapitation to lost limbs. The man to Parcher's left had a twelve inch splinter the size of a chair leg through his chest. His eyes concentrated on Parcher's before they rolled back and he slipped to the deck.

"Ammunition, goddamit!" the call came. Parcher was paralyzed.

Another crash, as an enemy ball hit. The ship quaked when the mainmast fell across the bow. Parcher knew enough to guess the *Lawrence* was surely helpless now. Those still standing had the look of fear, expecting another hit, but the *coup de grâce* never came. Only distant cannon fire. At length all hands were called on the main deck.

He could not believe what he saw. The ship lay dead in the water. Rigging was everywhere. Remnants of sail hung tattered on the spars that still stood.

An officer Parcher recognized as the first mate addressed the company, warning them of a probable boarding party to seize the ship. Pikes and short swords were distributed from the armory while the dead and wounded were attended.

"Where's the captain?" someone called.

Gradually word was spread. The commodore had been rowed away, presumably to the *Niagara.* The men began to grumble about the commodore's abandonment, but it wasn't long before the Niagara came racing downwind to engage the two remaining British ships that had somehow gotten entangled with each other in the heat of battle. The whole crew watched the commodore's pennant atop the *Niagara.* The ensuing exchange proved to be a decisive victory for the Americans

Shouts of "Hurrah!" and "Perry!" from the crew. All but Parcher, who could think of nothing but how close he'd been to death.

Thirty-nine

Andy

She felt she could wait until Monday to encounter David Wyse of the G&K Cycle Shop. If Barry were going to spook Wyse into fleeing, he could do so before she could drive there. Better have Terry with her, maybe a patrolman, as well.

She drove home to find the workers packing up for the day.

"Find anything?" she asked a fresh faced girl in Levis, flip-flops, and a *Red Hot Chili Peppers* tee shirt.

"Just the handle of what must have been a spade or hoe. We can't tell yet. The handle is rotted, but that's what it was."

The girl went off to join a car full of others her age.

At the dig she could see the handle was no more than a dark line in the lighter colored soil. The edge of a rusted piece of metal protruded at the end of it. A tool in a tool shed did not seem all that exciting.

She was dead tired and starved. Time to relax and think about how to approach her suspect on Monday. She really had nothing more than minimal evidence tying him to the murder—time, place, opportunity, but no motive.

~ * ~

Arnold Terry stood, hands in pockets, looking at Andy's week-end endeavors—over thirty-five colored pins pushed into a map on the wall. The map wasn't big enough for some of the outlying addresses.

"And the first one you followed up was a hit?" He gave Andy a smirk she was becoming accustomed to.

"I'm not ahead of myself, though," she said. "I need to follow up on his missing wife."

"Gotta say, things are starting to add up," he said. "What's her name?"

"Alice—Barry, or Wyse. She might be using either if she's not that collection of bones in Forensics.

"But you're assuming she is," he said

"It's as good as any assumption. If I can't locate her in Canada or the U.S., it's a *damn* good assumption."

"So…"

"So, I take two days looking for her. If I can't find her, I assume she's dead, and we pull in David Wyse, and give him the business."

Terry snatched his suit coat from the chair. "Lotsa luck. I'm off on another wild goose chase."

Andy got on her computer and pulled up the Interpol database. She punched in Alice's name and any other Barry or Wyse she could run down. Meanwhile she had a rap sheet ordered for David Wyse. It would be a long day.

~ * ~

On Thursday, Andy was convinced Alice Barry—or Wyse—did not exist. Repeated requests of Willard for another name she might have used were fruitless. The woman must be dead. Dead, and residing in an O.P.P forensics drawer. It was time to move on Mr. Wyse.

Her cell phone beeped. "Blake."

"Andy!" It was Lila Knowles. "Can you get away?"

"As a matter of fact, it's a good time. What's up?"

"Something to show you at the dig."

~ * ~

For three days Andy had put the thought of what might be at the bottom of the cellar out of her mind. The previous Sunday was spent as a welcomed reprieve from the chaos in her backyard. Grant came over around 10:30 for a leisurely breakfast of French toast. Talk of archaeology or skeletons in the wall was absent, replaced by Grant's interest in a future for Andy's son, Tim.

Now, her interest was intensified. Her front yard was more jammed with vehicles than ever. She parked on the highway.

At the site was the regular cast of characters plus a few she didn't know. One lady who looked familiar said, "Here she is!" She introduced herself as a member of the St. Joseph Island Historical Society.

Tremblay was, as usual, holding forth, but Lila emerged from the crowd to fetch Andy.

"Come see!" she said.

The group of possibly thirty parted for Andy to approach the cellar. There, a grad student was busy with a brush and trowel meticulously removing soil from around a leg and hip bone.

Andy was taken completely off guard. "Is it human?"

"Human, all right," Tremblay said. "A woman."

"You're sure?"

"The pelvis. No doubt about it."

Andy was mesmerized. Only one leg and a hip were exposed, but she visualized the entire person there in her family's backyard where she and her mother were both raised, not having an inkling of what lay only a few feet under the earth.

Tremblay put a hand on her shoulder. "Andy, I'd like permission to widen the hole. There is so little space to work in. To expose and remove the skeleton we should come at it from the side in a procedure called a pedestal."

Andy gave him an automatic nod of the head, still staring at the excruciatingly slow uncovering of the pelvic area.

"Is it a grave?" she asked anyone who would answer.

"Probably not," Tremblay said. "The body is not in repose."

"Meaning?"

"Either an accident or foul play."

"Oh shit," she said to herself, but aloud. "Just what I need. Another murder mystery.

~ * ~

All morning and the night before, Andy berated herself for not checking on an obvious lead for finding Alice Barry—her mother. Was there a mother somewhere? Willard Barry hadn't been forthcoming, but whomever gave birth to the girl might.

She didn't stop at the Detachment, but kept going north on 17N to the Barry house. When Willard answered the door, he was downright belligerent.

"What the fuck you want now, sister?"

"You can watch your language, Mr. Barry, or we can have this interview in a holding cell. I need to know the name of Alice's mother."

The question threw him. Andy sensed him drifting back to another time.

"Mr. Barry…?"

"Gladys, it was," he almost whispered.

"Gladys—what was her maiden name? What name would she be using now?"

He seemed to perk up. "Hillman. I got no idea where she is."

Andy jotted in her notebook. "Were you legally married?"

"Of course! What kind of damn question is that?"

"One more thing, sir—Alice's full name—she had other names?"

Again, he seemed lost in the past. "Merle, I think. After Gladys' ma."

"Thank you. If we locate Alice, would you like to know?"

Andy thought the old man might cry. His pale eyes glistened.

"You do what you want," he said and shuffled back inside.

~ * ~

The rest of the day was spent searching Canadian and U.S. databases for any combination of Alice, Merle, Wyse, and Barry for a woman of about forty.

She came up with nothing. It was time to pick up David Wyse for questioning.

Andy and Arnold Terry followed a black and White O.P.P. patrol car to the G&K cycle shop on the west end. Tony Crucianni and his partner would have the privilege of escorting Wyse in for questioning.

The shop seemed to be well managed, unlike some cycle shops Andy had seen that were hangouts more than anything else. They had no trouble finding Wyse. He was behind the counter in a grey work shirt with the names "DAVE" and "Service Manager" embroidered over the pocket.

"Mr. Wyse?" Andy said. If he was surprised at seeing O.P.P. shields flash, and a pair of uniformed officers at the door, he didn't show it.

"Guilty," he said, which Andy thought was prophetic.

"You have someone to watch the place while you come in with us and answer some questions?"

"What about?" Wyse's dark eyebrows matched his beard, and lowered into a frown.

"We're looking for Alice, Mr. Wyse. I'm sure you can help."

His face relaxed. "She's been gone for…"

"We know, David," Terry said. "We'll talk it over at our place, instead of involving your customers."

~ * ~

When it became clear to Wyse this was no simple follow-up to a cold case of a missing person, but that he was under suspicion for his ex-wife's demise, he stopped talking and asked for a lawyer. In the meantime, he revealed his mother-in-law Gladys Hillman had left Alice's father soon after the girl was born, and taken her to Gladys' home town of Calgary.

Alice showed up at her father's house when she was eighteen, a runaway. Wyse claimed to have met her at a bikers' party.

At this point, the questioning got serious, and Wyse stopped cooperating. A man Terry knew as a competent defense lawyer arrived, and heard the evidence against his new client. He told Andy she didn't have enough hard evidence to hold Wyse, which she already knew.

As Wyse and his lawyer walked out the detachment's front door, Andy said, "No problem. When the DNA analysis comes back, we'll have enough."

Terry agreed.

It wasn't ten minutes later that a call came in from Bay Street. "We have a match on your DNA—a missing forty-one-year-old woman."

"Bingo!" Andy said into the phone. "What name did she use?"

"Wanda Bergstrom. Last address, 2077 Goulais Mission Road, Goulais River, Ontario."

Who? "Goulais? Are you sure?" This didn't make sense.

"Would I kid, Detective? I'm sending the file to the Sault Detachment now. Have fun." The call ended.

The copies were received and delivered to Andy's desk. She looked at Wanda Bergstrom's picture. A young girl of sixteen posing for her G-1 driving license. A file with a request from a single mother for help in locating the girl after she ran off with a Paul Crowder.

Crowder had an ID as a construction worker, temporarily employed in the Goulais area at the time. Both had vanished—physically, and from public records.

Terry perused the file, said, "You don't suppose Wyse and Crowder are the same guy, do you?"

"One thing is sure," Andy said. "Wanda isn't Alice. I checked, and found Gladys and a daughter Alice living in Calgary while Wanda was in Goulais, according to this." She thumped the file.

"I'm taking a ride up there tomorrow. Want to go?"

"Can't. I think I've found my missing wife in a Petoskey Michigan shelter for battered women."

Andy threw the whole Woodruff—renamed Barry—file in her briefcase, and headed for home.

Forty

Nettie

April 1814
Sault Ste. Marie

It was Carrie's twelfth birthday, but Sunday was the traditional day for socializing. The lack of a church or mission in Sault Ste. Marie meant personal introspection for the devout and ample time for relieving the pressures of the week. The Johnston children had insisted on hosting the party at their home on the south side of the river. Those adults who could, made the effort to fete the popular girl.

Never mind this was a children's party. The adults were anxious for the latest news from Fort Michilimackinac. A lieutenant Robert Dickson had been dispatched with John Johnston back to the Sault to recruit native warriors.

Sault Ste. Marie was almost devoid of men, who had been removed to the fort for its defense. On the previous September, the Americans scored an enormous victory on Lake Erie, resulting in the

Detroit fort falling back into American hands. They now had command of Lake Huron, as well. The expectation of an attack on Michilimackinac when the ice broke up soon was strong. The new commander there, Lt. Colonel Robert McDouall, had arrived in February with ninety regular soldiers.

Lt. Dickson had a boyish face and a deferential manner to complement it. The girls and young women were vying for the handsome young officer's attention. But when Johnston introduced him to Nettie, he had time for no one else. He was obviously charmed.

"My colonel has put me in charge of a company of Indian warriors for the defense of the fort, ma'am. I have a problem, however, in that there are but a few of them left there after two years of occupation."

"So you are in command, but have no one to command?"

Dickson smiled, and offered a curt bow of respect for Nettie's mot. "Indeed! That sums it up. Mr. Johnston suggests you may be a help in that regard."

"Me!" Nettie scanned the room, as if to suggest he must be addressing someone else. "Mr. Johnston has his own contacts with the natives. Why on earth me!"

"Mr. Johnston claims you have influence with a certain Wa…Wabig…"

"*Waabigwanbindegoon*? Lily?"

"Yes, if that's what you call her. Mr. Johnston says she is a powerful elder with influence among your natives."

Nettie knew Lily was a shaman. She had healing powers, and was invited to councils for her respected opinion. "She may have some influence, yes."

"I'd be beholden if you would introduce me to her." He gave Nettie his best boyish smile.

"She is usually at our home across the river. You are welcome to call. Now, I believe it is time for the birthday celebrations." She extended her hand to him, and they joined the group of laughing children.

It wasn't long before the adults joined in the birthday games. Dickson chose Nettie as a partner in the three-legged race, resulting in a tumble on the Johnston lawn to the delight of Carrie and her friends.

By mid-afternoon, it was obvious Thomas, who had been in the background most of the day, was drunk, or nearly so. His voice rose above the others, railing about some perceived abuse or another. Nettie decided to try to calm him. He'd cornered a small group of uncomfortable guests.

"Thomas," she said, taking his arm, "they are beginning a new game. Come and be my partner."

"Can't you see I'm engaged here?" he snarled, and snatched his arm away. "Ask your young suitor!"

Nettie was mortified. Carrie and her friends stared at the scene.

Thomas tried to ignore his gaffe, returned to his corralled group, but forgot what he'd been talking about. His audience dispersed.

Carrie's face dissolved into tears. Nettie went to her, but the girl moved away to the edge of the lawn near the river.

Nettie decided it was time to go home.

Forty-one

May 1814

Thomas' erratic behavior was becoming commonplace. At home he was sullen and non-communicative, but in public he was apt to spout off at any moment. Nettie worried about his work. A slip of the tongue from Mrs. Logan, the wife of Thomas' superior, suggested they had been discussing Thomas as a problem to be dealt with.

On a morning in mid-month, Nettie thought events might come to a head when Thomas announced over breakfast he would not be going in to the warehouse.

"Are you ill?"

"Not in the least. I have the prerogative to do as I wish, and I wish not to go in to the office."

"Thomas, are things as they should be at the Company?"

"Of course they are, silly woman!" He stood, tossed his napkin down, and stomped to the parlor.

Nettie looked for an answer in Lily's expressionless face.

Carrie called, “Papa, don’t be mad—please!”

He was unresponsive. Nettie went to him. “Thomas, dear, something is troubling you, I’m sure.”

“Leave me alone.”

She was stung by the rejection, yet inwardly free of a sense of loss. She had long since stopped loving Thomas Gibson. They stood in the parlor, facing each other as strangers.

A tapping at the front door broke the tension. Nettie noticed a carriage through the window.

Lily answered it. In walked Martin Legère, dressed in Voyageur garb.

“*Monsieur* Gibson, Mrs. Gibson,” he announced. “I hope I do not intrude. We only this morning arrived from our overnight camp at St. Joseph.”

“What brings you here, Legère?” Thomas asked.

“A courtesy is all, sir. You are both well?”

Nettie said, “Well enough, Martin. And how is your venture doing?”

“Thank you for asking, Madam. The war has slowed all commerce, to be sure, but I am doing as well as I could expect. I now have a warehouse in York which I expect to be a major city after the war. Presently we are delivering four families and their possessions to the Minnesota Territory and The Forks of the Red and Assiniboine Rivers.”

Thomas sniffed. “All very intriguing, Legère, but I am needed at the Company office, so I must bid you adieu. Lily! My hat and cane, please.” He offered no more words, and was on the street for the short walk to the Company warehouse.

Carrie, who had watched the events since her father's breakfast declaration, came to Legère for an embrace. "I'm so happy to see you again, *Monsieur* Legère."

He was obviously pleased at the show of affection. "Nettie! She is as tall as you! I have borrowed a carriage I thought a ride on this fine morning might be welcomed."

Nettie said to Carrie, "Let's, dear. It would be refreshing."

"If you don't mind, I'll stay and finish my book. It's near the end, and I want to know…"

"Of course," Nettie said. Carrie was deep into Jane Austen's latest book *Pride and Prejudice*. She shook her head in wonder and pride in her daughter as she retreated to her room.

"Lily, I doubt we'll be long," she said.

Lily approached her, saying softly, "I think it may rain. If you are driving east, and you need a shelter, use my *wiigiwaam*."

There had not been as much as a cloudy day for a week. Nettie looked at Lily for an explanation for such a suggestion. Perhaps the old woman's eyes shone somewhat brighter.

"Thank you, Lily."

They took the same route as they had two years earlier. Legère was more animated than she had ever seen. He told her of his coup in hiring the best available men both last year in the west, and this spring in Montreal. He had eight canoes and plans for another eight when he returned east in the fall.

"It is a huge risk. I am counting on the war ending, and settlers rushing to get land grants in The Forks region."

The carriage hit a rut. Nettie reflexively grabbed Legère's arm. It felt good, and she remained that way, feeling a small thrill at this forward move. He stopped talking. She could see the tight line of his mouth and knew he was feeling the same sexual tension as she. The steady rumble of the wheels on the dry road accentuated it.

When it came, Legère's voice was hoarse. "Nettie…this year will likely be my last in a canoe. Others will…"

She put a hand on his mouth. "Don't say it!" Her mind raced. Not to see him again would be impossible to think about. She could not live with Thomas without even the infrequent hope of being with Martin Legère.

"Come to York with me." He said this, not pleading, but as an imperative. "We will go when I am back here in September."

The idea was delicious. I cannot wait that long, she thought. Then Lily's strange suggestion made sense. The wise old woman knew what both she and Legère wanted—needed.

"Up there by that bent tree—turn in." She pointed.

He obeyed, and the horse led them up a track until it could go no farther. Ahead was a dome-shaped structure covered in hides. It looked deserted, nestled in an attractive clearing surrounded by birch. Nettie had taken Carrie here many times to stay with Lily, learning the Ojibwa language and ways.

"Help me down," she said. He did, and she was in his arms. "I won't wait for autumn. I want you now!" Her own words amazed her, but had an electric effect on her body. She was burning.

He kissed her. The touch of his tongue on hers was incendiary. "Now!" She led him to the hogan, which was clean and orderly inside. A small bed of blankets on fresh hay filled one corner. In the semi-dark Nettie worked the buttons of her dress free. She pulled her chemise over her head, facing him, her breasts exposed.

He gasped. "I had no idea. You are…beautiful!"

"Hurry!" she pleaded, and attacked his shirt which he easily pulled over his head. They were soon on the cot, drinking each other in. She saw his erection and moaned, "Please now!"

~ * ~

They lay there. A breeze moved the flap at the door. The cool sweetness of the pine and maple forest reached them. It was mid-afternoon, and they had devoured the hours together, talking, making love.

"We must plan your leaving that man when I come back from the Assiniboine country."

"I cannot leave without Carrie. She'll have to be convinced."

Legère said, "She is wise. She will understand your decision."

"I hope so, I truly do."

The breeze grew stronger, bringing with it a drop of rain. Then they could hear it in earnest on the roof of the hogan.

Nettie laughed. "Lily knew what she was doing, after all!"

"We'll have to stay until it stops," he said.

She smiled and pulled him to her, the fire reignited.

~ * ~

The afternoon sun formed dappled shadows through the trees, as their carriage made its way home. Nettie resented every step the horse took that drew her closer to a parting with Legère.

"Three months at the most," he assured her.

Eventually the carriage drew up to the Gibson house. Legère dropped the reins, and gently took her face in his hands.

"It will be three months of agony," she said.

"Then remember this." He kissed her long.

She put her arms around her neck. "Go now. This is too hard for me."

She stepped down, unaided, waiting with her eyes closed until she heard the sound of him leaving. Slowly she walked up the flagstone path to her door.

From the slanted shadow of the entry stepped a figure to meet her—Thomas Gibson.

"So this is what the wife of thirteen years does behind the back of her husband and daughter." He was red-faced. Perspiration dotted his forehead. His chin trembled. She could smell the alcohol.

She tried to push past him, but he blocked her.

"Not here, Thomas!"

"Why not! You did not seem to mind a minute ago, kissing that ruffian for all the town to see."

"He is our friend, Thomas—a kiss goodbye."

"I am no fool! I know a chaste kiss, and it was not that!"

Years of holding back her resentment for his abusive behavior gave way. "Yes! Are you satisfied? Yes!" She pushed hard and passed him into the house.

He was on her heels. "You admit it!"

She whirled on him. "I would have told you later, but yes. Martin Legère is nothing you believe, and all you are not!"

"He is a rogue! A half-breed, ignorant river man!"

She bristled. "If that is what you think, then you are a fool."

"Mama!"

They both were startled to find Carrie, book in hand, staring at them with glistening eyes.

"Oh Carrie!" Nettie said. "I'm so sorry…"

"Go to your room, Caroline," Thomas ordered.

"I am not an infant to be sent to my room." A tear broke loose and ran down to her lip.

"Something is wrong, and I am sure to be involved. It seems to be my affair, as well."

Nettie went to her, speaking softly. "Carrie, let me work this out with your father, and I will come to your room and tell you everything."

Carrie shifted her gaze from her father and back to her mother, gave a curt nod and left.

Thomas' eyes were downcast. "She was always more yours than mine, and now you have shamed her as well as yourself. The whole town knows of your assignation with that man."

"Assignation! It was a ride in the country!"

"Nonsense! How do you think I came to hear of this? You were seen leaving with him—alone. People think the worst, and it seems they were right. I was besieged at work with derisive joking. I am humiliated and you will be the subject of gossip in the entire region by evening."

Nettie took this in. He was right. She'd hoped to avoid a prolonged scandal by telling him in September, but now there would be three months of avoiding the stares and questions. She could no longer live in the same house as Thomas Gibson, but what choice did she have?

"I want to end this marriage," she said.

Thomas blinked, apparently not expecting the blunt declaration. He made no reply, but went to the brandy decanter, retreating with it to the rear of the house.

Nettie went into the kitchen to find Lily stemming freshly picked string beans. "You heard?"

Lily laid her knife down and folded her hands on her lap. “I did.”

“Oh Lily, I’ve made a mess. I wanted to wait until September to tell him I was leaving. Now I cannot continue to spend another night in this house. I don’t know what to do.”

Lily stood, put a finger under Nettie’s chin. “But I do.”

Forty-two
Parcher

July 1814
Aboard USS Caledonia
Lake Huron

Parcher sat on the floor of the tiny cell across from the ripe bucket of his own excrement. He watched the water in his bowl slosh gently with the roll of the ship. His nose and cheek bone were still swollen from the beating and hurt like hell. He'd sworn he would never be dragged into one of those lake ships again, and had done his best to keep his word. Naval Marines had found him in a tavern south of Detroit on his way home to Ohio. That was four days ago.

There was the sound of the cell bolt sliding and the door opened, revealing the boots and white trousers of a Marine guard. "Crawl out of your hole, Parcher, and join your mates."

The corporal was one of the four Marines sent to fetch and persuade him to return to duty.

He glared at the man. "I won't forget…"

The corporal cut him off. “Keep your threats to yourself, you damned deserter. I would have had you shot.”

Parcher knew the man was right, hating him for it. He was lucky not to be hanging from a rope.

After the assignment of militia to bolster Commodore Perry’s fleet on Lake Erie, the men returned to duty at Ft. Meigs. Parcher was so happy to be back on dry land, he stopped complaining for a while.

But fate had an evil trick to play. He was one of those “volunteered” from the Ohio Militia for duty on this, a task force of five ships headed north somewhere to attack a nameless fort lost to the British two years ago in 1812.

The Marine led him through to the fo’c’sle, the crew’s quarters, a dark bay crammed with over forty hammocks swinging with sleeping bodies.

“There are three men to every hammock sleepin’ in shifts,” the Marine said. “You’ll have to find someone to share with, if any of ‘em will have ye.” He left Parcher there to shift for himself.

“Yer kit is over there, Bertie,” a voice from one of the hammocks said, “next to the bulkhead.”

“Name’s Albert, God damn you,” Parcher hissed to the anonymous voice.

There was sniggering among those not sleeping.

“I’ll try to remember that, Bertie…oh, Albert.” More chortling.

“Let the devil have you, then!” Parcher climbed the ladder to the deck. The fresh air was a relief, but the July sun bore down with palpable weight. The deck was alive with working sailors and troops trying to stay out of their way. Parcher stood at the port rail where he could see the distant shoreline to the west.

"What ship is this?" he asked a sailor working at a capstan.

The sailor eyed his swollen face and possibly assumed where this man had been for the last four days. "The Caledonia. We're a day north of the St. Clair River."

Parcher looked through the rigging to starboard, and saw the expanse of water that was Lake Huron. Other sails dotted the surface.

"Them's the Niagara and the Scorpion," the sailor offered.

Parcher remembered the names from the battle last year on Lake Erie where Admiral Perry had driven the Niagara into the British line, forcing all seven ships to surrender. It was now the flagship of the fleet, Commodore Arthur Sinclair.

"You! Sailor! Get back to your work, man!"

They both whirled to see the Army's Major Holmes on the poop. Parcher knew him from Ft. Meigs, a hero at the battle of Longwoods.

Holmes was in command of the three infantry companies plus the Ohio militiamen, spread out over the five vessels, and seemed to know Parcher well, calling him by name. "Private Parcher, come here."

The sailor dropped his eyes to the deck, as Parcher went aft. He saluted, looking up to where Holmes was standing on the raised deck.

"That you do not have a bullet in your head is by my grace and the situation of my needing every man I can lay hands on for this engagement. As far as I am concerned, your life is as good as forfeit. Any step out of line by you will result in a belated firing squad for your desertion. Have I spoken clearly?"

"Yes sir," Parcher croaked.

"Dismissed."

Parcher did an about-face, and somehow in his rage made his way forward through the crowded deck. Damn them! Damn them all to hell!

Forty-three

Nettie

July 1814

St. Marys River

The aching across her shoulders began to build as Nettie paddled, the ruins of Fort St. Joseph now in sight. In the rear, White Deer added his strong strokes and the light craft leaped forward. Between them were stowed some of Nettie's clothes and provisions for a week.

After hearing Lily's plan, Nettie had gone to Carrie's room to find her curled on the bed.

"Caroline, my darling girl, I want to talk to you as a woman."

Carrie sat up on one elbow. Her eyes were dry of tears, searching her mother's face for a sign of candor.

Nettie reached for her daughter. The two sat together on the edge of the bed. "I have stopped loving your father for some time now. Worse, I have stopped respecting him. It is no one's fault, it is just how our lives have developed."

Carrie said, "I know, Mama. Papa is not easy to love even when he is not drinking rum or brandy."

Nettie continued. "Dear, I think I have loved Martin Legère for a long time. I do love him now, and know he loves me…and you." She waited for a reaction, but Carrie said nothing.

"I have promised to leave your father, and move east with Martin. We want you to come, too."

"When?"

"In September, when the Voyageurs return from Assiniboine."

Carrie put her arms around her mother. "I love the way Martin treats you. I love him, too. I know you haven't been happy."

"Dear Carrie! What a gift you have just given me!" She kissed her daughter. "But I cannot live here until September. Lily has a good plan. White Deer will take me to the Askins' house to live until Martin returns."

"On St. Joseph? Of course! The house is empty. But how will he find you?"

"He'll come here for me. Lily will tell him."

"…or I will," Carrie said

"You?"

"I cannot leave Papa alone. He needs someone for a while. We owe him that. I'll come with Martin in September. That will give me time to say goodbye to Papa."

Nettie was awed by the maturity and judgment of her not-yet-thirteen-year-old daughter. She harkened back to herself getting married at seventeen, certainly no more adult than this girl.

Forty-four

Andy

The trench allowed the archaeologists to dig around the skeleton, exposing it completely. Still nothing of the remains had been removed.

The skeleton was mostly face-down. Arms and legs were in varying positions with only the right arm pinned under the spine. It was remarkably intact.

Tremblay was ecstatic. The students were obvious in their pride, their Joe-college jocularity subdued by the enormity of what they had accomplished.

Andy stared at the shape at the bottom of the pit, not looking at a skeleton, but of a woman. She remembered Tremblay's proclaiming this to be either an accident or foul play. There was little doubt about it. That person was thrown into the cellar either dead, or unconscious.

The blade of the rusted spade—as it was since deemed—had been removed and tagged. She could see the rusty mark where it had been next to the body. *The murder weapon?*

Tremblay was standing next to her. "We got a fix on that brass bird we found." He reminded her of the small piece found while screening the dirt from the floor of the foundation. "It's from a cockade worn by a regiment of the Ohio Militia in the war of 1812."

"How did it get there?" Andy said.

"How indeed. There is only one reasonable possibility. The American army was fortified with militiamen from Ohio when they raided Sault Ste. Marie and burned Fort St. Joseph. One of those men was here at the time, which was only a few days."

"I can't bear to think what would have happened to a woman here at the time."

"The fort was abandoned. Supposedly no one was here," Tremblay said.

"But we now know that wasn't the case, don't we?"

She turned to the sound of her name being called

"Andy! Can you spare some time?" It was Lila Knowles holding a manila envelope and a binder.

Andy sighed inwardly. She was tired, and had the damned Wyse case on her mind. "Sure. Let's go inside."

The day was hot and the parlor felt cool. They sat across from each other—Andy with a glass of ice water.

Lila opened the thin three-ring binder, and turned it around so Andy could see it. "I told you it's easy to trace families with all the tools the internet offers these days. I've taken the liberty of tracing yours, just from the little you've told me."

Andy looked at the chart on the first page. Some of the names she knew. Most of the others were completely foreign.

"This is your complete pedigree chart. You can study that later. Turn the page."

Andy flipped the page to reveal a similar, though simpler chart with fewer branches.

The heading read:

Line of Maternal Descendancy from
Caroline Gibson to
Andrea Blake

It described Caroline as married to a Henri Passeau with at least one daughter, Andrea.

Andrea was indicated as married to Robert Carney, the couple having a daughter Bess.

Bess had a daughter with one Hector McVey whom they named after her mother.

Bess McVey married Arnold Bledsoe. Among their children was a girl, Mildred...

who married Earl Blake. They had three daughters, one of whom was Andy, herself.

"This follows only your ancestors who have remained in present day Algoma over the generations," Lila said. "Curiously, the line is all maternal. You told me your mother's maiden name was Bledsoe. The LDS database in Salt Lake City has your line back to your second great-grandmother, Andrea Passeau."

"Andrea!" Andy couldn't contain a chuckle, despite her original lack of interest in all of this.

"I had a little trouble with the next generation. It seems Andrea's mother, Caroline Gibson Passeau lived in Montreal for a time. A most fortunate thing, because church records are our main sources of lineage, and there were no churches in the early nineteenth century Sault village. We found her record, and Andrea's christening at Christ Church Cathedral in Montreal."

"So how does this stuff relate to that foundation in my backyard?"

"Caroline's father was connected with the Canadian fur trading company that was burned when the Americans sacked Sault Ste. Marie the same time they burned the fort here. He returned to Montreal in 1814 with his daughter, but there is no record of her mother's death."

"Quite a lot of effort here, Lila." Andy thumbed through the pages of the notebook containing details on each individual.

"Believe me, it was less work than it looks. I do this as part of my work for the Foundation. I didn't have to leave my computer."

Andy crossed her legs, leaned back and sipped her water. "Why do I have an idea this has something to do with that manila envelope?"

Lila laughed. "My! You *are* the detective." She retrieved the envelope from the sofa. "Andy, I want to get a cheek swab from you. This is a DNA kit. We're sending samples of the skeleton's DNA. There's a reasonable chance the body is that of Annette Gibson. It was the right age for Annnette to be in 1814."

"So you think that skeleton is my…" She counted back generations on the chart. "…third great grandmother?"

"I'd bet on it," Lila said.

Okay, what the hell! Andy thought, as Lila was removing the swabs from the kit.

~ * ~

The trip north to Goulais wasn't bad, just a half hour north of the O.P.P. station. She turned left on Highway 552 looking for Goulais Mission Road. The address was just a short distance from the highway, a small, but neat cottage with 'Bergstrom' hand-lettered on the mailbox. A woman was in the garden on hands and knees pinching back dead blossoms. She rose at the sound of Andy's jeep on the gravel.

"Mrs. Bergstrom?" Andy held her shield out.

"I am, dear. Can I help you?"

She was about sixty, but might have been mistaken for older. No makeup, sun weathered skin, kind eyes. Her wiry grey hair was pulled back in a ponytail; a few strands were loose over her damp forehead.

"You can, ma'am. I'm following up on the case of your missing daughter."

The woman closed her eyes, as if warding off another round of fruitless hope.

"I understand she was last seen with a Paul Crowder. He hasn't contacted you over the years, has he?"

"Goodness no. Why would he? We certainly had no love for each other."

"Can you tell me about him?"

"He was here from The Soo, a construction worker on the development that went on then near the Lake." She pointed east, in the direction of Lake Superior. "Wanda met him at some party, and thought he was God's gift."

Andy got out her notebook, motioning for the girl's mother to continue.

"Well, he *was* a charmer, I'll give him that. Seemed to be quite good at quoting scripture."

"That doesn't sound too bad. Why didn't you two get along?"

"They insisted on marrying. I was against it, so soon as it was, and I suppose he resented me for it. They moved into the Bunkie," she indicated the small trailer in the rear of the property, "until his work at the development ended. After they married, he made no effort to help around here. I was working myself, cleaning vacation cottages. Goodness knows I could have used the help."

"So they left together?"

"Said he had work in Blind River. Last I ever heard from either of them."

"You wouldn't have a picture of Wanda, would you?"

Mrs. Bergstrom wiped her hands on her smock as she trudged into her home. She returned with two pictures. One, a graduation photo, cap and gown included. The other a snapshot of Wanda and a young man in his twenties arm-in-arm in swimsuits, the horizon of a large lake in the background.

"That's Paul Crowder?" Andy tapped the picture.

"That's him. The police never found him. If you do, you'll know what became of my girl."

~ * ~

Andy drove back with the image of Paul Crowder messing with her head. He had a moustache and long sideburns, and the eyes, so familiar! It was driving her nuts. Then she remembered where she'd seen those eyes, and couldn't get back to town fast enough.

Back at her desk, she punched in a name for a background check. Just as she thought, no credit reports, driver's licenses, property taxes; nothing before eighteen years ago.

She took a copy of Crowder's photo to one of the officers who was proficient in using the O.P.P. software for facial modification. "Take away the sideburns and 'stache, will you?"

He easily zipped them off, revealing a clean-shaven visage.

"Now thin the hair a little, the hairline a little farther back." She watched as the face emerged. "You know that ridge that goes from your nose to your upper lip?"

"The philtrum," he advised.

"Make it more pronounced."

A new lip was substituted from the many available.

"That's it. You're a genius!"

The officer accepted the compliment with a shrug, and printed her a copy.

Andy found Terry working his computer.

"You look smug," he said.

"Not really. Happily chagrinned is more like it." She picked up her phone, and punched in the name of David Wyse's lawyer, and watched Terry's face as she told the man "You can advise your client he is no longer a person of interest in our investigation, and the O.P.P. thanks him for his cooperation."

"You were so sure," he said.

"Not as sure as I am now. Let's get Tony Crucianni and his partner in on picking up this piece of crap."

Forty-five
Parcher

USS Caledonia
July, 1814

Lake Erie was bad enough, but at least Perry's fleet was rarely out of the sight of land. Even then, Parcher vowed he would never again set foot on a boat of any kind. But this Lake Huron was so vast! He'd found two others from the militia to share a hammock, but was otherwise not likely to be found below decks. The thought of being down there when the ship was sinking was unbearable. He spent as much time as allowed staring at the thin layer of clouds that promised the existence of land to the west.

The Caledonia was now well north of Saginaw Bay on the east coast of The Michigan Territory. The officers and noncoms began to confirm what the rumors were saying: they were seven hundred men strong, sent to recapture an island fort with a long Indian name, Parcher could never get it right. The fort was key to protecting British and Canadian trade. Taking the fort would cripple commerce so vital to the Canadian economy and their war effort. It was said the Caledonia was a captured ship that had been instrumental in the loss of the fort they were planning to re-take. It would be sweet revenge.

Their first action would be to cut off the fort's supply from the east through Georgian Bay. It would be well into the second week in July before any engagement took place. Meanwhile, the Navy found make-work for its cargo of soldiers.

It was on one of these work parties, chipping old paint, and applying new, that the sergeant in charge spied Parcher at the rail, and commandeered him.

"Soldier! What's your name?"

Parcher didn't recognize the man, though he was a militiaman, like himself. He responded, but took his time about it. "Parcher, Sergeant."

"Take this scraper and follow me, Parcher."

Christ! He'd tried his best to keep his head down, and off those work details.

"Get to work on this section along the scuppers. I want it down to the wood."

"All that?" It looked like a week's work.

"You'll scrape until I tell you to stop, Parcher. It's a long sail to…" He stopped, studying Parcher's face. "Where you from, Private?"

"Pretty much all over, I guess."

"Swear to Old Harry, I know you from somewhere."

"Could be," Parcher said. "Don't think I know why."

"You ever been in Cincinnati?"

Parcher's defense mechanism kicked in. Something was wrong. "Uh, no."

"'Cause you look like someone I been lookin' for a long time. You sure you never traipsed up and down the Ohio's North Bend?"

"I'm from Baltimore. Only came to Ohio a while back."

"So you don't got a couple of friends named Barton and Fletcher?"

The mention of the two names sent a shock through Parcher's body, and he saw the sergeant knew it. That's almost ten years ago! Who is this man? "No, can't say as I do."

The sergeant said nothing, but continued to search Parcher's face.

"I'll get to that scraping, then," Parcher said, and bent to his task.

~ * ~

After two days of fine weather, the fleet turned east. Clouds rolled in, covering the sky like grey flannel. They had entered Georgian Bay, and a fog began to hinder visibility.

The Caledonia anchored in a place Major Holmes said was Matchedash Bay. From the deck, Parcher could see some of the smaller boats nosing in and out of the inlets, but Caledonia and Niagara stayed well offshore of the rocky coast.

A day passed with neither apparent contact with the enemy nor discovery of their base. On the second day, several men, including Parcher, were ordered into longboats on a patrol up a nameless river, searching for a supply depot of some kind. It came to naught, but Parcher got a good taste of insect life in the virgin forest of Canada. The ship did not seem so bad upon their return.

The following morning, the order to weigh anchor was heard and the fleet was underway to the west. All this time Parcher could feel that sergeant's eyes on him. Finally, he mentioned it to a regular from the US 24th Infantry during mess.

"Ya mean Sergeant Sauer? Ain't noticed him as spyin' on anyone."

Sauer! Corporal Saur! Now Sergeant. Parcher let his spoon clank in his bowl. He'd never forgotten the name from the day those green soldier boys, years ago back in Cincinnati, were bragging about shooting Fletcher, and how Barton had been killed by the men in the flatboat. Corporal Saur, they'd said, was the one who'd vowed to get the one who got away that day on the Ohio River.

But he didn't get my name. Or did he? *Does he just think he knows, or is he playing with me, and plans to turn me in once we're off this floating jail?*

Parcher dumped the rest of his potato soup in the slops, and went back on deck. He wasn't hungry any longer.

~ * ~

By mid-month, the fleet had traversed Georgian Bay to its western limits, arriving on the eastern shore of what was said to be St. Joseph Island where a British fort was situated. They turned south, traveling under topsails only, while sounding for the bottom. One of the gunboats had already had a close encounter with a huge submerged boulder. Ten fathoms could instantly change to a few feet in these waters.

They rounded the southern tip of this very large island to encounter an archipelago of smaller ones to its south. After a few miles of shoreline passing on their starboard, *The Niagara*, leading the fleet, furled sails.

Caledonia and the other ships closed up, and did likewise. Parcher could see the corner blockhouse of a stockade. This was the British fort, but the *Niagara* did not receive nor give fire. He watched as a longboat was lowered. An officer and perhaps a half dozen men rowed to shore seemingly in complete ease.

Forty-six

Nettie

July 1814
St. Joseph Island

From the Askins' porch, Nettie could see the old Indian, Blue Feather, on the shore, gathering freshwater clams. Three weeks earlier, when she first arrived on the island, he was the sole inhabitant, a Cree Indian who one day decided he'd had enough of the fur trade, and chose this island as his last place on earth.

The Cree didn't speak English, French, or for that matter, Ojibwa as far as Nettie knew. He was a true hermit, but didn't seem to resent her presence. In fact, she would sometimes receive a gift on her doorstep of a fish or freshly killed squirrel. She wondered if some of those clams might show up tomorrow morning.

Despite the fact she was counting the slowly moving days until Legère showed up, life alone on St. Joseph Island was pleasant enough. White Deer had returned twice with supplies since her arrival.

He'd brought news of Carrie, Thomas, and Lily. They seemed to be getting along, except for word that Thomas' drinking was no better. He was not terribly abusive, but becoming more and more withdrawn. Lily thought he might lose his position at North West Company.

This day, she reckoned it was the twentieth of the month, her few chores were over. She'd weeded the Askins' small vegetable garden, and bathed. She carried an old rocker they'd left onto the front porch to enjoy the fine day and cool breeze funneling down the channel from St. George Island.

Looking out onto the serene water, she recounted the many pleasant memories in this house with Madelaine Askin. Once, back in 1811, the resourceful Madelaine, at the request of Capt. Roberts, headed up a group of women from the Island and the Sault to sew warm coats from blankets the captain had procured from the South West Company. The poorly equipped 10th Royal Veteran Battalion faced that winter with no other option. They were of plaids and other colors not in the least regulation. Later the garrison at Michilimackinac copied the idea. Ever since they were known as Mackinaws.

Nettie was smiling at the vision of those soldiers in their gay colors. Then, she could scarcely believe her eyes. She had day-dreamed for a minute, no more than ten, opening her eyes to view a large ship easing to a halt. An anchor was splashing into the water directly in front of the fort. And the flag! The flag was one she'd only seen in illustrations, red and white horizontal stripes with a blue field…American!

She felt paralyzed, unable to move from sight, but somehow found herself inside the house watching the scene through the window. Other ships now! Hundreds of men on their decks. The largest ship was lowering a longboat. *They'll be here! Enemy soldiers!*

A rap on the rear door nearly stopped her heart. She whirled, and stared at it, unable to speak. Slowly it opened. She searched the room. She had no musket nor other means of protection. Then it swung open, inducing a deep sigh of relief.

Blue Feather stood in the frame. He pointed to the thick bush to the north of the Fort. He's telling me to hide. And then he was gone. *Think! Where? I cannot live in the trees like that old man.*

Slowly, her senses returned. *The gardens!* They were well away from the fort on that bay to the east. Those storage huts would be good shelter. She grabbed a basket, filled it with as much food as it would hold, and started for the open rear door. At the last minute she lit the lantern she used for the privy, and took it along. It would be dark tonight. The sky had been moonless for the past few days.

~ * ~

She emerged into the clearing that, apart from the fallow gardens, looked exactly as it had on that unforgettable day of lovemaking with Martin Legère. From where she stood, she could see no sign of a ship on the bay or beyond. Still, she was careful to follow the tree line around and up the rise to where the two small buildings sat. She chose the larger. It was unlocked.

Inside, dead flies and some mouse droppings on the floor were the only indication of change since her last visit. Gardening tools, a small table, chair and cot. It was ideal.

Let the Americans have the fort!

Forty-seven

Andy

The door swung open. This time it wasn't Gwen, but the Reverend himself.

"Paul Corinth, or Paul Crowder, you are under arrest for the murder of Wanda Bergstrom Crowder, do you understand? You have the right to retain and instruct counsel without delay..." She went on reading his rights from memory, enjoying the look of despair on his face, the face that matched the computer rendition to a T. "You are not obliged to say anything, but anything you do say may be given in evidence. Do you understand? Would you like to speak to a lawyer?"

He looked over his shoulder at the sound of his wife's voice. "Not yet. I prefer to talk to you somewhere else. I'll come with you now."

It was a stroke of luck. Paul Corinth had no wish to face the wife of his reconstructed life. It gave them time to talk to him before his counsel arrived. Once in the interrogation room, his picture with Wanda on the table before him, he amazingly confessed, relieved to have the load of guilt taken away.

Wanda never got the hang of playing the pastor's wife. She developed a bit of a fast reputation for herself in Blind River where Crowder was trying to start up a fledgling church. But in spite of her, he got it going, especially after she left him for another biker from Toronto. He decided to change his name when he met Gwen. She was everything Wanda was not—pious, shy, and virtuous. The ideal first lady of a parish.

He got a reputation as a stirring speaker, and when the 'People's Church of Our Lord' in Sault Ste. Marie had a search for a preacher, he got the job. It was an unbelievable coup. Unfortunately, Wanda showed up. She was into drugs, and wanted money. Paul didn't have it, he said.

Wanda threatened to expose him to Gwen and the new parishioners. That was enough. He agreed to meet her in the abandoned house nearby and get her the money. It was an agreement Wanda should never have made.

~ * ~

The lawyer who finally showed up was irate, claiming Corinth/Crowder's rights were violated, but four officers had been there for the reading.

"The lawyer should have taken his wrath out on his client. We had only circumstantial evidence that linked Crowder to the murder," Andy admitted.

"Yeah," Terry said. "You're one lucky crime fighter."

Forty-eight

St Joseph Island

Her food was running low. White Deer was due to come with more in a few days, but not if the Americans were staying. *Are they going to occupy the Fort? Possibly. They've been here two days now.* Nettie had to consider that eventuality. What could she do?

One thing was certain. If the Americans stayed for any length of time, she'd have to move. Someone would certainly discover her. She had learned a lot about frontier life in the past seven years, but not living in the wild, finding food in the bush.

Food. The thought drew her attention to the root cellar she had yet to explore. Anything down there was likely spoiled, but it was worth checking.

The wash stand had to be moved, which she set aside. The door was set flush to the pine floor of the cabin, but made of the stouter planking. She pulled on the recessed ring. The door swung up heavily on its hinges and against the wall.

In the dim light of the single window, she could see nothing but a dirt floor about five feet below. There was no ladder. She'd have to climb down there to see clearly.

Nettie turned up the wick of the lantern which she kept lit, not having thought to bring a flint. She descended, taking the lantern along. The place was a disappointment. Other than an old cloth sack, it was empty. Nothing. The cellar was barely larger than the size of the opening. She knew her disappointment was irrational, but couldn't help it.

Slowly, after reaching up to set the lantern on the cabin floor, she climbed out of the empty hole. As she turned to retrieve the lantern, light poured in from the front of the cabin.

The silhouette of a man was framed by the door. Her first thought was White Deer, but the shaggy side whiskers and hulking body killed the idea.

Then an unfamiliar voice said, "Well hello…" and she knew this was not a friend come to rescue her.

~ * ~

Parcher

July, 1814
St. Joseph Island

The *Caledonia's* captain and Major Holmes were ferried back from the *Niagara*. Commodore Sinclair had a meeting to discuss the situation. It so happened the fort was abandoned. A warehouse belonging to a prominent American fur trader was there, as well as a few abandoned houses outside the confines of the stockade. Strict orders not to harm the Americans' property were given.

They were to use the fort as a base while a raiding party continued upstream to the Falls of St. Marys where the Canadians had a major trading post. At least that was what Parcher made of it when the news filtered down to him.

~ * ~

For two days he'd been kept aboard the anchored *Caledonia*. Some of the men were sent ashore to help loot anything of value at the fort, but not he. On the afternoon of the second day, the raiding party returned. Some of the raiders had been from the *Caledonia*, and were boasting how they burned the warehouses of the Canadians on both sides of the St. Marys River and destroyed a schooner as well.

They were telling stories of the successful raid when Sgt. Sauer clapped a hand on Parcher's shoulder. "Parcher! You're coming with me."

The thought that Sauer was arresting him for something that happened ten years ago flashed through Parcher's mind. "What for?" was his reflexive response.

"You'll find out."

Parcher followed to where two sailors and a longboat waited alongside.

"Get over the side and on the boat. You and me are going to check that cove we passed gettin' here."

As the sailors rowed to shore, Sauer explained the mission. Some small structures had been noticed at the rear of an open field facing the cove. It was a likely chance there were munitions stored there, it being a likely place for an enemy to make a landing. The sailors would wait while the two soldiers inspected the buildings.

When the boat was beached, Sauer got out waiting for Parcher to follow. Parcher began to march up the rise to the two buildings about four hundred yards away. Half way there, Sauer said, "Hold it."

Parcher turned. "What?"

"I didn't bring you along for this one man detail. I want to get you alone, away from the ears of the others. This is just between you and me—nothin' to do with rank."

Parcher was pretty sure he knew what was coming.

"You know and I know you were one of them pirates what probably killed that settler on his barge. There's two men back in Ohio who'll say it was you, if need be. I'm bettin a skunk like you is wanted for other things. I'm not sure what I'm gonna do, but I know this—you do whatever I want from now on. Consider yourself my boy. Got that?"

Parcher was livid, could feel himself being boxed in. Over Sauer's shoulders he could make out the sailors smoking by their boat. "Seems like I have to, for now," was all he could think to say, after a long pause.

"Now get up there and check those shacks while I have a smoke with them gobs."

Walking up toward the cabins, Parcher racked his brain for a way out of the mess he found himself in. Could Sauer really find those witnesses? For now he decided to do Sauer's bidding. There was always a way.

He went to the first cabin, a structure possibly twelve by sixteen feet with walls of hand-sawed planks. Its door was ajar. Inside, a wheelbarrow, its wooden wheel split in half, blocked the entrance. Behind was a collection of tools, stakes—gardening equipment! Not quite a munitions bunker. He pushed the old barrow aside to look closer at the array of junk, then left.

The second cabin, about twenty paces away, was slightly larger in size and more solidly built with a foundation of local stone. A stack of rotting hay bales was piled along one wall that had no window.

He tried the door. It was unlocked, and stuck slightly as he pushed it in. What he saw was the last thing he, or anyone else, would have expected. Slowly he stepped inside, and shut the door.

"Well. Hello!" he said. "Ain't you the pretty thing?"

Forty-nine

Nettie and Parcher

St Joseph Island

The man smelled of mildew and male sweat, reminiscent of her voyage from England those many years ago. Her lantern caught the dark features of his face. A bully's face with piggish eyes, frightening eyes.

He was talking to her, but she was petrified, too afraid to register his words. That seemed to make him angry.

When he reopened the door, she thought he might leave, but he only looked back toward the shore, closing it again. She tried to speak, but couldn't.

He smiled, but not a friendly one. Then he tossed his hat on the chair, and was unlacing his breeches. Her worst fear was confirmed. *No, no.*

Survival kicked in. Nettie searched for any means of resisting. While he was fumbling with his laces she found the spade in the corner. With all her might she swung it, hitting his head a glancing blow.

The man went down on his knees, screaming in pain. She took another swing with the spade, but this one was anticipated. A big hand shot up, and caught it on the shaft. The spade was pulled from her grasp.

He was shouting at her now, spittle flying from his lips. She made a move for the door, but a hard hand slapped her hard in the face. It sent her reeling back onto the table.

Now another voice at the door. Arguing, a scuffle, then the door was shut once more. He was back at her with his tirade. She tried to get up and past the man holding the spade—swinging the spade.

She felt the blow, but not the pain.

~ * ~

It made no sense at all, this pretty woman served up in her own little house for Albert Parcher to play with. She was scared to death, and that just made him want her more.

"How long has it been, you without a man, missy? Hey? Speak up. Think you're too prissy for Albert Parcher?" He opened the door to see Sauer still talking to the sailors, then shut it.

"Now let's you and me have some fun, little lady." He grinned at her. Tossing his hat aside, he began freeing his laces, conscious of his hardening member and months of life without a woman.

The blow was a surprise. He saw it coming, but had only enough time to prevent being hit full in the face. He went down on his knees to shake it off.

She swung at him again, but this time he was ready, catching the shaft, and jerking it free from her grip.

Her face was contorted in to a mask of consummate hate. "Who do you think you are, you fucking sow? You're the same as all the rest of your sex. You're just my whore of a mother, all the prick teasing sluts and whores in the state of Ohio."

He was screaming. The door opened. Sergeant Sauer was there.

"Parcher! Let her be!"

Parcher lost control. His ears were still ringing from the blow to his head. He saw Sauer only as his ticket to jail or worse. The spade was still in his hand, and he let Sauer have it full in the face. Sauer went down, falling backwards out onto the ground.

Still enraged, he focused his attention back on the woman. He hated the sight of all she stood for, all he never could attain, transferring all his failures onto her, then struck her with her own weapon.

Voices sounded from the beach. The sailors. He saw them starting up toward the cabin. The woman's body was still. *A murder charge.*

Think!

He rolled the woman into the open root cellar, tossing the spade after her, then banged its heavy door shut. *The lamp! Burn the place!*

The lantern was full. He emptied it onto the summer-dry wood of the cabin walls and furniture. It was like a tinder box. He turned the flame up, and crashed the lamp onto the pine floor. The result was almost explosive. The whole interior was instantly engulfed. He barely made it out over Sauer's sprawled body on the grass.

The sailors were shouting, running. His only escape was into the thick bush behind the burning cabin.

Fifty

Parcher

From the heavy thicket, Parcher watched the sailors drag Sauers' lifeless form away from the fire. The heat must have been intense. The sailors had their shirts pulled over their heads in order to get close enough. One of the sailors had Sauer over his shoulder as they stumbled back to their boat.

Parcher continued to watch the blaze until the roof caved in with a shower of sparks, taking the walls with it. There was nothing left of the place but glowing embers and white smoke from the ring of stones that had been the foundation.

The fire temporarily diverted his attention from thinking about what to do next. From his brief experience ashore at Georgian Bay, he knew this was harsh country. But others survived here, and he would too.

He soon discovered that may have been an optimistic thought. There was no place for him to go but farther into the thick bush. His idea was to circle around to the fort. There might be something there for survival...food, a knife, temporary shelter, *something!*

The sky was overcast. He shortly lost any sense of direction, but he had to keep moving. Fallen trees impeded his progress, undergrowth clawed at his shin. Tiny biting flies soon found him.

Now he was breathing hard, thrashing and cursing his way through the bush. The going was impossible. A small clearing ahead raised his hopes until he recognized a gnarled tree he was sure he'd passed. He was walking in circles.

Exhausted, he slumped against a large pine. There was a whistle. *A bird?* He looked to see a man in leather trousers and shirt. A large blue feather hung down in his long black hair. He was holding something—a bow.

The arrow hit Parcher exactly in the solar plexus, knocking the wind from him. He recovered the blow while shock set in to mask the pain that would have followed if he'd lived.

He looked at the shaft protruding from his chest, unbelieving. The man was walking toward him with a knife.

Albert Parcher was losing consciousness. He barely felt the blade on his scalp at it was torn from his head.

~ * ~

Aug. 1814
Sault Ste. Marie

"Hurry, Caroline. I want to be rid of this place."

Her father's words stung. Carrie loved this house. She knew she was stalling. Packing her few things in that chest was such a final act.

Thomas Gibson, on hearing of his wife's infidelity, decided then and there to return east, taking his daughter with him. He would wait for the first available transportation.

Attempts to locate her mother on St. Joseph Island after the American assault were fruitless. She had disappeared, or worse, been taken by the invaders.

Carrie pleaded in vain for her father to wait another month, at least, but a canoe returning to Montreal was here, and he meant to take it. She had no choice in the matter.

She went to her mother's room, despairing of the clothes and other possessions still in the drawers. Many of Nettie's toiletries were there on the dressing table, neatly arranged as if waiting for her return.

Carrie turned to leave, then noticed something under the chair. Her mother's single earring. *She must have lost it just before she went to the Island to wait for M. Legère's return in the autumn.*

She picked it up. Yes, it was her favorite, given to her at her wedding.

Carrie returned to her room to open the canoe chest, removing the small, wooden box decorated with the design of the red fox. In it were some of her cherished memories.

To them she added the earring, vowing to return to this house one day.

~ * ~

September 1814
St. Joseph Island

The rain pelted like grapeshot on Legère holding the oilcloth over his head. It splattered on the darkened ashes inside the ring of stones that had been the burned tool shed.

He'd arrived at the Sault to find the Gibson house empty. The Indian woman, Lily, the family called her, said Nettie had fled to the Askin house, waiting for his return. She could hardly bear to tell him of her disappearance following the American raids

A search party to the Island found nothing except the burned fort and ransacked houses. It was hoped she'd escaped to Michilimackinac or Drummond Islands, but it was not to be.

"I believe the American devils have taken her," Lily had said, but Legère had to see for himself.

The fort was burned, the houses, including the Askinses' burned or completely gutted. Nothing of value was left. Something drew him to the place on the small bay where they had spent that summer afternoon, but there was no clue here in the grass, or among the sodden ashes of a lifeless tool shed.

Big Henri urged him to believe she would find him in York. It was a slim ray of hope. He would hold on to that.

It was all he could do.

~ * ~

Andy

She felt the DeHaviland jet bump down at Windsor International Airport as Porter Airlines flight 668 landed. Grant had an important meeting with the Ontario Ministry of Transportation about a sizeable equipment leasing contract. He promised to fly down to pick her up when she'd finished her business in a week's time.

Andy had taken the 4:50 afternoon flight. Just before leaving home, Buck Tremblay caught her. "Here, stick this in your bag. We found it under the skull, a keepsake for all the trouble we've caused you."

She was late, or she'd have opened the small package there. She tossed it in her carry-on.

Andy thought of all she'd have to do in the following days. Most immediate was her formal separation from the Windsor Police Service. She still had her old shield, pistol, and a pair of handcuffs. She wanted to assure the deal O.P.P. made with the City of Windsor about transferring her pension was understood. Finally she had a host of friends to say good-bye to.

She wanted to sell her Subaru. The Jeep Grant loaned her was so perfect for twelve month duty in northern Ontario she convinced him to sell it to her.

Finally, the condo had to go on the market. That could take a week or a year. She'd have to find a realtor.

The cab dropped her in her driveway, steps from her door. The driver politely waited until she was in, dragging her wheeled bag behind her.

Inside, the place looked eerily foreign. A scent, or lack thereof, from no habitation. It occurred to her there was nothing to eat in the house. She'd have to go out again. *Damn!*

Slowly she unpacked, and put things away. When she got to her carry-on, the package from Buck Tremblay was there. She sat down on the bed and opened it.

Wrapped in tissue, was a small lump. The tissue unfolded to reveal, of all things, an earring face down on the paper. She lifted it by the shepherd's crook finding, and turned it over.

Andy gazed in disbelief. How had Tremblay come to have this? *It was under the skull, he'd said.*

She went to her closet, flipping through jackets, slacks, and dresses for the sweater. From its pocket she found the little wooden box with the red fox design, and opened it. From it she took the gold chain and pendant, both box and pendant gifts from her grandma Bess. The pendant and earring were identical. Someone had made the pendant from an earring, she could see now where the finding had been. A jeweler's mark on the back of each was the same.

What was her name? She found the notebook from Lila Knowles.

Annette (Nettie) Duncan Gibson
b. 2 Feb. 1784 Carlisle, Scotland
d. Unknown

Andrea Blake held the two pieces, thinking of the woman in the cold pit on St. Joseph Island, and cried.

Meet

Richard Whitten Barnes

Richard Whitten Barnes is a native Chicagoan, graduating as a chemist from Michigan State University. He is now retired from a career in international chemical sales and marketing, which has taken him all over the world. Barnes is a veteran of the U.S. Army 82nd Airborne Division and an avid sailor. He lives in Lake Wylie, S.C., but spends summers with his wife Marg and dog Sparty at their cottage on St. Joseph Island, Ontario, on the shores of Lake Huron.

FORGOTTEN ROOTS is his sixth novel.